P9-DGV-422

MAYUMI AND THE SEA OF HAPPINESS

Jennifer Tseng

MAYUMI AND THE SEA OF HAPPINESS

Europa Editions
214 West 29th Street
New York, N.Y. 10001
www.europaeditions.com
info@europaeditions.com

This book is a work of fiction. Any references to historical events, real people, or real locales are used fictitiously.

First Publication 2015 by Europa Editions

Library of Congress Cataloging in Publication Data is available
ISBN 978-1-60945-269-8

Tseng, Jennifer
Mayumi and the Sea of Happiness

Book design by Emanuele Ragnisco
www.mekkanografici.com
Cover photo © Paula Daniëlse/Getty Images

Prepress by Grafica Punto Print – Rome

Printed in the USA

CONTENTS

MAYUMI AND THE SEA OF HAPPINESS

FALL

It began at the library. While the young man waited quietly to be helped, I stood neatly in thrall to the world outside the window. *Momijigari* was ending; leaves were falling in drifts like snow. Blackcaps were eating the trees, striking the bark with their beaks then rapidly chewing it, in that annual burlesque of sheer appetite I've always found vulgar. When I turned, he cleared his throat and asked for a library card. He explained with darting, downcast eyes that although he'd been coming to the library with his mother since he was a child, he'd never had his own card. There was something in his manner—softness, reverence, a hesitation in the face—that is peculiar to a son close to his mother. Doesn't intimacy foster reverence more completely than anything that can be taught? As I handed him the form and then watched as he filled it in—his fingers fumbling a bit with the tiny pencil—I didn't think of having him yet, I simply gaped at his beauty. I had the thought: *he is out of reach*, a thought that, had I been younger, might have spurred me on, but in middle age, warned me to retreat.

He pocketed the card and walked lightly out the door. I typed his information into Athena, that cunning, square-faced virgin into whom every librarian daily enters strangers' private information. He'd written an up-island address in a neighboring town, on a road with an old-time name I had never heard of. We live on a voluminous island. There are worlds within the woods I will never discover. I have lived here long enough to know that obdurate truth.

He was not calligraphically precocious. No, there was nothing particularly pleasing about those small, awkward letters, but they were perfectly legible. And why did I, even then, feel a twinge of pride at that? His name was followed by two surnames joined together by a hyphen. The way he had spoken of his mother seemed to negate the presence of a father, as if the world through which they moved belonged only to them. He told me her name. Divorced, I thought. A divorced mother whose child bears her name is exceptional. His information agreed with that on her record (hardly considering why, I immediately cross-referenced their accounts), except for his hyphenated surname, of which she possessed only half.

Our first transaction became emblematic. I had so little and yet it seemed to me so much. Disturbing really how little it took to excite me. We were, both of us, adolescent in this respect. I was like a young boy who cannot stifle his own pleasure, even when he makes a strenuous effort. Surely there are worse lots in life. But (even now) I race ahead. For though I confess I pored over the penciled facts of his existence, it was with some measure of ease and detachment. For on that day I still believed I had no chance. By "no chance" I don't mean of having him—my mind never worked that way—but merely: no chance of attracting his attention. I read over the young man's form with the curiosity of one who loves books, information, a good story. I was a librarian after all, nearsighted, spectacled, sitting at a desk, legs crossed, mind adrift, a woman who, at any given moment, would have rather been reading.

I read every small chance I got, in the basement stacks while sipping my milk-sodden tea or at one of the picnic tables while crunching perhaps too noisily on sesame seaweed or tamari-baked nuts. Snow or shine, I carried an open book on the ten-minute walk from the library to the apartment. If I was awake when at last my young daughter Maria fell asleep, I read, and if, by some mixture of good fortune and great effort, I woke before her and could leave our bed undetected, I crept directly to my books. I read on the porch of the nursery where she spent her weekday mornings, four of which I spent working at the library, a precious one of which (Fridays) I spent on the floor, in various fetal positions, reading.

That first day I must have forgotten him (How difficult it is now to fathom!), walked my usual route through the museum garden, then on to the state road with a book in my hand. At the slight break in the trees that was our road, chances are my steps became heavier. Upon arriving at the apartment—a lean, towering shack reminiscent of the Once-ler's, built with nothing but Var's ingenuity and scraps from wrecked houses on a patch of land left to us by his grandmother Chica—likely I went upstairs to read, if not silently to myself, then aloud to Maria with whom I shared, among so many things, a love of books. (Var also loved books but disliked both being read to and reading aloud.)

For Maria, simply reading the book was never enough; she wanted to act the story out with me afterwards. She played the starring roles and I, mildly content to be the root to her flower, supported them. I didn't mind. It was a kind of reading, I told myself, a way of becoming closer to the text and to Maria. She was never a child who could be lured to sleep by the sound of a book being read, such sounds brought her to life. Though exhausting (it was usually I who drifted off, even as I read), I found it to be a beautiful tendency, a sign of good health that one's eyes should open rather than shut at the sound of a human voice telling a story.

We read in the bedroom for there was no front room. At the top of the dark, narrow staircase, instead of a parlor or a sitting room, one was met by our version of an unclean butler: the foul gape of the dim, squalid bathroom that, after hours of scrubbing, never looked clean. I had no choice but to perform, with a kind of futility, my ablutions within it. Every night it greeted me, a stained towel draped over each of its rusting arms, and filled me with a dirty sense of despair. (In these moments I tried to be grateful for the running water. One feels ashamed to grumble when one's husband builds the house with his own hands, but Var was not a carpenter but a wood carver, simply a man determined to put a roof over our heads. I have a weakness for determination and a love for the makers of this world.)

Neither my mother nor my father would have tolerated such an affront to civility and cleanliness. The "washroom" was much too close to the entrance of the apartment and ruined beyond rehabilitation. They would have removed it and started afresh or—and this would have been my father's preference—they would have moved. It would have been intolerable for him to live without a reading room and he loved to discover new places and things. He was not bothered in the least by leaving a familiar place for he loved so much to arrive at a new one. I shared my father's aversion to filth and his love of books, but I lacked his adventurous spirit. He had been correct when he complained I always took the path of least resistance.

Several days later, the young man returned to use his new card. Strangely (for in most instances I held fast as a steel trap to the scant details I had), I don't remember what he checked out, only that it was not a book but a film, more than one, all comedies, which was to become his habit. He asked, with a serious face, to borrow one of the computers. Conscious of his beauty (dark eyes lit with cunning, eyebrows threatening to merge, hair chaotic and elegant as storm waves), yet betraying nothing, I said of course, happy to be giving him something and with so little effort. There were several public computers scattered throughout the library. He chose the one closest to me, in full view of the front desk. I'm convinced he chose the shortest distance between himself and the machine without giving our closeness a second thought. I too was not disturbed by his choice or his proximity. They reinforced my claim to obsolescence.

I resumed working, greeted other patrons, then left to fill and tidy the nearby shelves. On my way back to the desk, I observed him working intently, wearing a pair of headphones he must have brought from home and put on when my back was turned. (The library headphones were silver and small, his were large and made of black leather.) He appeared to be writing. As I strode past him I felt a pang of curiosity, the first of many. What could a young man of his age be writing? (In the beginning I didn't allow myself to consider him as being any age below eighteen. I chose eighteen less because of his physical appearance than for that number's magically permissive quality—the one so sure and solid next to infinity turned on its head. Yes he was at least eighteen I told myself, probably somewhere in his twenties.) Perhaps he was composing an essay for a college application. Or perhaps he was already in college and had a term paper to finish. Or, and even as my mind formed the sentence I knew it was absurd, perhaps he was a writer working on a book. I knew even then he was no writer. The next day he borrowed the same computer again and continued writing. I too worked without feeling any sense of interruption.

* * *

I have lived on a series of islands and I began as an island: I, an obscure piece of earth, floating choiceless within my mother's sea. The first island I encountered outside of England was Alcatraz, home to the notorious prison off the coast of San Francisco. I was eight. My parents and I had journeyed to America under the auspices of visiting a distant cousin of my mother's. (Deeply anti-American, they would have been quick to deny any interest in sightseeing.) Of the fog for which San Francisco is well known, I remember nothing; to my pale, unaccustomed eyes, most days were blindingly sunny.

One mercifully gray day, we rode with the cousin on a ferry across the bay. The boat paused at a safe distance so that we might behold the grim monstrosity while the guide recited a history complete with highlights of various prisoners' failed attempts to escape. I liked the idea of being placed in the sea as punishment and into a building so fortified. Were not the island's inhabitants as protected from the world as the world was from them? How quiet the grounds must have been, how gray and solitary. As a child, I envied the men their setting. I did not pause to imagine the cells stuffed with rapists and murderers. Only years later did I imagine such terrible things. Only after I met the young man did I wonder if the prisoners could hear the blue crashing of waves from their cells, the way I could hear the yellow school bus from my bedroom.

There were other boats—sailboats, speedboats, freight boats—out on the water with us. Then I imagined we were all moving toward Alcatraz, my child's mind believing there were no journeys other than our own. We spent so little time at the cousin's house and I remembered so little else from the trip that for years afterward when I pictured her, I pictured her on Alcatraz Island. I believed all Californians lived there on the water, at once surrounded by beauty and trapped in a prison.

The island on which we have settled has much in common with the English countryside: sheep grazing upon greenery, stone walls, gray skies, the mysterious expanse of the sea. Though here one is more apt to notice the hush of fall than the hush of winter, for it arrives on the thundering heels of so many departing guests, those patrons of paradise, their traveling housekeepers and gardeners, young nannies and builders, fit instructors of sailing and swimming.

One morning in September we wake to find them gone, the town as it was. Stillness, trees, a few neighbors. The wind howls as if wounded by all the departures. Leaves fall to the ground and then, like the visitors, they too float back across the water or up to the sky. The days grow darker. The bravest swimmers have their last swims. Our eyes soften, our lids become heavy. School begins and the streets empty further. By November, no foot traffic is visible through the glass. Gardening and construction vehicles, fuel trucks and delivery vans begin making their way up-island to invisible seaside compounds and modernist castles in the woods. Periodically one hears buses on the state road, a few cars, the doomy clap of a hunter's shot at dawn, the cinematic clip of a horse's whinny. The waves of the sea are near but not audible (unless there's a storm, in a storm one feels as if the entire island is a ship and we are all of us together at sea on some perilous but temporary journey).

The air is cold enough to turn an orange but such trees don't grow here. Little fruit grows here. The soil is difficult. We have apples of various sorts (though not nearly enough to feed our inhabitants, every apple in the store is imported from the mainland). Diminutive peaches. Child-size pears. Autumn olives. Beach plums. A minute crop of blueberries, raspberries, strawberries, melons. There must be a place more extreme than this, a part of the world that is completely fruitless, a place where there is nothing to pick. Of tree fruit, nothing. Of melons, none. Of berries, not even one.

One by one, the shops and restaurants close down. Gardens are put to sleep. A portion of the population flies south. There is virtually nowhere to go (unless you count the woods, within the woods the possibilities are endless). If you don't mind being preached to, there's the corner church on Sundays. If you don't mind sitting out in the gloom, there's the general store where people go to mail letters, buy coffee and food. On the porch they read papers, watch passersby and the street, sometimes a tractor or a bicycle, a gang of motorcycles, a presidential motorcade. The store opens at 7:00 and shuts at 6:00. The porch is lit all night. The town restaurant is open on weekends and will soon shut completely. It is a dry town. The closest thing to a public house is the library, which is open seven days a week and till 9:00 on Mondays. Our "winter hours" begin in the fall. Like the Mishima novel about a boy who spies on his mother's lovemaking, the island has two seasons. Summer swallows spring and winter obliterates fall.

For the first time in months the library is quiet. *It's so quiet*, people say. Some wrap their coats about themselves more tightly and are frightened by the sudden emptiness, while others smile Mona Lisa smiles, exuding happiness and secret knowledge. In the great absence of all the departed visitors, we become acutely aware of one another. When I say *we* I'm referring to strangers. The reverse is true of familiars. At least it was for us. As the island grew quiet, so did the shack. On Fridays when Maria was away and we were alone, Var and I retreated more deeply into our own thoughts. In the silence we forgot one another more completely. But strangers and acquaintances—librarians and borrowers, shoppers and clerks, those milling about town or sitting in cafés—sense one another for the first time.

I was no exception. I was as common as the weather, as was he, as were we. Show me a middle-aged woman who lacks desire and I will show you a liar. Show me an unusual young man and I will strip him down to commonness. I have no intention of making public excuses. I do find myself looking within for reasons I might give, if only to myself, for my own behavior. I obsessively recount the past in search of my missteps. At the outset I was able to tolerate his proximity with relative ease.

I insist I would have proceeded along my ethically-sound

trajectory had it not been for two things. You may say it is arbitrary to reduce it to two. That there were a slew of factors—my temperament (sensual but prone to fits of sadness), my history (born and raised in England of a Midlands housekeeper and a Japanese expatriate economist, an immigrant at eighteen, an orphan at twenty), my circumstances, (deep isolation, an inactive marriage)—goes without saying. When I say two things I mean two thorns that, when I least expected it, pierced me.

* * *

The next time he seemed to be in a hurry, which irritated me slightly. There are times when I resent being drawn into the vortex of a stranger's stressful day, I resent being an ameliorative figure with whose efficient help another item on her to-do list might be triumphantly crossed out. His manner, newly brisk, had lost its former softness. He spoke in a rush. These were, I learned later, symptoms of his nervousness, but at the time I read them as signs of someone making demands. He had the look of one who has been protected from manual labor. His black hooded sweatshirt with its white soccer emblem, his black jeans as crisp and clean as my father's gray suits.

Pressing too far forward against the counter, with a note of insistence in his voice he said, "I was told if there's a movie I want you could get it for me in a week." I felt a flare of irritation. It surprised me, my capacity to feel such annoyance with someone I knew so little and had up to then only admired. All at once, as if the lenses in my glasses had changed, I saw him as a teenager. I saw the protruding lump of skin that held his chewing tobacco and gave him the look of someone suffering from a sublabial tumor.

"That depends," I said curtly, "on whether we have it in our collection or will have to borrow it from another library." I felt supremely detached from that distorted face of self-seeking youth. It was a moment I would often revisit, a moment whose power I would try and fail to retrieve, the moment I saw him as simply another patron to attend to.

As the moments passed and he became less nervous, his soft manner returned. He said the title of the film, one I recognized (with a maternal spurt of pride in his youthful refinement) as being a classic, the actors of which preceded even my generation, and in the same instant I realized the young man's voice was utterly familiar to me but I couldn't place it. The smell of his tobacco, which to my mind tasted faintly of toffee, suddenly reached me. I had handed him a request card to fill out and he was already handing it back to me. I was conscious of how little time was left for him to speak before our transaction would end, but he must have managed to say a few more words and I to hear them for I heard the voice again and this time identical to the gravelly, rough-throated voice of my favorite film star. At the sound, my lenses changed again; I could no longer see him as ordinary. Like a thorn in a fairy tale that bewitches the one who is pricked, his voice pierced me.

The second thorn was more difficult to isolate. Perhaps it was his dark eye darting up to meet mine or its swift flight down to the card; perhaps I had taken subconscious note of his anxiety or had harbored the recognition all along. Regardless, what pierced me was knowledge: I had gained his attention. His hand trembled slightly as he held it out to take the new card. With that, I went flying off track like a boy's slot car, only to find myself being lifted up and placed onto another track. Though I could sense the dangerous curves and revolutions looming ahead, I drove on, cleaving like a magnet to the new track, powered by a hidden electricity that I can only describe in retrospect as joy.

As soon as the door shut behind him, shamelessly, in a fever, I related the incident to my co-worker Nella, whose untidy desk was nearby. She had been the only other librarian to see him. I appealed to her in much the same way that a mourner, once her loved one has departed, appeals to the living for anecdotal information, anything that might keep the memory of her loved one alive. Though unlike such mourners I was ecstatic. For my beloved—far from being dead—had just been born. When at first I asked Nella for her opinion of him she yielded nothing. It was only when I pressed her further that she finally surrendered in a disinterested voice that he reminded her of Var—a disappointing remark that was of no use to me.

While Nella was on break, I accosted my supervisor Siobhan (the quiet, sardonic head of circulation with whom I was quite close) and described, in painfully hushed tones, the scene afresh for her. I pulled the young man's record up so that she might see his lovely, hyphenated name in full and so that I might receive the thrill of seeing his name being seen by another. Such were my dessert-like pleasures in the beginning.

Siobhan's first reaction to my news that I had developed a "patron crush" was a dubious question: "Is that legal?," her face flushed a little by the possibility. I answered promptly in the affirmative and carefully framed my narrative so as to underscore its element of pure fantasy. Mine was a fantasy I wouldn't dare pursue and what I told then was the truth.

Here I must add that Siobhan had always been a moral compass on the staff. Though far from hindering me, this fact somehow heightened my sense of excitement in telling her. Virtuous as she was, Siobhan was no miser with affection; there was in that upright heart of hers a tendency toward openness, her heart so dense with compassion that I nicknamed her Pema. (She later retaliated by calling me The Lowly Lady Nabokov, never guessing how very lowly I had become.) When I came to the bit about the young man's voice, she let out a little gasp. We shared an appreciation of the same film star! Her open heart opened further still.

The procuring of a sympathetic audience was perhaps my

first misstep. Though at the time my logic ran counter to that: Wouldn't I, by revealing myself to others, be ensuring my own accountability? Surely I wouldn't dare approach a young man in broad daylight under my co-workers' knowing, watchful eyes! Such logic dictated the more co-workers I told, the better. There were only three out of eight librarians to whom I failed to confess. One was a man whose sad eyes, in the presence of children, shone with a pedophilic twinkle and who wore, but did not activate, a hearing aid that resembled a doll's liver; he was a man who might have understood all too well my predicament but with whom it was difficult if not impossible to discreetly share secrets. Another librarian had a schedule whose shifts rarely overlapped with mine, though if our shifts had coincided I might still never have confessed, for my feelings towards her were cool and it was always with heat and affection that I spoke of the young man. The last was someone I was quite fond of, someone to whom I often considered confessing but whose sense of propriety won out in the end. She became, for me, an emblem of Reality (Moral Implications, Possible Jail Time etc.) incompatible with my Fantasy, whether lived out or not. All the rest knew and I rather think they enjoyed themselves as I brought them along for a ride on my shiny black track.

A week passed. Every morning I left the apartment at 9:00 under the pretense that my shift began at 9:15 when in fact it began at 10:00. The senior librarians prepared the library for the public and I was merely expected to arrive before the doors opened. During Maria's infancy this omission had seemed the easiest way to procure time for myself and once I had built the time in, it was difficult to give up. Not once did Var question me about it. (What a pleasant change it was from our usual battles over time! What freedom my small deception afforded me!)

I walked in my cross-trainers down the state road. (I had

become the kind of woman who walks to work in hideous yet comfortable shoes and changes into another slightly less hideous, considerably less comfortable pair when she arrives, the kind of woman who ensures that she has something, however trifling—a stroll in comfortable shoes while reading a novel by twilight—to look forward to at the end of every day.) Most mornings, instead of going to the library, I turned left on Music Street then left again on a small dirt road that led to the woods.

The trail in was tunnellike; the trees on either side arched to meet one another. It was a private trail leading to private land. As soon as I set my foot upon it two large dogs barked distantly yet viciously in response, giving the torpid ox of my pulse its daily whipping. The NO TRESPASSING sign nailed to one of the trees gave me a start as well, though I had once been warmly invited by the owner to walk there for the purpose of showing Maria the "magical fairyland." Still, I felt I was violating an unspoken agreement. The owner had never said outright that I could visit it alone. I speculated hopefully that if the woman had a sliver of a heart (surely people who used the phrase "magical fairyland" were endowed with at least that), if she had known the extent to which her forbidden preserve daily drew the iron weight of my body out of bed like a restorative magnet, she would have forgiven my trespasses.

The last bit of tunnel was downhill and at the bottom the trees gave way to a large rushy pond upon whose surface there was often, gliding serenely, a glossy profusion of ducks that then fled in a frantic green and black flapping. A wooden bridge carried one over the pond's edge, over the top of a waterfall. One could follow the trail down to a stone bench at the base of the falls or follow it deeper into the forest and cross over a series of modest bridges—most of them single planks of wood or flat stones, all of which crossed the small river that traversed, like a black artery, the body of the forest, bringing fresh blood to some remote, unseen heart.

The owner had set out candles and wind chimes along the way, presumably for the enjoyment of children and/or romantics. The long series of bridges ended with one very long plank that led to a wooden deck complete with wooden bench, large candle, and stone statue of the Buddha, a place where such visitors could give thanks for their good fortune.

When I visited the fairyland alone, I rarely got as far as the Buddha or even the planks and the stones. I walked from the top of the waterfall down to the stone bench where I sat, (suddenly Buddha-like myself), and watched the water flow. What bliss! What *aananda*! I could have stared at the waterfall for hours though I typically had seven minutes before it was time for me to report to the library, my fear always that, while I sat bathing in oblivion, my watch would stop and I would unwittingly be late.

* * *

By the time the young man came in again he had incurred fines totaling $12.00. I had the sorry job of informing him that he had exceeded the $10.00 limit and would not be permitted to check out materials until he paid. He was attempting to check out *Fast Times at Ridgemont High*, which struck me simultaneously as trash and (for a boy his age) a cult classic. (Queer how trash that endures comes to be regarded as classic.)

As gently as I could I said, "The limit on fines is $10.00. You could pay $2.00 and bring food in for the food pantry for the rest next time." Eager to give him a way out, I realized too late I had offended him.

"I have money," he announced and quickly withdrew from his pant pocket a black leather billfold, the sort that fathers carry. His nail-bitten fingers shook as he slid the crisp ten and two ones from the wallet and handed them to me. The bills looked as if they'd earlier been removed from the inside of a child's birthday card.

"Thank you," I said, feeling already a pang of guilt. "You know we don't charge fines for books," I teased. "So if you ever check out a book, you won't need to worry about fines."

He half smiled and said slowly—he almost always spoke slowly—in a voice that brought to mind a chain being dragged through a gravel pit on a dark night, "We have so many books in our house, I can't imagine ever needing to borrow one from a library." He looked down at the green book request cards and a wave of hair fell like a small curtain over his eyes.

Did I detect a bit of defensiveness in his reply? Had I overestimated my own power? I thought for the first time of the sociology of illicit affairs between adults and minors, parents and children, teachers and students, employers and employees. The term *power differential* returned to me from textbooks I had read during my college years. It seemed that I had intimidated him simply by being who I was, the vision of myself as "a middle-aged librarian" suddenly clear to me as the now familiar lump under his lip. (Was I really middle-aged?! If I lived to be one hundred, technically I wouldn't reach the middle until fifty.) If only he knew I was the last woman on earth who might be impressed by the existence of money in his wallet. Not for a moment had I doubted his capacity to produce such an emblem of maturity. Nor did I doubt his level of literacy or care if he ever checked out a book. If only he knew that I had complete (though completely unfounded) faith in his intelligence. This was an essential part of what drew me to him: my profound sense of the person he was, the person I would certainly discover if only I had the opportunity.

And yet clearly this intuiting was not mutual. On the contrary he perceived me as someone to whom he must say: *I have money. I read books*. Was this the much-writ about power differential at play or was it merely one young man's insecurities? It was impossible to tell, so I resolved to try to be more sensitive the next time. We hadn't even touched hands and I was beginning to learn that one of the virtues of having a much younger lover is that one is poised to be patient. One enjoys the kind of loving tolerance one has for one's child. The awareness that he or she hasn't lived, and so can't possibly know, underlies everything. Before we had uttered one another's names, the power differential bred mercy.

* * *

The young man began visiting the library approximately once a week, a frequency that, it occurred to me later, likely corresponded to the avoidance of fines if it corresponded to anything. At first, to my anxious, inquisitive mind, he seemed to alternate between Mondays and Thursdays, but in truth there was never a perfect pattern. His only fairly reliable habit was that he nearly always arrived five or ten minutes before closing, so that there was never as leisurely a feel to our interactions as I would have liked. Between encounters, I would pine openly for a glimpse of him with certain of my co-workers. When he happened, inauspiciously, to visit the library in my absence, Siobhan would discreetly let me know and bring his record up so that together we might view his current items and comment upon them.

I confess I watched the door, my black head swerving like a tire each time it opened. I avoided being assigned to the children's room and the basement, for these were sections of the library he never visited. It was difficult enough when I was assigned to the main room to somehow ensure, without drawing attention, that it was I who helped him and not another librarian.

On one occasion, I was on the phone and saw him coming. I worked to extinguish the conversation so that I might be released to greet him. He was still a fair distance from the desk and walking at a moderate pace. There was no reason why I shouldn't be free in time. I persisted in keeping my answers clipped, my tone final, but there was no end to the maniac's list of questions. I considered hanging up. It is physically painful to be torn between one's professional obligation to a disembodied voice and the desire to move closer to one's approaching Adonis. I felt the pain in my chest. As if a high pitch was being struck; my glass heart threatened to shatter. Heroically, with a smile on my face, I fought to end the conversation and was about to emerge victorious when the library director, stylish, effective (though, unaware as she was of the young man's special status, tragically ineffective for my purposes), smiling broadly, held out her hand to take his card.

The unrelenting caller chattered on. I gave up, it was too late anyhow, so I surrendered to being a receptacle for his words and used the phone pressed to my ear as a cover, a perch from which I might surreptitiously watch the young man as he waited in fidgety silence for the director to check out his films. In the end, this mishap proved beneficial for I saw that he was tensely aware of me for the duration. His dark eyes glanced sideways in my direction as I held the phone and at last crept up to meet mine. We smiled hello. We were too far away to be in conversation.

The director remarked, referring to the comedies he was borrowing, "I bet you'll have fun with these!" We were friendly librarians. Whether or not she was being flirtatious, whether or not she found him attractive, I couldn't be sure, but it was difficult to believe otherwise. That she was happily married to a stone butch by the name of Tony and old enough to be the young man's grandmother did nothing to alter my blind vision of him as universally irresistible. (Biologically speaking, I too was old enough to have accomplished such a feat, though I would have had to have been a very early bloomer and I had been nothing of the sort. Perhaps this, I thought with satisfaction, had been the reason all along for my retarded development. Of course boarding at the Hatfield School for Girls hadn't helped.)

This incident provided me with yet another reason to disseminate my secret to the staff. After he'd gone, I lightly informed the director—who was a playfully good sport—of the young man's special status. She apologized extravagantly and promised in typical mensch fashion that next time she would leave him to me (assuming she would recognize him, which, as it turned out, she would not). The well-meaning director's oblivion aside, my colleagues (Nella in particular, who could easily have had a second career as an air traffic controller so strict was her visual command of the front walkway) were immensely helpful during this initial phase of the relationship.

Despite my daily vigils I was surprisingly slow to detect his approach. I was a worker who tended toward engrossment regardless of the frivolity of my task. I was easily captivated by the filling out of forms, the slicing of paper into squares, the placing of books in their proper order. And I was so intent upon the thought of his arrival that I often missed the actual moment he arrived. More often than not, it was Nella who alerted me as she glanced out the window over her blue-stemmed glasses, a slight frown on her face, "Your prayers have been answered."

Imagine my alarm when a week later it was I who saw him approach through the picture window, accompanied by, of all people, his mother (Siobhan had been quick to identify her as such just a few weeks before). I was at once overjoyed to see him and mortified by the prospect of encountering him in the presence of someone who would be a walking, talking reminder of the chronological chasm between us, a woman who would have every right to hate me if she knew my thoughts.

"My God," I said to Nella under my breath, "he's with his mother."

She looked coolly at the winsome pair and then at me without expression. Firmly, she pressed the bridge of her glasses into place as if to say: *Everything's fine. Don't panic.*

Before I had time to think further, Mother and Son were in the front door. I needn't have worried about those first few minutes of contact for as they passed the front desk the young man kept his head down like a convict while his mother managed a strained smile and said hello. She was very pretty (one could easily trace the lineage) though discrepantly ill at ease, exuding as she did an odd combination of beauty and unhappiness (shades of Rachel Ward's bone structure displaying the tentative, agony-shaped sulk of Emily Dickinson—any heterosexual priest with a pulse would have found her appealing). It was the first time I had seen either of them in the company of another. As they made their way toward the DVDs, I stifled an urge to run out of the building. I suppressed my mounting anxiety in an effort to quickly reason out the best way to handle our impending encounter.

They were lovely together. Both dark-haired and dark-eyed. I felt the inappropriate urge to photograph them. She stepped up to the counter and he hung back a bit. I was reminded of the way a mother is tied to her infant in the early days; when the infant cries, the woman's insides contract. The thread was still there between them, I could see it in the way she led and he followed, the relief with which he allowed himself to be released from the obligation to speak. It surprised me that he was clearly more relaxed in her presence than he had been alone. One hears stories of teenagers estranged from or embarrassed by their parents. In this respect, he was more like a younger child who constantly tracks the mother for comfort and is on edge when she is out of sight. He seemed, if anything, grateful for her protection, for the opportunity to be in proximity to me without the pressure to converse, near me and yet safe from my advances.

They spoke in soft, teasing murmurs.

"You haven't seen this?" he laughed, pointing to one of the films.

"You know I don't sit around all day watching stuff." She seemed to be hinting at the fact that he did, but either he didn't notice or he didn't mind.

"I know," he said, backing away another step, looking at the carpet and smiling. "I just thought you might have seen it," he trailed off.

They shared the habit of never focusing on one object for very long. Her eyes flitted from the stack of films to the pencil can to my face, as his scanned various points on the carpet. She smiled at me briefly. It was an anguished smile but there was a scintilla in her eyes that lit my affection, which I suppose I'd been quietly holding out to her like a piece of kindling all along. I carefully stamped the films and handed them back to her. I couldn't help wanting her to love me.

"These are due November 26," I said too warmly, like one pretending to be a librarian for the purposes of gathering intelligence and currying favor. I was a phony, an interloper, a spy! I was a prurient woman who wanted a mother to love me so that she might entrust her son to me in order that I might undress him, mount him, do with him as I pleased. At the same time I knew she could never agree to such an arrangement, that I could never reveal my true intentions. This gave her the moral high ground (for she was herself while I was an impostor) which made me love her (and want her love) even more.

My only wish at that moment was to be granted a future transaction with the young man sans his loveworthy mother. How modest our desires become in the presence of certain emblems of Reality. Indeed in our case, the emblem of the Mother was the most devastating. He did not look up to say or nod goodbye but kept his restless eyes on the carpet as they went, the two of us already criminals in our way. He the convict with his head down in shame and I the spy, friendly in my disguise, not yet caught, my crime just beginning.

And so it was with us; we met on a more or less weekly basis, sometimes alone at the counter, sometimes surrounded by staff and patrons and phone calls, on occasion in the presence of his mother, always in public and always at the mercy of external forces. Our interactions lasted a few minutes at best and outside the perfunctory words exchanged between any patron and staff member there seemed to be, on the average, room for one additional sentence, a meager tidbit for an appetite such as mine. I began to prepare sentences in advance, thinking hard upon how I might get the most out of each one.

It occurred to me that the most suitable sort of sentence for one whose pangs of curiosity were as sharp as my own was the question. Question composition became my pastime, a meditative practice I undertook while shelving, while affixing labels to the spines of books, while feeding patron records to the steel teeth of the shredder like so many privately swallowed desires. My practice was not confined to idle moments at the library (even as my hands busied themselves, there was an element of idleness to my brain) but continued as I walked along the highway, as I stood at the small stove frying noodles for Maria and Var (I began, perversely, cooking Var's favorite foods as a form of penance for sins I hadn't committed), as I lay next to Maria, waiting for sleep to release me from one reality and take me to the next, my eyes, without glasses, straining to see the stars whose magnificent designs might bear for me some message. *What makes you happy? What makes you laugh? What do you wish you could change?* The practice ceased when he appeared and resumed when he was gone. Certainly I must have thought of other things between encounters, but I can't now remember what.

I quickly ruled out the obvious, questions the answers to which I could not have wanted more, but could not, without violating one or more laws of etiquette, ask. They were the questions that cut with dizzying speed to the chase: *Are you available? May I kiss you? May I make love to you now in the stacks?* I gained new respect for those men who thought little of posing such questions on a regular basis and to complete strangers. The very men I once felt assaulted by now struck me as boldly in touch with Fate and the Implications of Time. If not now, when? The bomb of time was ticking!

In trying to slow my frantic pace, I had done a series of calculations, all of which returned the same discouraging result. There was no time for a leisurely courtship, a long engagement, a four-year college career. Within a year, the trim figure I had managed to maintain would surely sag, my skin's elasticity would, without warning, snap. Within five, I would be infertile. Within ten, my hair would be white. Within fifteen, I'd be old enough to withdraw money from my retirement account. There was no time for patience or common sense or delayed gratifications of any kind. The time was now and there was much to be discovered.

There were the questions pertaining to his person. *What's your favorite film and why? Who's your favorite filmmaker? Are you close to your father?* There were the questions pertaining to his whereabouts. *Where do you live? Do you have a job? Are you in college? Do you have plans to leave the island?* All of which I intended to ask at some point but which seemed too mundane, necessary but not revealing enough. In the beginning I felt I shouldn't waste my one question (though perhaps I might squeeze in two) on any query that didn't reveal something intimate about him or that might result in a "yes" or "no" answer.

Everything was different in real time. I had finally settled on a question, one I hoped would extract the maximum amount of meaning while necessitating a minimum amount of effort on his part: *Would you rather be: a) a filmmaker, b) a film critic, or*

c) a film star? With the utterance of a single letter I stood to learn something essential about his self-concept and his conception of the world, not to mention something about the nature of his relationship to film. (I had become convinced that he was no ordinary viewer of films but watched films with purpose, with a certain destiny in mind. That is, I fancied him a filmmaker. Not one who currently makes films but one who will grow up to do so. Part of the appeal of youth is its immense sense of possibility.)

My theory was corroborated when, during his next visit, he borrowed neither a film nor a book but *The Odyssey* and *Crime and Punishment* on CD. As I watched him set the plastic cases sheepishly (as if I would be judging his selection) on the counter, my sincere and totalizing surprise erased any memory I had of my well-rehearsed question.

Unable to stop myself from smiling, I picked up *Crime and Punishment*. "What brought this on?" I asked.

"Oh," he said, smiling in return his mother's pained and pretty smile. "That one's for Mom." His omission of "my" preceding the word "Mom" tugged at my wildly beating heart. It seemed to me people who omitted possessive pronouns were capable of great intimacies, those that defied context and transcended possession. I opened the *Odyssey* case and scanned the barcode. He nodded slightly toward it and as he did so that small curtain of hair fell before his eyes again as if to indicate that any impending disclosures would be accompanied in equal parts by concealment. "Have you seen the movie *O Brother, Where Art Thou?*"

"I have," I said, racking my brain to remember the plot. "A long time ago. I saw it when it first came out," I added, wanting to sound like part of his circle, someone who would see the film immediately upon its release, instead sounding the bell of alarm that I was going to movie theaters before he could read.

"I read that *The Odyssey* was their inspiration for making

the movie. So I want to check it out." He had the look of a Romani who has been sent to prep school, well-scrubbed but out of place, eyes loaded down by memories of a childhood spent in Transylvania dreaming of films.

"Very nice," I said. Kindly, staid librarian thinking bold, prophetic thoughts: *You will be a filmmaker. You will fall in love. I see artistic accomplishment and forbidden love in your future.* "You'll have to tell me how it is. It's been even longer since I've read *The Odyssey,*" I said, withholding the phrase, *It was before you were born.* "These are due December 3," I said, less to inform him of our policy than to elicit his customary rough-throated *thank you,* the aural pleasure of which I felt I should thank him for.

It was our most protracted exchange. He had asked me a question. He had confided an interest. My inner rib cage was trembling, hands, trembling. Every centimeter of my face was flushed, my hairline and earlobes ablaze. I was so short of breath, I wondered if I had not become an instant asthmatic. Nella, working circumspectly at her desk, gave no indication of having heard anything. I suspected she'd heard everything. Like the only witness to a heinous crime, I felt the need to flee the crime scene.

"I'll be right back," I said. She looked up from her papers just long enough to raise one eyebrow conspiratorially. I walked briskly to the children's room where Siobhan was processing ILLs and stood rose-faced and trembling in front of her desk.

"Help me to calm myself!" I commanded in a whisper, afraid that I would involuntarily cry out or erupt into uncontrollable laughter or break into enthusiastic song if someone did not bridle me at once.

Siobhan took her tortoiseshell glasses off and let them hang on their woven cord.

"What's goin' on?" she said, parodying her Midwestern drawl for my benefit. I blurted out the gist of what had happened, the effect of which was not unlike finding that one's deeply transformative and endlessly complicated dream may be summarized in a single sentence.

"Oh yeah," she said. "I saw your friend. You like that big, dark eyes, dark, wavy hair thing, huh?"

At least she had recognized him. It was more than I could say for the director, who, it occurred to me, might do well to get her eyes checked. "He's a cute kid," Siobhan conceded and then opened her stack of green cards into a fan and began to fan me. "You better cool off, lady! I can feel your heat from here!" Easy for her to say, she at least had the occasional "afternoon delight" while her teenage kids were at school. (*Honey, if I didn't have that, I wouldn't have a marriage!*)

"I think he fancies me," I confided, my thoughts roaming lustily in several directions at once.

"He better not!" Siobhan herself quivered now the way the red needle of a fine moral compass tends to quiver in the presence of moral drift. She gathered her cards into a tidy stack and smacked the desk for emphasis.

"Why not?!" I was in no mood for deprivation.

She set her cards down, reached for a scrap piece of paper and wrote the following message in pencil: *Because you are married and he is the same age as my son!* Siobhan had discovered that the young man was a "friend" of her son's on Facebook and that he too was a senior in high school, age seventeen. Prior to this discovery, our difference in age did nothing to deter me for I had conveniently, grossly underestimated it, my most delusional estimate being twenty-nine. Now I turned away from his actual age the way one turns away from an overly graphic image. Why contemplate statutory rape laws and prison terms when no crime had yet been committed?

She returned her glasses to her face and picked up the green cards. "Aw, you're not fun!" I said, borrowing a phrase coined by Maria.

"Just sayin'," she said, tapping me on the wrist with the pink eraser end of her Ticonderoga, "probably better keep this one at the visual level. You know what happens when the other senses get involved."

My problem precisely. I didn't know any longer! And which was worse, that I had forgotten my other senses or that they were beginning, all too quickly, to come back to me?

* * *

The many hours I spent in bed I spent with Maria. We slept entwined or draped upon one another in the form of an x, ear to ear or head to foot or as spoons in a farmhouse drawer. She never slept alone as surely as Var and I never slept together. He was too light a sleeper to sleep with another.

Maria was no solitary sleeper, no relinquisher of my flesh. No matter what the positions of our bodies were in sleep, she managed to hook a part of herself—a foot, an ankle, an elbow, a knee—over me so that I couldn't move, so that I would remain near enough for her to hear my heart beating for the duration of the night. Our closeness did not prevent us from dreaming we had lost one another. I would dream for hours of wandering a city in search of her, only to wake to find her atop me. She had nightmares of being kidnapped while lying in my arms. Our closeness never made us complacent. We understood each other's value; we understood that even the one closest to us must be sought.

In the beginning my greatest resentment toward Var was his refusal to free me of Maria's company. But after a few years of that fruitless bargaining, I began to prefer her company to that of most others, including his. There was still the matter of solitude, which I craved, but the very idea of trying to obtain it by way of Var was as questionable to me as asking one's warden for a cake on one's birthday. Even if, against all reasonable expectation, the fellow appeared at the door of one's cell with Black Forest cake on a white china plate, one might not feel inspired to eat it. There might be trickery involved, manipulation, the possibility of poison, and of course, the matter of one's pride. And so Var lay in his solitary room while Maria and I held each other till morning.

After the appearance of the young man, I no longer fell asleep in tandem with Maria nor did I creep out of bed to read once she was sleeping. When I was sure she wouldn't wake, I allowed myself the pleasure of thinking about him. The nervous darting of his eyes, the toffee taste of the smell of his tobacco, the sound of his rough-throated voice reporting on the many books in his house. I could easily imagine him alone in a room. Once he existed there, I could join him. We could do as we liked. Without having laid a fifth finger upon me and in only a few weeks' time, he had given me more pleasure than Var had in years. There was something obscene and unjust about this. For the two of them were equally passive in these matters, but the young man pleased me simply by being himself. As I lay in the dark enjoying my body's pulsations, this injustice was not lost to me and I became accustomed to the small volume of tears that would run out of me as soon as my body was still again.

Yet in the morning my sadness would be forgotten. I would wake with a fresh sense of purpose as I prepared myself for another day at the library, another day on which I might encounter him. Although I had failed to pose a single question from my ridiculous queue, I was pleased with, even a bit alarmed by, our progress. The sensation of being on a dangerous and terrifying track, racing toward a joyful collision, persisted. I felt alternately like a daredevil piece of the finest machinery and a child's toy being controlled by an unseen operator. I had come a long way since my days of self-assigned obsolescence. Indeed I was speeding along with a new sense of satisfaction, feeling unusually primped, alert to beauty, and exhilarated by the pursuit. But the truth was, I wanted more.

I could see that not far up ahead, a piece of the track was missing. I could not reach the infuriatingly lovely black loops and twisting figure eights I saw in the distance without first finding or building the missing pieces of track. There was a gap to be filled, a chasm to be crossed. How I went about it seemed of the utmost importance. If I hurled myself across the void too recklessly, I might shatter into bits when I landed. If I went too slowly, I might drop into the chasm without making it safely across. How could I reach my hand across the library counter and touch him? How does one do something inappropriate in as appropriate a manner as possible?

* * *

Inspired by Nella's comment that she had seen the young man there one Saturday, I, rather inanely and with the fervor of a religious devotee on pilgrimage, began to visit Main Street as often as I could, with the hope that I too might be so blessed. As soon as Maria had finished her afternoon snack I would ask, with as much story time animation as I could muster, "Would you like to go to the city?" Having once visited New York, she knew there were no cities to be found on our island, that the city to which I referred was nothing but a quaint street with a few shops and cafés, a city only in comparison to the hush of our rural world. "Oh yes!" she would say, fluttering her eyelashes and swatting the air with one hand, in imitation of any number of animated heroines she had encountered. "I just love the city!"

I would take on the aspect of a gallant prince, bow deeply and offer her my hand. We would walk thus, down the highway to the bus stop where we would wait for the #2 bus to take us down-island. Our favorite bakery, Colette's, whose almond croissants rivaled New York's (someday, I promised, I would take her to Paris, though I did not know how), was the only bakery on the island that stayed open year-round.

During these "city" excursions I pampered her. We split the mountainous croissant down the middle and I allowed her a glass of steamed milk. As we sat facing each other at a table next to the window, I tried continually to take her in (her large brown eyes that were shaped much like the almonds on our pastry, her soft Gerber mouth, the well-spaced little row of teeth that had the look of a toy picket fence, the cheeks that retained the plump exuberance of a nursing infant's). I looked at her directly and listened intently to her stories, barely looking down as I poured yet more milk into my tea, but all the while I was keeping an eye on the street. Yes, all the time she was talking about the lonely dinosaur family that had secretly survived extinction and the cat named Castle-Diamond whose daughter Shukana could talk, I was watching for the young man.

Once the croissant had disappeared, we would turn our gazes to the street (we also shared a love of people-watching, of gazing raptly out windows) and for a few minutes I was free to search openly for him under the guise of watching the sparse parade of humanity. But she would soon grow tired of this passive receptive mode, eager to go out and I, intent on prolonging the outing, would succumb.

As fate would have it, the shop with the largest windows to the street was The Toy House. Attached to a bluebird-blue gingerbread cottage, the storefront was an indoor porch made almost entirely of glass, conveniently fortified with every type of toy you could imagine. One could stand inside the shop and discreetly look out at the street, shielded by a mottled mob of dollhouses, stuffed panthers, red-handled jump ropes, silver harmonicas, clown-shaped punching bags, Tinkertoys, croquet sets, rubber balls, kaleidoscopes, badminton sets, and the like.

What would I have done if he had paused in front of said window? (But how unlikely! He was, after all, too old for toys!) If, by some erratic stroke of fate's otherwise steady hand (pushing me firmly as it were, into the store with Maria, the street barren behind us), I were to find myself inside the shop looking at a dollhouse, myself on one side of the glass, the young man on the other, our eyes suddenly meeting through a tiny curtained window, would I will myself, chameleonlike to blend with the toys? Would my Liberty print blouse become, to the untrained eye, simply another busy pattern in the window? Or would I signal to him? Press a finger to my lips and a note to the now lightly steamed window? Or would I step toward the door, Maria's hand in mine, to expose myself for what I really was: a mother with a tote over her shoulder, shopping for the toy that would stand as payment to her child for another excursion to the "city" endured?

Only once did I catch a glimpse of the young man out in the world and it was not on Main Street but on the state highway. I have always been slow to notice when someone is noticing me and I am becoming increasingly obtuse with age (though there is also increasingly less to notice). I was walking along the side—looking back now I see I made a pitiful spectacle of myself—wearing my long black coat en route from the library to the apartment. He was driving in a little gray car toward me. As the car passed and he saw me, his double take was so dramatic that even I understood he was trying to catch a second glimpse. The absurd swivel of his head recalled that of a battery-powered doll and reassured me of what I had never quite been certain was true. I was ecstatic.

This encounter left me with the false impression that I would soon see him again, the sense that he was nearby, that if I stayed where I was, I would, inevitably, encounter him. Though not an avid traveler, I did, on occasion, go across the water for social and professional purposes. Seeing him outside the confines of the library caused me to regard such excursions as foolish distractions. In its geographic specificity, encountering the young man was akin to encountering certain celestial occurrences. One can't very well observe the aurora borealis while standing in the southern hemisphere. The island glowed green with a rose-shadowed light that outshone the larger blue world. Indeed my local attendance was required.

I knew I had lost my former grip on Reality when I declined an invitation to present a paper on Japanese and Japanese American Floating World Literature at The New School in New York for the sole reason that I did not want to leave the island. Var, as if sensing disaster, offered to drive me but I refused. I was no longer compelled to do anything that required standing on a piece of earth that was not connected to the piece of the earth on which the young man too was standing. To be off-island would nearly nullify my chances of encountering him. I wanted nothing of networks, of connections to the main. What seemed formerly interesting or important now struck me as an absurd waste of time. I wanted only to be stranded on what I had come to view as an island of possibility.

Chilling to think he did not even know my name (unless he had taken notice of the letters imprinted upon my gold-tone name tag and I hoped that he hadn't, so mortified I was to be wearing a magnet affixed to my chest) and there I was (un)planning my career around our next encounter. Yet sometimes it bore the clarity of a mathematical equation. Leave the island equals leave the young man. Stay on the island equals stay with the young man. The choice was simple and clear: proximity or distance. I, who had had my fill of distance and had been sickened by it, chose proximity, chose the island, chose him.

Meanwhile, he had not appeared at the library in weeks. My hardy optimism was not blighted in the least by this drought.

Every day I prepared to meet him, convinced that I would. My interactions with the library staff suffered. I tried, casually, to speak of him. In his absence my failed attempts were not so much perceived as suspect as hardly perceived at all. Siobhan, on the other hand, who was not to be fooled, was losing patience with my inability to speak of anything else. After all, what exactly was there to talk about? I was alone on my marvelous black track, doomed to drive the same loop repeatedly. I alone felt the thrill.

* * *

"You know," Siobhan remarked one afternoon, "I have to say I did a double take this morning when I saw Var." I smiled to myself at the mention of double takes. In its utterly singular preoccupation, my mind had become an islet. No matter how far one wandered, one was never far from one's starting point.

I was becoming increasingly absentminded. For the third time in as many weeks, I had forgotten my lunch and Var, without coaxing, had agreed to bring it. He was a reader who seemed to pride himself on never setting foot in the library, preferring instead to line the walls of his narrow room with mold-ridden books from the town dump. When, in the early days of my library job, I would ask him if there was anything he'd like me to bring home, he would say: *No. I have my own library.*

"What do you mean?" I asked her. It *had* been kind of Var to bring the lunch, so kind that it caused me to feel suspicious. Could he be checking up on me? My heart convulsed slightly at the thought.

"I mean my first thought when I saw your husband walk through the front door was: Well, who's this cutie?"

"Oh God, don't say that." He had given me an odd wink as he'd handed over my cloth bag, as if the two of us shared a secret I had somehow forgotten.

"And then I realized it was Var!" she laughed. "He's a pretty good lookin' guy, that's all!"

"I'm afraid I don't see your point." My patience for Siobhan was thinning. I had no desire to fritter away our shift together chatting about my husband's good qualities.

"Just sayin'," she slipped into her sunshiney drawl—all the more reason not to take her seriously.

Clearly, the young man's protracted absence had disturbed Siobhan's loyalties. Not only had she begun warning me against the perils of seeking pleasure outside the confines of marriage, she was now blatantly rooting for Var.

In recent weeks, she had been inserting Var-related comments here and there, (either reframing an anecdote in such a way that it redeemed him or regaling some positive attribute of his come to light), all of which were based on secondhand information whose source was myself. She let slip bits about the severe consequences of extramarital affairs, also based on the flimsiest of hearsay, shoddy bits that in summary reminded that those who committed such reckless offenses often *lost everything in the end.* She must have felt it was her duty as a friend. Then too there was the irrepressible librarian in her who could not stand by and watch a human being in distress without leaping to her aid, whether that person could not find the coin slot on the copier or was on the brink of domestic destruction. The most conscientious librarians don't know when to leave well enough alone.

I grunted at Siobhan's comments like a wild, uncomprehending native who must feign ignorance to gain advantage when her island is being attacked. I heaved sighs of boredom during her sympathetic portrayals of Var and moaned in disgust when she complimented his appearance using an exaggerated drawl. But being the public servant that I was—trained to listen, trained to respond—despite my defensive display of indifference, I could not help but carefully file her pleas and warnings under the heading, "Things I Should Probably Consider But Would Rather Not...To Be Considered at a Later Date."

Indeed just three days after the third forgotten lunch incident I returned to the file, though that implies it was a voluntary act. It would be more accurate to say that one evening while lying in bed with my eyes closed and my ears tuned to the wind, Siobhan's gibberish came back like civilizing words to colonize me. She was a very good friend after all (one of my only in fact), one who undoubtedly had my best interests at heart and whose opinion I rated highly. Would it not be folly to ignore her?

I considered what she had said about Var. It was true. He *was* rather handsome.

His most attractive feature was a pencil-thin moustache that drew attention to his sensuous lips, which, despite the fact that they seldom uttered words, kept rather busy nipping the tips of toothpicks, kissing the lips of coffee mugs, nibbling on *brigadeiros*, all the while muttering a steady and audible but unintelligible stream of Portuguese verb conjugations. I kept, in a letter drawer, along with a motley assortment of letters, an old photograph that accentuated his moustache. His lips are parted; he's in Rio on holiday using a red tripod pay phone, the remaining pods vacant on the crowded street, as if waiting even then for Maria and me to claim them, wearing a black T-shirt and a vintage black baseball cap bearing the insignia of a Japanese team. He has a gorgeous, masculine lacquer of self-containment spread over him, the very same lacquer that caught my solventine eye in the beginning and which later resisted all my efforts to dissolve it. I don't know why I approved so heartily of his particular moustache for I had never liked a moustache before his, in fact I have a general aversion. My father, whose skin, like my own, was nearly hairless, raised me to believe that moustaches were accessories befitting movie villains and crooks, not proper gentlemen. On those rare occasions when, beyond our safe parlor of honest, smooth-faced men, we encountered a man with a moustache, as soon as the bandit had departed, my father would shake his head and tsk loudly. In a low, husky voice, he would remind me to beware of such men, to remember that moustaches symbolized evil. And when I laughed, he would issue a warning, "Don't you know? The man with the moustache is the man who will do you harm," his words years later sounding less like the ravings of a superstitious immigrant and more like those of a lucid prophet.

I concentrated on the photograph in my mind, paying special attention to Var's moustache and lips for the sake of my own pleasure. Suddenly Siobhan's ghost appeared to the left of Maria's outstretched arm, her friendly, clean-haired presence palpable as Maria's. I jumped. "A photograph?!" she laughed. "You're kiddin' me, right?" I sat up and squinted my eyes in the dark. She was gone. Maria's lips were quivering, as they often did when she dreamed. She pursed her lips to a point, raised her eyebrows, then snickered. I smiled. She had been performing the same comic sequence since infancy.

I slipped out of the bed. More out of some inexplicable loyalty to Siobhan than to Var, I knocked on his door and offered myself to him.

I saw what I read as the faintest hints of astonishment and happiness flicker in his eyes. He moved quickly to accommodate me, lowered the single mattress (which he kept propped against the wall) onto the floor and pushed his desk of apple crates into a corner next to a wooden statue of Jesus he'd recently been commissioned to carve. His space was more like a hallway than a room and the air within it smelled toxically of the musty books he so regularly deposited there. He switched off the overhead light and turned on a lamp that sat like a cat on the carpet. I reached to turn it off but he intervened.

"I want to see you," he said. I undressed and laid down on the narrow mattress.

"I'm cold." I reached for a quilt that was stuffed between the Jesus and the wall. I covered myself with it. It too smelled like a musty book. I lifted the quilt and he slid in next to me fully clothed. He undressed himself awkwardly under the covers (he was a man who looked fit as a result of doing nothing and yet was modest as a nun), pausing to fold each article of clothing while lying down. I made note, not without irritation, of how quickly his desire for order superseded his desire for me. I tried to put the thought out of my mind. I thought instead of Siobhan, her sunny expressions and her good intentions, the way her fine, shiny hair bounced to and fro during brushings. Pem's "heart advice" would have been to take a deep breath and *Welcome Everything*.

It was no use. I could not welcome everything. I was like a house whose most beautiful window (the one next to the jasmine, overlooking the lake), whether due to paint or time or season, would not open. And to his credit, I suppose, Var was not the sort of man who would force open a window. He was the type to wait for the weather to change until he tried again or for another man to open it. So I remained intact and alone. I offered to placate him using other means but he politely declined and so I went to back to bed, wondering if I might not have been better off with the photograph, if not my simple yet stirring memory of the young man's face.

* * *

As it began to seem less and less likely that he would make an appearance, I turned my attention to the young man's mother, less in resignation than in search of an outlet for my devotion. Like most obsessive readers, I was no stranger to sublimation. If I could not observe the young man in earnest,

I would observe his source. I would sublimate. What was more, I could speak of her freely without the appearance of speaking of him. His mother became my alternate subject. My research, in the form of avid island newspaper reading, seemingly casual yet literally rigorous interviews with patrons, a few relatively barren yet somehow intense googling sessions, and one field trip, yielded the following:

Violet made her living selling luxury foods to the stranded rich. She ran a charmingly ramshackle shop on the highway called Plum Island Provisions whose dusty farmhouse exterior concealed a treasure trove of exotic snacks for millionaires. Like the only bar aboard a great ocean liner, it was a lifeline to a certain way of living.

She sold, in addition to her own cheeses, imported food (French cheeses, Swiss chocolates, English biscuits, Chinese tea, Italian flatbreads, Vietnamese rice wrappers, tamarind, harissa, lime pickle, mango juice); vegetables that grew behind the shop; fresh fruit pies (The strawberry rhubarb was especially good, I had tried it once at a dinner party years prior, likely when the young man was in kindergarten.); artisanal bread baked by a friend off-site; and a smattering of locally-made foods such as honey, sausage, popsicles, and ice cream. When it came to the shop's inventory, there seemed to be no reigning manifesto but pleasure, which only added to the puzzle of her being and, perhaps by extension, to that of the young man.

Siobhan and I had taken note of Violet in the previous year. She had been one of our "patrons of interest" long before I had discovered the young man. She stood out among library patrons as someone who seemed lovely from a distance but was in fact unfriendly at the counter. She was probably in her late forties, somewhere between Siobhan's age and mine. We were both drawn to her, but found that our attraction to her was one-sided or at least not reciprocated. Whether because we were perceptive or slighted or both, she struck us as unhappy, even suffering, and in predictable librarian fashion we wanted to help. But she did not seem to want our cheerful greetings, small town chitchat, clothing compliments, and book recommendations. We took our cues respectfully, we withdrew our attention from such misplaced "help" and turned instead to studying her mannerisms and reading habits. The appearance of the young man had further heightened our interest. In his absence, she was the next best thing.

It was her habit to deposit a few items—never more than three or four—in the return bin before going in search of more. She was silent, unsmiling, the solemnity with which she deposited her books that of a spy making discreet but important deliveries. I tried perpetually to catch her eye but her pause at the bin was nearly nonexistent. It was as if she were blind to me, intent on her simple mission to the exclusion of everything else.

Unlike her son, Violet always went directly to the basement. Within minutes of her arrival she vanished among heaps of old novels, free from my curious gaze. I enjoyed the delicately unnerving sensation of knowing his mother was standing on the floor below me, paging through books. Which one was she holding now? Was she nearly finished searching? (She struck me as a woman who opens a book in order to find something.) Such questions tempted me like flares from the dark stairs. I longed to follow them but I refrained.

In those moments I felt a bit like a spy myself. Using the Conscientious Librarian disguise as my cover, I lunged to help patrons, I snatched Violet's books from the return bin and studied them. I accomplished innumerable pointless tasks in order to prolong my stay at the front desk to which I knew, with some guilt and even some pity, she was obligated to return and where I could at last meet her face to face. She was far too polite to ignore me within the context of a book-borrowing transaction and so it was within the narrow confines of these fleeting encounters (as thrilling as those I had with her son and yet doubly complicated, the difference between them like the difference between pornography and Victorian literature with an erotic subtext) that I, on duty and in public, plunged my pan into the cold river of friendship and brought it up again and again, each time hopeful, if not certain, I would see gold.

One Thursday, when I returned from lunch and saw the three self-help audio books in the bin, I knew at once they belonged to Violet for I had checked them out to her myself the week previous. The words *Peace Is Every Step* sent a shudder through my groin.

"Is she still here?!" I accosted Siobhan.

"Basement," she whispered.

Siohban leaned down to take Violet's items from the bin. "What do you think she does while she listens to these?" she asked as she scanned in *Smile at Fear* by Pema Chödrön. I had wondered the same.

"Probably she makes cheese." I laughed. I had pictured her countless times in a green apron with yellow ties, preparing gourmet lunches for the young man.

"Can you really learn to love yourself while stirring hot cow's milk on the stove?" Siobhan closed her eyes and brought her fingertips to her temples.

"Is that really how cheese is made?!" I gasped, mildly disgusted. There were many things (cheeses, butter cakes, Afghani slipper bread, child-rearing, current events, the disastrous results of extramarital affairs, et cetera) that Siobhan had superior knowledge of.

"Close enough."

I wondered if Violet had sent the young man to the library to borrow *Crime and Punishment* or if he had chosen it for her.

"She seems to have moved beyond her Dostoevsky phase," I said, thinking more of him than of her, though I was beginning to have difficulty distinguishing between the two modes. Siobhan must have known and indulged me.

"No more guilt, my Lowly Lady!" she cheered. "It's time to love yourself while making Gouda!"

"What do you think she has to feel guilty about?" I asked, feeling a shiver of guilt myself. But before Siobhan could answer, I heard Violet's tread on the stairs and shushed her.

"She's mine!" I hissed.

"What?" Siobhan asked. She hadn't recognized that light-footed ascent.

Violet approached the desk like a woman who has lost her luggage. She wore a brown sweater and carried nothing but a look of concern which quickly changed to one of disorientation as she began to speak (as if she'd left her map in one of the misplaced cases and was lost without it, would continue to be lost without it until one of us came to her aid). She addressed us equally, first Siobhan, then me, her eyes finally resting on the smooth, green lake of the counter.

"I wonder if one of you might recommend a good novel?"

As soon as her question was uttered, I lost heart. Mine indeed. Ravaged by cowardice, tormented by my hidden conflict of interest, I looked wide-eyed at my own hands and then at Siobhan. She cast an uncomprehending glance in my direction and then answered with the unflappable calm of the uninvolved, "This is our resident literary librarian. She's the perfect person to help you." Siobhan turned to me and patted my shoulder.

Violet thanked her and then gazed at me, waiting for my perfection to show. We managed to make our way to the basement (as if she needed me for that), the ungraceful lurchings and silences of our descent embarrassing but merely accessory to the terror of the literary underworld to come.

I reached the foot of the stairs feeling coarse and ineffectual, unworthy of my task. Before I could even begin my self-soothing Conscientious Librarian routine, Violet put in eagerly, "Maybe you could just recommend one of your favorites?" Patrons short on time often suggested this method, failing to realize that we were two different readers whose preferences would likely have little or no overlap. It was a mild nuisance, not to mention, ironically, a waste of time. In this case I allowed myself to receive Violet's suggestion as a compliment, a sign that she saw some affinity between us, as if she was sure to love any book I loved.

As I perused my mental catalog of favorites, a dangerous well of possibility opened before me: sensuality, deception, obsession, the many forms of inappropriate love. Books containing these themes now took on a sinister quality. I did not want to be misconstrued, to inadvertently communicate a message. Or, if I was doomed to communicate (was it possible not to be?) I wanted to communicate innocence, anything but my own guilt. And yet I *was* innocent. I had done nothing. It was only with my mind I had sinned.

"What kinds of books do you usually enjoy?" I was stalling for time, having realized that to rule out sinister subject matter was to reduce my list of favorite books considerably.

"Well, I've read lots of classics but it's been years since I read something contemporary."

Yes, I thought with a rush of sympathy. And by now those contemporary novels have become classics.

"What are some of your favorites?" I asked. I imagined something old-fashioned in which guilt, shame, and anxiety figured prominently. Or perhaps, if she was feeling adventurous, one in which a prisoner is set free.

She hesitated before answering and in that moment's hesitation I noticed that she was eyeing my name tag, though her birdlike gaze did not alight there for more than a few seconds before it flew to the nearby shelves.

"I've always liked *Crime and Punishment*. I like *Wings of the Dove* and *Anna Karenina*."

So she had read the Dostoevsky before. She was a rereader.

"Have you read *The Lost Daughter*?" I asked, thinking that if one stretched one's imagination it had something fundamentaly in common with *Crime and Punishment*. "The author is living, though no one knows her true identity. Elena Ferrante is her pen name. She's a complete recluse."

"People on this island can relate," she said.

"Yes." I imagined a reclusive life in which my sole companion was her son.

"She lives somewhere in Italy," I drifted.

"I love Italy," she whispered, perhaps drifting a little herself.

"Why?" I imagined tins of amaretti and flatbread for sale in her shop.

"Oh, everything. The food, the churches, the weather." I'd never cared for spaghetti or popes, though a Mediterranean climate had its appeal. Italy had never interested me. That is, not until now. Violet could have said the London squats and I would have been intrigued.

"It's this way," I pointed, and began walking toward the F's. She followed. I handed her the book.

She glanced at the cover and blushed, then quickly turned the book over. The cover photograph was of the backside of a doll whose dress was unbuttoned to reveal her plastic bottom. "Thank you," she said, reading the back cover. "I think this will be just the thing for me. What's your name?" she asked, for we had never been formally introduced. And when I didn't answer immediately she added, "Where are you from?" The latter was a question some people asked after hearing me speak. My accent was slight but those who listened carefully could detect it.

I lifted my sweater toward her slightly so that she could better see my name tag. "It's Mayumi," I said. "I'm originally from England."

My name means "truth, reason, beauty" or, depending on the *kanji,* sometimes "linen" or "bow." I felt a dim pang of self-consciousness at the thought of these exalted meanings, none of which I seemed equal to.

"Whereabouts in England?"

"Stockingford."

"Do you miss it?"

"No."

"Do you visit?"

"Not often. I don't like to leave the island."

"I understand."

It was my turn to give a Japanese nod. I was at a loss as to what to do with my body, afraid that if I opened my mouth I might let slip an incriminating sentence: *Your son's so attractive!* And yet I also felt a teenage desire to impress, which only further undermined my ability to speak. It seemed better to say nothing than to offend or disappoint.

"Thanks again for the book. I hope I'll be able to finish it in time." Gingerly, she pressed her lips together.

"You can always renew it," I said, hurrying forward in my mind to our next encounter, my next chance. As if she'd known I hadn't needed to be told, she left without telling me her name.

It was one of those fall days that bears more resemblance to summer or spring, the colored leaves like bright flowers, the sky blindingly blue. The world, as I ran through it toward the apartment, surrounded me in shelves of color. There was the cocoa ash of the soil, the fields of hay marked by occasional scarlet, the gray umber trunks of the trees, their green tops just beginning to be dotted with red, yellow, and orange. The sky burned with sunshine, its bright white clouds dense as flames, the air ravished by an invisible sun. And beyond everything, also unseen, lay the darker blue shelf of the sea. I felt closer to him now and, of course, closer to her. I hoped she would like the Ferrante. *Come back to me, Violet*, I said to the day, *whatever you do, come back.*

She returned, wearing the same brown sweater, to thank me for the recommendation. "I liked it a lot. I think I'll get another of hers," she said, and walked self-sufficiently to the F's.

"I'm so glad," I said, keeping my eyes on the spine to which I was affixing a sticker and then a clear piece of tape. "I haven't read that one. You'll have to tell me how it is." At last I looked up.

"I'd like that," she said. She smiled the smile of pleasure shadowed by pain and I thought I saw a gap between her top teeth. She paused in front of the desk with *The Days of Abandonment* in her arms; she was enfolding it the way I had many times imagined her son would enfold me.

A woman with only one sweater, I thought, is typically austere or practical or of little means. I wondered which, if any, applied to Violet. I began to dream of knitting her a new sweater using a warm cherry yarn and a fine gauge stitch, although I did not know how to knit.

"Shall I check it out for you?" I asked, trying to imagine how she would look wearing the finished sweater. Indeed, a warm cherry would suit her.

"Oh no, that's all right. I'll bring it upstairs." Like a girl on her way to a literature class, she clutched the book more tightly and hurried away.

We were no longer strangers. We were coterminous, like distant neighbors whose common boundaries were the young man and a woman who had yet to reveal her true name.

* * *

Although I love books and although I have obviously devised ways of benefitting from my position, I am, in many ways, ill-suited to being a librarian. Though I shelve cart after cart without complaint, though I give excellent recommendations and can intuit a patron's needs, I otherwise have few, if any, of the appropriate talents. My ability to lose myself while engaged in mindless tasks notwithstanding, I don't like to smile when I'm in a foul mood, I'm prone to carpal tunnel syndrome (nowadays everything in the library is done on computers), I don't feel the need to pick up the phone during the first ring (or at all frankly), nor do I want so desperately to please others that I will skip a lunch break in order to do so. I care little for best-seller lists and book reviews, I fail to watch PBS, to listen to NPR, to read *The New Yorker*, not to mention mainland newspapers. Indeed I am embarrassingly out of touch with what is popular in the book world. I have a strong musical voice that lends itself to whispering on occasion but for which the daily imperative is a prison. My most glaring deficiency is that I am not detail-oriented, although I lied unwittingly during my preliminary interview and described myself as such. In truth, before being initiated into that Mansion of Minutiae, I had no idea the true meaning of the phrase. Put another way, I had no idea how well the librarian's vocation lends itself to existential crisis.

The entrance of Mother and Son into said Mansion enhanced my vocation and its meaning considerably. The seasonal Japanese restaurant worker who accelerated my pulse every summer and fall, the one-hundred-year-old woman whose barbed comments regularly stung me, the savage children whose despicable manners once annoyed me, now had a tranquilizing effect. All patrons now had a tranquilizing effect. They belonged to a race of people who were *other than the young man*. In their presence, I was unassailable. I exuded confidence. Behavior I might once have found irritating now amused me if it touched me at all. I was overwhelmed by a new sense of ease, with every breath conscious of my remarkable lack of nervousness. All of this was in contrast to the feverish, heart-racing state of wanting and agitation I experienced in his presence.

No longer was the library a saltbox of Time, Patience, and Tedium that I approached with a sense of duty and occasional hesitation. Now it was a fulminous palace of Fate, Beauty, and Possibility waiting to be entered. Existential crisis averted, meaning revealed, weather uncertain, engine revved, for the first time in years, I was eager to go to work. I saw myself lurching forward, careening when necessary, pressing my foot casually yet heavily upon the gas, daring even, on occasion, to lift my hands from the wheel. And yet the word "wheel" misleads, for I was not driving but being driven. (Indeed I did not even have a driver's license!) But by what or by whom? A boy in high school? The power differential be damned, whatever the force, I could not stop it. And why should I? No crime had yet been committed, not a single offense taken. My joy was everywhere evident.

Who dares to block joy's tidal wave? Who if they try can stop it? But I defend myself, a useless exercise. Then it was like reading of love in a book. One feels the many pleasures without inflicting any pain. In the end, no one is hurt or saved but the solitary reader. When one closes the book, life resumes. The husband continues to irritate, the child continues to breathe heavily in her sleep, her skin persists in smelling like cake, her washed hair of flowers.

Prior to the young man, I had avoided my own reflection (unlike Maria who climbed and then sat for hours upon the dresser like a cat, luxuriating in the sight of herself, rapt with her own facial expressions, her own ability to move: a sly squinting of the eyes, a feline flicking of her tongue, the tart raising of her bare backside up in the air). Now I peered curiously into the mirror, I lingered in the moments during which I changed out of my white flannelette, a gown given to me by my chaste Aunt Tomoko. I gazed at the back of myself in particular, at once with a mother's loving eye (I had become much less critical of the human form since becoming a mother) and with the shy yet avid eyes of the young man, recalling expressions I had seen upon his face across the counter. To my surprise, I, he, we, liked what we saw. I began indulging in daily showers, a habit I'd given up the day Maria was born. I primped myself like never before (not that I had a very impressive primping history) and felt an irrepressible sense of buoyancy during the hour before going to work.

More than ever, I read. I visited other libraries (another old habit revived), perhaps searching for the book that would inform me of what to do next, perhaps hoping to find that in one of these parallel universes, the young man still existed. There is a library in every town on this island. I fought the urge to borrow sensational nonfiction paperbacks pertaining to our situation, as well as reference books containing relevant laws and legal precedents. It was, I reasoned, too risky; no one understands better than a small-town librarian how little privacy borrowers possess.

I would wander the stacks of the strange library in search of nothing in particular, sometimes choosing a letter of the alphabet to guide me, sometimes a subject like dark matter or French cooking. There were days I chose a book because I liked or disliked the cover or because I liked or disliked the author's name. Other days I would go straight to a beloved book and borrow the book that was to the immediate left or right of it. Books are not so different than people. Often the person across the room with whom you first lock eyes should be bypassed in favor of the quieter, less charismatic person standing next to them. What's more, one's longing for a stranger can be a longing for someone invisibly connected to that stranger.

As if to practice understanding said stranger, I began reading books in translation. Like a schoolgirl for whom passion is a novelty, I read love stories. I read more than one book in which a pair of lovers meets for the first time on a train. In one, translated from the Greek, the two encounter one another on a commuter train. Daily they observe one another until at last one morning they speak. In another, translated from the Spanish, a man is traveling cross-continent and for several hours he observes intently a woman sleeping across from him. How I envied these lovers their proximity to one another, their being at liberty to observe!

Then again, had the young man and I met on a train, I might have wished we had met in a library (one is doubly afloat in an island library, surrounded by water, surrounded by books), in a sanctuary that never arrives late or suddenly, one that never departs slowly, only to disappear out of sight. In its intimacy and safety, a library is the opposite of a train. It is that which remains, that which holds people (children are the exception here) while they are, for the most part, not in motion, that which holds people while they dream, while they resist travel even as they read of other worlds.

The young man was like one of these exceptional children. He never paused for long in front of any bookshelf, he never sat in an armchair and fell asleep, only twice did I see him sit at a computer terminal for more than ten minutes. To be writing intently while wearing headphones does not compare to being asleep. The beloved's degree of oblivion dictates one's freedom to observe. And I, busy with my endless sequence of minute tasks, I, in my furrowed brow and compulsive friendliness, could not have been further from the man who sits idly in his train seat with a smooth, placid face, inspecting alternately and at his leisure the landscape to his right and the sleeping woman before him.

In fact, it disturbed me to think of having met the young man on a train, for there were no trains on the island. Residents who wished to visit the mainland traveled by ferry or, if they were endowed with wealth, by propeller plane. There was once a railroad but it was destroyed over a century ago, dead before either of us was born. Many islanders, especially the young who cannot come and go as they please, have never seen a train, much less traveled on one. If I had met him on a train it would not have been *him* at all but another version, perhaps a Londoner or a Bostonian. I had no interest whatsoever in meeting any such foreign replacement. In the end, every book I read left me in the place where I'd started: on the island again. In the apartment, in the woods, at the library. No trains, no daily observances, no sign whatsoever of the young man.

* * *

One night in the parking lot, Siobhan finally posed the question that even I had begun to consider but did not want to hear.

"What if he never comes back?" she asked. I feel a strange tenderness for her now, a gratitude in retrospect for her willingness to be so direct with one so convoluted.

"I haven't the faintest idea," I snapped, sounding haughty and imperious yet feeling bereft. "I'd rather not think of it in those terms if you don't mind."

"Terms?" she queried. "I'm not talking about terms, I'm talking about reality. There's a fifty percent chance he'll come in, a fifty percent chance he won't. All I'm sayin' is what if he doesn't? What if that's the outcome?" She was standing on the asphalt next to her car and I was standing at the opening in the trees that led to the museum garden. We always parted ways there.

She was trying to take me by the hand and lead me to a precipice, to the edge of a darkness I dared not fall into. The image of my small life without the young man was one of a library with its doors locked, or, simpler and more terrifying, that of a book with half its pages missing.

"He'll come back," I said with false confidence as I moved toward the trees. But then, unable to leave it at that, I stopped and asked, "What makes you think he won't?"

"Nothin'. Just that he hasn't been by in a long time so I'm thinkin' maybe he's gone off to college." His mother must have known but I couldn't bring myself to ask.

"But it's the middle of the academic year."

"Okay, or maybe he just moved away. Maybe he got a job on the mainland. I don't know. I just want you to be prepared for what might happen."

"I *am* prepared," I said, startled by the sound of my own conviction. "I couldn't be more prepared for his return."

As Siobhan climbed into her car, I felt a moment of envy for her practical outlook, immediately followed by a surge of pity for her lack of relationship with the young man.

"But what if he never comes back?" she asked once more, her well-tended hands resting gently on the steering wheel. "Or what if he does? Then what?"

"He'll come back," I said, my vision of his return now so exact that I felt no need for verification. "And when he does, I'll be at the ready."

I said this as if speaking of a storm for which I had long been preparing. My hatches were battened, my provisions set aside; whether the storm was on its way or simply imagined, there was nothing left for me to do but wait.

WINTER

Somewhere the last leaf let go its stem and the snow fell fast upon all of us. The director took down the "Island Memories" calendar and replaced it with "Our Oceans' Most Endangered Species," whose local publisher had zealously donated copies for each of the librarians. I went on dutifully making miso and noodles, taking my sly morning walks, I went on ecstatically composing crass questions. I went on processing books with such fixed passion that when at last my young Odysseus returned, I was oblivious to his entry, so engrossed was I in the covering of young adult paperbacks with plastic laminate—my bland, unbeautiful weaving. Unnerving to think that he slipped past while I was smoothing an air bubble out with the bone folder. If it weren't for Constance Whiting, who softly cleared her throat as she pressed the January issue of *Elle* like a cold lover to her cashmere bosom, I might never have seen him browsing the DVDs with his startlingly large back to me. Though the library thermostat was set to seventy-six, I felt chill. My many daily observations and nightly recollections notwithstanding, I wasn't altogether sure it was him.

Beneath his black, unbuttoned coat, he was wearing an unusually filthy white T-shirt untucked, filthy jeans, and a stalwart pair of muddy blond boots. He had the look of a day laborer. His hair was longer, more disheveled than I had ever seen it, and most startling of all, when he turned to the side, was his girth. His chest, his back, his torso, were a man's. If it was him, he had grown. Anyone who has known a child will recognize the sensation, the absolute shock and disbelief one feels upon encountering a child who has, since your last encounter, changed so drastically that he no longer looks like himself.

Nella shuffled in holding a chocolate bar in one hand, a large bag of cheese puffs in the other, and distractedly surveyed the circulation area. She, who had once been of the "I don't need a break" variety, seemed to have made a resolution to reverse her previous behavior. Indeed it was the time of year to be resolute. Before she could reach her desk, I intercepted. I appealed to her in as much of a whisper as my excitement would allow. "Help! Is that him? I can't tell!"

Nella peered over her glasses at the him. She knew exactly who I meant. "Let's find out." She quite generously set down her snacks, walked purposefully to the DVD corner and began to straighten Drama, which was adjacent to Comedy, the section in which the youth in question stood browsing. She shifted a chunk of movies decisively from one shelf to another then pulled two DVDs in a rather convincing show and came back. "Dreams really do come true," she admitted briskly, sat down, and began at once to unwrap her snacks.

Before I could process her report, the young man appeared at the front desk. I felt keenly that the encounter I had been longing for with such fear and trepidation would take place too quickly. I felt the violent onslaught of its ending before it began. There was now no mistaking his face. I was lobotomized by the sight of it. I could not recall a single question from my absurdly long queue nor the appropriate sequence of words one ought to use to greet a patron. Neither did he say hello, which did nothing to help. (I would soon learn that he never spoke first, that the deference of speech was for him a form of politeness, his way of showing that I was to lead. Like a dancer's pause or a dog's crumpling to the floor, his silence was an act of submission.) As I tried quickly to take in the latest revisions to his being (the filthy shirt, the broad chest, the manlike flanks, the enormous boots—I learned later he'd been working in his mother's garden) I also saw the young man I knew (the trembling fingers, the distorting lump, the dark eyes darting from object to object and then at last to meet mine). I wanted to shout with all the joy and fury in my librarian's heart: *I thought I'd never see you again!* But instead I said in the lowest voice possible, "Have you ever been to the waterfall?"

He smiled a slightly defensive smile accompanied by a grainy chuckle, as if there might be a trick to my question.

"I don't know," he managed (looking back now I see he had to summon at least as much courage as I did!) and then added craggily, "I've been to *a* waterfall. I don't know if I've been to *the* waterfall," revealing at once uncertainty and a charming predilection for contradiction.

"Do you like waterfalls?" I asked rather idiotically, my mouth no longer mine but that of some ventriloquist's dummy.

Quietly, as if I had shamed him into it, he said, "Yeah," and hung his head in the familiar convict style of the previous October.

In the rush of silence that followed, I saw within myself a cup marked *complacency* and a cup marked *disappointment*, the contents of both spilling over. I saw that I had been staring impassively for years at the spectacle of my own pain overflowing, as if at a hideous waterfall. Now I turned my gaze toward the young man. As I spoke to him awkwardly, imperfectly, and yet effectively, saying only what needed to be said and in the hushed tone that was, in truth, rather counterintuitive, if not repellent to me (had I not renounced the library-like setting of my English childhood for the star-spangled vivacity of America?!), I saw that there was within me also an empty cup marked *pleasure* and I resolved at once to fill it. I refused to be thwarted. I heard myself say, "Tomorrow at 9:15."

There was a hint of alarm in his eyes and I feared he would ask me the question *why?* but he did not. I waited for him to answer. The alarm receded like sunlight into the dark of his eyes. Later I would learn that he was seldom good at camouflage but when it came to the concealment of fear he was virtuosic. His look of fear was brief but I caught it and was unnerved by it. Perhaps because I was so frightened myself, I had not imagined I would frighten him. When finally he consented, I wasn't sure if he had conceded as a minor to an adult's request or if his answer had been driven by free will.

Having acquiesced, he stood erectly, moved his head back, his chin slightly down, his eyes to the carpet. He took a step back from the counter without taking the films. I pushed them toward him.

"Your movies are due in one week!" I said, now a pert Sybil, desperate to resume a more perfunctory mode.

His face looked drained of blood, a physical change which, though unsettling, did nothing to diminish his beauty. (On the contrary it gave him the look of an invalid, one who does nothing all day but lie in bed and desire.) I felt a double dart of guilt, one for having ambushed him in public (possibly within earshot of Nella, who, though she showed no signs of having overheard my proposition, had the ears of a bloodhound), another for wishing that he would now get out of my sight so that I might recover in solitude. He grabbed the DVDs and nodded goodbye, as if any further utterance might induce him (or me) to vomit.

His departure was a relief. I felt a stringent need to be counseled which became more stringent still when I realized that it would not be wise to speak of my foray with anyone. I glanced back at Nella who was making a flyer for the Saturday craft. I tried in vain to read her face. It was inscrutable. Her left hand delved noisily into the cavernous bag of puffs while her right hand clicked the mouse. She might have continued these actions for the duration of our encounter, absorbed by her task, or she might have used them as a cover while listening intently. I was no stranger to such tricks of the librarian's trade.

Of course it mattered little whether Nella had heard me or not. Nella, with her ever scanning yet half-mast eyes, her perpetually cocked ears and her silence, her insistence on a slow pulse, a flat heart rate, her refusal to fret over any library matter, should have been the least of my worries. What my lobe-less brain failed to compute that afternoon (paradox being an inaccessible concept to one as denuded of reason as I had become) was that by reaching out to the young man, I had made myself an island. With each passing minute I drifted further from the main, further from the familiar shore upon which Nella's hand was partaking once more of the flame-colored pile as she contemplated clip art and fonts for her flyer, upon which Siobhan in the next room, with her long, graceful fingers and their fine, tapered nails, was gently setting still more green cards into the wooden tray in service of those whose desires required additional research, upon which our director, in the basement below me, her energy unflagging as that of a hired horse, stayed late most nights, cataloging new acquisitions, writing grants, making phone calls, paying bills, reassessing the budget, signing off every two weeks on the time sheets that would pay me my due. The shore upon which I too had once occupied myself with the tools of my trade—bone folder, X-Acto knife, scissors, book tape, scotch tape, paper cutter, paper shredder, countless rolls of stickers, and plastic laminate—was swiftly disappearing. I had crossed one chasm only to discover another. Between the receding shore of my former existence and the tiny green earth of my new life rose a dark, watery gulf. But I had yet to discover it. I was stranded in my joy.

When at last my shift was over, I ran to the apartment brimming with happiness. As nonsensical as it may sound, I couldn't wait to see Maria.

She was in the garden. As soon as I saw her red coat I ran toward it. "Ave Maria!" I cried out.

"Mama!" she shouted. I knelt down and held her. She wriggled away. "Mama! Did you bring me something?" It was my daily habit to bring her a book. In my trembling, lobotomized state, I had forgotten.

"Oh no! I'm sorry, love, I didn't have time." My first lie. (I didn't count the lie I had invented in order to procure an extra fifteen minutes for myself each morning. That was an innocent lie, invented for innocent purposes.) I don't know why I didn't simply tell the truth and confess that I'd forgotten. It was the beginning of my use of treachery to establish the appearance of truth.

"But you're supposed to bring me something!" she whined.

"I know, I know," I said quickly, too happy to get bogged down. "I'll bring you two things tomorrow, I promise!" Though as yet I had committed no wrong, my guilt had already ignited in me a need to make reparations.

I wanted to tell her. I wanted her to know why I was happy. It was a stupid and dangerous desire to be sure. I quelled it.

"Will you put me in the tree?" she asked, sensing that I would do virtually anything for her.

"Yes!" I ran with her to the other side of the garden and lifted her onto the lowest branch of her favorite oak tree. A translucent net of fog passed over us, barely visible against the silver sky. "It's such a lovely afternoon," I said, squinting up at her. She growled at me, the way she did whenever I spoke to her directly while in fact preoccupied with other thoughts. I growled back and held her ankles. "Maria," I crooned.

"I'm not Maria. I'm a leaf monkey. That's a monkey the size of a leaf!"

At the top of the tree, there were three orange leaves, fluttering page-like in the wind. This surprised me for in my unscientific, melancholy state I'd thought every last leaf had fallen to the ground. But these leaves were still alive, their colors vivid as pumpkins. I felt the way I had at age eleven upon walking out of the optometrist's office for the first time, at last seeing the world as others saw it: a world so crisp and colorful it was cartoonlike, a world with the look of a dream.

I began to climb; my climbing always pleased her. She clapped her hands and then laughed as she lost her balance and then quickly clasped the branch once more. "You look so big!" she observed.

I hoisted myself up to the branch above her and sat astride it. "I'm a big mama."

"It's a little tree."

"It's not that little."

"Yes it is," she insisted. "You're not that big. The tree is little."

"Do you always see things as they truly are?" I asked playfully.

She looked off in the direction of the road. "Yes," she answered gravely. "Yes I do."

That night in the dark she asked, "Did your mother love you?" We were looking up at the glowing stars that the previous tenant had pasted pell-mell to the ceiling. It was not the first time she had posed this particular question and at bedtime which, in general, was the time that she reserved for her most pressing inquiries about mortality and love. Before I could answer her she said, "I want to be under your arm." It was a phrase she uttered nightly and always as I slid my arm under her warm body, I felt the urge to correct her sentence—for my arm was under her and not the reverse—but then as I pulled her closer to me, my arm curled and wound its way around her until she was indeed "under my arm." Nightly I realized her sentence was correct and so was silent. "Did your mother love you?" she asked again.

"When I was a little girl you mean?"

"Yes. When you were a little girl."

"I don't know," I said. "I suppose."

"But she must have loved you. You were her little girl."

"Maybe," I said. "Probably you're right. Probably she did, but I don't really know for sure."

"I know she did."

"Really?" I smiled. "How do you know?"

"Because you love me."

"You're right, I do."

"Do you know why?"

"Why?"

"You love me because I'm here. If I weren't here, you'd love another child. You love me because I'm here and I'm here because you love me."

I was silent, not so much because I disagreed but because I had found the less I spoke, the more quickly she fell asleep. "Really!" she said loudly, as if I didn't believe her.

"Okay," I said softly and kissed her head, the smell of which after nearly five years still brought me to a new brink of pleasure. "How did you know that?" I asked sincerely.

"I was born knowing a lot of things."

"Yes, you were." I wished then, rather selfishly, that I could ask her for the answers to other questions, questions about right and wrong, devotion and happiness, questions about what, if anything, would happen tomorrow between the young man and me. But I said nothing. We lay there for a few minutes in silence, perhaps contemplating together all there was to know in the world, and then her breathing slowed and became more audible. I picked up one of her hands and let it fall.

Sedated by the mere prospect of pleasure, I slept heavily, my subconscious journeying nine hours to some never before seen glittering underworld, a place similar in location and intensity to hell and yet belonging visually and emotionally to heaven. When morning arrived, I swam directly to the surface of my dreams, bypassing countless sensual diversions en route, and burst like someone who has nearly drowned, panting and short of breath, into the bright bedroom air. Reality flooded my lungs like oxygen. I began at once to accomplish my morning duties. The sooner I accomplished them the sooner I would be released. After I had left Maria safely at the nursery, I prepared myself (as I had been taught by both my parents to do) for the worst: snow falling upon an empty street, no cars, no people, no birds, no one, not even a leaf waiting for me, and then I walked to our assigned meeting place.

* * *

It surprised me to find the young man standing on the very corner I had suggested. I could hardly believe that my words from the previous day had produced such an effect; I felt a touch of the conjurer's power. He was wearing a dark blue hat marked by white snowflakes, the sort with earflaps that one puts on one's child in winter. He looked heartbreakingly out of place, standing as he was so near to the school bus stop and yet frightfully far from that childhood destination. Part of me wanted to rush forward and warn him against people like myself, against the perils of meeting a stranger in broad daylight on a corner such as this, and part of me couldn't be trusted.

As I drew near I saw that his eyes were sleepy slits, his upper cheeks puffy as peaches. He had the look of one who is not himself until noon. He smiled the family smile of happiness and pain. I smiled too, a smile that has taken some time to leave me, a smile that I can still retrieve in full.

"You came," I said.

"I told you I would," he sounded ever so slightly wounded. The words *power differential* returned to me and I quickly renewed my efforts at sensitivity.

"Oh, I didn't doubt you or your word. I just meant I can hardly believe you're here. It's so good that you're here. I can hardly believe it." At this, he stepped behind the pole of the metal street sign, as if to hide himself, though it was far too slim to even begin to camouflage his new girth. "Shall we walk?" I asked a bit too brightly, sounding like an English biddy who is in her element early in the morning. (Though I was soon to discover that almost anything I said was liable to sound mature if not biddy-ish when uttered in his presence. It was part of the undeniable charm and awkwardness of our situation.)

I cast my eyes around quickly as we set off. Behind us, in the town hall lot: the clerk's green pickup, the accountant's blue hybrid, and the assessor's black SUV. I glanced furtively at the windows on the second and third floors. The church lawn opposite us and the museum garden across the road were empty.

We walked down the left-hand side of Music Street in silence, the young man at my left kicking first at old chestnuts and then at acorns as we went. I wanted to reach for his ungloved hand, the fingertips of which hung miraculously down from his black coat sleeve like five tips of flesh in a confessional, yet I also felt vexed to watch for oncoming cars. I hadn't anticipated the feeling of utter exposure our walking together on a road would produce. I've made a mistake, I thought. I've gone about this improperly. As if there were a proper way to go about it. I had neither the audacity to reach for his fingertips nor the strength to face onlookers. Instead, I looked down at the light dusting of snow that had fallen during the night. I was glad to be cold. I wanted to feel the rigors and harshness of the world. I wanted to feel the cold bite my skin with its sharp teeth, the way one wants a pinch when in need of a confirmation of reality.

I led him onto the small dirt road. It was a relief to be off the paved one. If my ears had not deceived me, not one car had passed. We paused for a moment on the land bridge, watched the still water on one side, the rushing water on the other. When finally we arrived at the waterfall I began to wonder, with a twitch of anxiety, what we would do. We continued up to the trailhead. As always, the NO TRESPASSING sign gave me a jolt. I hoped, with the fierceness of one who has been kept waiting a long while, that the kind owner of the fairyland would not appear. It was mildly distressing to walk her snowy trail accompanied by someone other than Maria, to hear the unfamiliar crunch of the young man's boots behind me, and when I looked down and back, to see the two sets of prints—his large boots behind my smaller ones—in the light snow.

"Do you hear it?" I whispered, librarianlike. It was Maria's line. I stopped in my tracks and he came very close to walking into me but he didn't.

"Yeah," he said, very near my ear now. I began walking again, more briskly this time, suddenly frightened by his proximity. Despite all my motherly concern about his safety, was I not also possibly in danger? However young he was, he was also, after all, larger than I, and perhaps capable of violence. When we reached the pond, I did not linger to look across it or down at the falls, for I was plagued by the fear that he might, in a moment of insanity, push me roughly into the frigid water. I wanted to get off the swaying wooden bridge and onto stable ground again.

We followed the trail down into the forest then curved around to the river's edge. The sound of water was all around us; we could not help but stare at the dazzling spectacle. He sat down on the stone bench and watched it. I stood behind him. After a few minutes I felt more at ease. My fear of violence subsided. He said nothing about the waterfall but did not take his eyes off it. Finally I sat down next to him and attempted to explain myself.

"I come every day to this waterfall. I used to sit here and watch it and think about my pain cascading endlessly over the rocks and twigs, my pain being carried down from the pond to the river and away. But since I met you I only see pleasure flowing there. Even if you never agree to see me again I want you to know that you've changed the way I see the simplest things."

I couldn't tell whether he was wincing or smiling or both. He was silent except for a few huffs of air that came from his mouth. "Perhaps I've said too much," I said.

"No," he said at last very softly and with astounding tenderness, as if during the course of his short life he too had once gazed at the spectacle of his own pain. "You can say anything." He broke off bits of a stick and threw them into the water. They raced away with the current.

I stood up. "I've got to go. I'm afraid I didn't plan this very well. I was out of my mind yesterday."

"It's okay, I'm late for school anyway." He said this bashfully as if embarrassed by his youth and its requirements, then kicked an acorn into the river with the finesse of a World Cup football player. High school. Dear God, I'd almost forgotten.

"Oh I'm so sorry, how unthinking of me, I've completely lost my head. Honestly, I've become an insane person!"

"It's just cooking. I know how to cook already so it's not a big deal." Recklessly, I thought of him and Violet listening raptly to Dostoevsky while stirring a vat of Gouda.

"Will you be punished?" I asked, a bit fearfully, for I knew little of American high schools.

"No," he laughed and shook his hair out of his face. His skin was a balmy, tempting color, of pale fruit waiting to darken.

"Can you come tomorrow?" I asked rather boldly, for what, if anything, had he gained by coming today?

He nodded immediately and seemed even to suppress a smile. I thought I detected a bit of impatience in his eyes and it occurred to me that he was expecting me to make all the arrangements. It made sense I suppose. We both knew full well what I was old enough to be and if I wasn't going to protect him from the world of adult perils and pleasures, I should at least guide him firmly across the waters and onto the isle. "We'll meet here tomorrow," I said, pretending decisiveness. "Tomorrow's Friday. It's my day off."

His eyes went dark. He tilted his head forward slightly. "Okay," he said, looking briefly at me and then at the river. He didn't move from his place on the bench, as if at once afraid of joining me and anxious for tomorrow to come.

"I'm going to leave you here. You'll be all right won't you?"

"I'm not a child," he said in that masculine, slow-winding voice that had so effectively ensnared me from the start. It was certainly *not* the voice of a child, I thought as I ran up the snowy trail, leaving him sitting alone in front of the waterfall.

It wasn't until I was running across the land bridge that I realized I'd left my cloth bag containing my lunch and my ballet flats in the apartment, in all likelihood on the kitchen counter. I experienced a giddy surge of gratitude that I did not have the kind of husband who would observe such an oversight and then immediately deliver the forgotten lunch to his wife's workplace. So there were benefits after all to having this kind of husband! I laughed aloud as I ran, I didn't care about the lunch, I could buy a bar of chocolate and a bag of cheese puffs when the time came, I could buy two bars of chocolate for God's sake. What on earth did it matter?! I would stomp through the stacks happily all day in my boots, leaving traces of melted snow everywhere.

I arrived at the library breathless. It would have been

humanly impossible for Nella not to have noticed my unusually radiant mood, though she betrayed nothing, asking only the question she asked every me morning, "How's Baby?" the two words sounding such a new key of hilarity that I burst out laughing, thrilled with the double meaning.

"Baby's great, *really* great!" I said, glossing over the discrepancy between what I was feeling and what I could safely express with chitchat about Maria's growing repertoire of Petula Clark songs. "And how's Penny?!" I posed my customary question with unprecedented enthusiasm, for on that morning I understood more completely how important one's objects of affection are to one. Penny was Nella's one-year-old puppy—a copper-colored spaniel that would only return home to the sound of a penny whistle, of which Nella had a fine collection. There was talk of dog food and of Penny's ankle, which had plunged into the hole of a crumbling sidewalk and been twisted that very morning. All of it was immensely interesting to me and yet was simultaneously of no consequence, as was everything that happened that day, so absorbed I was by thoughts of the young man. The memory of our morning encounter was like a passage in a book that brought me more pleasure each time I read it. As I walked from station to station performing my duties, I was rereading.

Soon the UPS driver arrived with a shipment of books to be processed, which I welcomed as objects that would stand in for Reality as I dreamed. At noon, the director emerged like a stallion from the basement (where she had no doubt been working at a galloping pace since dawn) to remind us of various upcoming events and projects that begged our attention. She cantered across the street to the general store and returned with a cardboard tray full of cups of deliciously strong coffee paid for out of her own pocket, which were as much liquid incentives as treats for the staff. I added a slow spoonful of honey to mine and a splash of cream whose snowlike swirl into the round black sky held my attention for several minutes. So the day unfolded.

Siobhan did not work Thursdays and though I regretted her absence, some last remnant of my rational mind observed that even her absence was something to be grateful for. I saw my situation clearly now. I had landed alone on a new island. I had gone ashore and was surrounded by seas neither she nor I could cross. But I did not care to dwell on such matters and so I turned my energies instead to greeting the library public, the patrons who read and worked and whiled away their winter days there.

They were the very young, the lonely, the old, the highly literate, the thinkers and daydreamers, those prone to escapism and those committed to learning a skill, those who could not afford to heat their homes or to own a computer, those who would not have thought to purchase such a machine if they could have, too busy were they building houses or catching fish or knitting sweaters or planting seeds in rows, those in a hurry, for whom every minute meant money gone, and those who had all day, all the rest of their days really, to squander. Our island is a haven for misfits, a retreat for those marked by fragility or age or simply an incurable love of beauty; its forests hide fugitives, the mute, the unusually self-sufficient, the deranged, the damaged, the wild.

I waited on each with equal passion and authenticity. There was no end to my patience with the most tedious of requests, no end to my detachment from the misfortunes of computer malfunctions and missed ferries, the grief of stranded children, and the injustice of overdue fines. It was confusingly paradoxical. Far from inciting me to commit a social crime, the young man had thus far reformed me. He had, in a single morning, made me a gentler person. In less than an hour, I had been illicitly transformed into a kind and joyful woman.

This mind-bending paradox persisted throughout the day

and on into the evening. It followed me like a shadow up the stairs into the apartment where I found myself bestowing a flurry of extra kisses on Maria's plump, cake-scented cheeks, leaning in to Var's room to place a kiss on his startled lips. It was a sincere kiss. My invisible cup of pleasure was being filled. Day and night it would flow on, I could sense this was only the beginning. I could afford to be kind. Though that implies a kiss driven by pity and it was a kiss fueled by joy, unstoppable, indiscriminating, full of love. For Var was no longer the emblem of my despair, a thief draining my cup, he was simply a craftsperson who lived in the apartment. To be fair and honest and more generous still, he was the father of my child, he had given me my beloved Maria and for that I would always be grateful, for that I could always manage a kiss.

I cooked a tasty Indian dinner and then cheerfully did the dishes which, like the books, stood in for Reality while I dreamed. I washed each dish tenderly. I was generous with the soap. Never before had I seen such lather and the smell—lavender mint—was heavenly. I was washing Maria's enamel cup, trying to recall how he'd looked while laughing at my fear of school punishment, when the phone rang. Overtaken by the irrational hope that it would be him, (he possessed neither my phone number nor my name), I slapped the phone off its hook with my slippery soap hands.

"Hello?" I panted out the words, as if I had just run the length of a high school gymnasium to answer. It was the library director, wanting to know if I could please cover for her in the morning.

I was very fond of the director, so fond that I often agreed to cover shifts when it was in fact rather inconvenient for me. To work tomorrow of course would be beyond inconvenient. It would be heartbreaking. I set my right hand down on the counter and studied it, literally bracing myself for the wave of guilt that would rise in me when I said no. "I'm sorry, I can't.

I have a doctor's appointment in the morning and a friend coming to visit after that." Surprise. The lies came easily.

"Okeydokey!" she said, "I'll try Nella. Have a great night!" I stood admiring my plain, ringless hand. No wave of guilt had risen in me. The sea of me was placid. It made no sense. I had always felt guilty saying no to the director, even when I had the most legitimate of excuses (Maria has a fever, I'll be off-island, my cousin is visiting from England, my aunt is visiting from Japan etc.). And yet now, on what was to be the eve of my crime, I felt absolved, exonerated by the prospect of my own pleasure.

When I woke the next morning it was snowing. The garden with its bare branches and dead leaves had become, by a curious reversal of fate, a bright picture of purity, its many withered stems and yellowed blades mercifully covered by a thick layer of sparkling snow. Snow, as mothers who live in cold climates know, in addition to having the power to beautify and to cleanse, acts as a sleeping powder upon children, indeed even upon Maria for whom car rides and stories read aloud had the effect of stimulation. The snow might have well have been falling directly upon her through the ceiling, so still and heavy her plump body had become. She had removed her pajamas and kicked off the quilt during the night. The soles of her feet were pressed lightly together, her knees were open, her arms overhead. I felt distinctly the importance of external factors working in my favor. Like some distant ally come at last to my aid, the snow released me from the bed, it muffled my movements as I dared with uncharacteristic ease to open and close the dresser drawers. I went so far as to leave the room and take a shower—something I'd never have the audacity to do under normal circumstances for she was too light a sleeper. What a pleasure it was to stand under the rush of warm water, to feel the water clean my face, to be alone with my body and my thoughts of what might soon occur, and then to return to the bedroom wrapped in a towel to find her still sleeping.

I sat on the bed next to her and unwrapped my towel. I applied to my legs and elbows the good quality lavender oil, which I normally reserved for her highly sensitive skin. I applied to my wrists and neck a solid perfume of rose and vetiver. I combed my hair slowly though it hardly needed it. A hand run through once was sufficient. As gently as I could, I looked at my face in the mirror. With the exception of my very black hair, I did not look seventeen, but neither did I look forty-one. Though my face held evidence of age and suffering, it held too the same bone structure that had gotten me this far; my cheekbones were high, my lips well shaped, my eyes clear with conviction. In appearance, I am very much my father's child. Indeed, the only trace of my mother's phenotype that survived the making of my face was her sea blue eyes, which peer out like nervous European tourists from my otherwise Japanese face.

Maria woke whining, as she often did, angry that I was not in the bed with her.

"Maaaaaaa-Maaaaaaa!" I turned away from the mirror and sat down on the bed.

"I'm here!" I said and held my arms out to her.

"You were supposed to be watching over me!" she complained and slapped my arms down before turning her back to me.

Now the typical morning began. I was there to meet it. I didn't mind. I felt in myself the strength to meet anything. My cup was already being filled as I handed Maria her socks and underpants and then dressed myself, as I stood before the stove to prepare her morning soup and then my tea. As soon as she had eaten, her mood improved. It happened every day like this. Meanwhile, Var slept on, oblivious to her transformation. Today I felt only pity and tenderness for them both: her for being possessed by such a violent hunger upon waking and him for daily sleeping through its fulfillment. Snoring and twitching, he was animallike in his den, as possessed by his need for sleep as Maria was by her need for breakfast. Like a family dog, he was part of us and yet excluded from certain of our activities.

I held Maria's mittened hand tightly as we walked. We passed the hundred-year-old church, the general store, the pomelo yellow house with the well in front, the swan and her cygnets gliding across the mill pond, and a field formerly green, covered in brown and white sheep, now blank as a fly-leaf.

"Kiss me," I said and knelt down before the little wooden gate of the school. Immediately she took my cold cheeks in her woolly hands and kissed my lips with gusto. Since the first moment she had pounced upon my swollen breast and drawn blood, she had shown herself to be an aggressive and passionate lover. "Maria," I began. I felt the need to say something to mark the occasion, to express both my happiness and my guilt, but before I could finish my sentence she slipped through the gate and was running to greet a friend.

During the walk back to Music Street—past the field of sheep, past the pomelo house, the swans, the store, and at last the church—I had time to reconsider my day's itinerary. Instead of turning right down that light-filled, tree-lined street, I could return to the school to observe the children, help the teachers grind the flour and knead the bread, or I could cross the state road to the library and put in a few extra hours (though extra hours were typically discouraged) or I could go to the church and confess my sinful thoughts, not to the priest, who was likely not in, but to the imported statues who presided over the stained-glassd nave and to the rays of sun that streamed colorfully through them or—and this was the least appealing choice of all—I could continue on to the apartment, where I could read a book in translation about foreigners in love, Var's many emissions accompaniment to my act of martyred devotion.

I lingered at the corner of Music Street and the state road holding the metal signpost. I circled the pole briefly, as if to show someone, anyone—the priest who might have been crossing the grass from the church to the refectory, a town employee who happened to be standing at an upstairs window looking down, someone in a car driving past who was extraordinarily observant—that I felt, if only for a few moments, a painful pin of hesitation, along with several preemptive stabs of regret. Then, overcome by the tedium of my other choices and by the hot feeling of pleasure that traveled briskly through me when I gazed in the direction of that snowy, forbidden street, the dirt road, the woods, I let go of the sign and walked quickly toward our meeting place.

I saw, even before I saw the young man, that the first icicles were beginning to form on the waterfall. A row of frozen phalli seemed a chilly portent. I sat down on the bench next to him (though not touching him) but could not speak, so struck down was I by the realization that despite my modern American hairstyle, my explicit fantasy life, and my shamefully inappropriate invitations, I was, at heart, a tea-loving English librarian, the result of a well-mannered curmudgeon and a prudish ex-nun, who could not possibly make advances upon a man in a public place, most certainly not a man as young as the one in question. The pinprick of guilt I had felt at the crossroads coursed through me like a hideous transfusion.

And yet I was also calm. I suffered calmly for I possessed within myself a faith, born of desire, that everything would right itself in the end. Meanwhile, the sight and sound of the water persisted like emblems of pleasure that, as time passed and we watched, were rushing away from us.

I conferred briefly and to the point with myself as with an

unfamiliar woman upon whom everything depends: *Is this truly what you want to do?* I asked. *Yes. Are you willing to take responsibility for your actions?* (Siobhan's voice.) *Of course. Do you realize the gravity of the situation? I do!* Ecstatic as a deranged bride, all my thoughts turned faithfully toward consummation.

As if ethical considerations were not enough, the snow softly and steadily continued to fall; had I been bold enough to linger with him at the bench, we would have soon found ourselves covered like two iced dolls upon a cake.

"Shall we go for a stroll?" I said aloud. By then he must have thought I had lost my nerve.

To show the young man I meant business, I strode ahead of him, returning to the trail we had carefully come down on. Instead of turning left back over the pond I walked tentatively right through a dense tunnel of trees I knew led to a gated garden, and beyond that, a house. It was a path I generally avoided but I turned to it now like an old, forgotten book, with the hope that I might open it and find something new.

He walked closely behind me. I had already begun to expect this. The sight of his snowy footprints following mine no longer filled me with fear for my personal safety but I felt a faint sense of menace at the thought of our imprints being seen together, the fact of our leaving evidence behind, however fleeting. I was intermittently startled by the simple fact of his presence, of which his footprints were a stark reminder. I was like a reader on a train who is so absorbed by her book that she slips in and out of contact with her surroundings—one moment forgetting her destination, the next jolted by signs of its imminent proximity.

Like spring, winter has its share of newborn openings and fresh paths. In the absence of leaves, another world is illumined; the ancient ways become more evident. Walking through the tunnel of snow-lined branches was like traveling inside a long cage of the most intricate ribs. The cage was still, black trimmed with white, while we were red as a beating heart within it. The pond was on our left. I scanned the trees on the right for openings. I took the first one I saw. The young man was silent. He was an excellent follower. Not once did he fall behind or encroach too closely upon me. I searched for shelter of any kind; I would have settled for a large tree. I wondered if he knew I was plunging ahead aimlessly with nothing more than a libidinal sense of purpose to guide me.

The path narrowed and rose up. I sensed we were nearing something. At last I saw, at the top of the next ridge, a small gray house backed by a stand of towering black trees that all leaned slightly to the left like meddlesome spectators. Miss Marple-like, I scanned the path in front of us for footprints but it was smooth. I turned back to look at him. "Here," I said, nodding as if to say, "Here is the place I was looking for," when in fact I meant, "Here. It will have to be here. There is nowhere else."

He nodded as if he had heard and understood both versions. The attentive quality of his silence moved me; it seemed suited to the priesthood. What a frightfully attractive priest he would have made. I smiled at the thought and waited for him to join me.

I felt the need to pause before the house. It was a Cape Cod cottage with a chimney and one snow-covered window on each side of the door. Snow had collected as well on the front steps. The threshold looked like a wedding cake.

"Do you want to go back?" I asked and turned to look him in the eye, that dark evasive eye. I felt morally obligated to give him a last chance to escape.

"No," he said quickly and shook his head. As he did so, some of the real snow that had fallen onto the snowflake pattern of his hat fell to the ground. "Do you?" he asked. It was his first question of the day, his second in our short history.

Slowly, methodically, I repeated his question to myself. I did not charge forth unthinkingly. Indeed, I proceeded mindfully as a Buddhist; his posing of the question only infixed my desire for him.

"God, no," I said. I had never been so sure of anything in my life and I was not decisive by nature. I placed my black boot festively upon the frosted steps. The door was fastened with a simple iron latch. As I lifted it, though I reminded myself repeatedly that the path had been smooth, the steps white, I could not rid myself of the feeling that we were on the verge of intruding upon someone.

The door opened easily and quietly. There was no one inside. The only sounds were the soles of our boots scuffing the wood floor. He began at once to remove his hat and coat, which alarmed me, I could not help but read his movements as foreshadowing. The thought of him soon shedding the rest electrified and petrified me.

Petrification being closer to my natural state, I stood in my coat and hat and inspected the house's interior. It looked as if it were intended for one rather ascetic occupant. There was a small wooden table and one wooden chair at a window on the left. In the back left corner, a black wood-burning stove. A modest kitchen on the right and at the back and above us, a loft built crudely by hand.

I could have stood there all day gawking at the house's unwrought interior, studying its architecture, speculating about its owner, had the young man not began to stomp the snow off his boots, in a manner that was uncharacteristically rambunctious. He seemed at once nervously excited and full of hesitation. It was only my fear of him losing patience that finally drew me up the loft's treacherously steep stairs. Despite being raised in a home in which the wearing of shoes was banned, I couldn't bear to take my boots off prior to ascending. It seemed entirely too suggestive. (What's more I had a fear of slipping in my socks and falling to my death in advance of our encounter.) At the top of the stairs I removed my boots. Dutifully the young man followed me but left his boots on.

The house smelled mildly of Murphy's oil soap and cedar, the loft of dust and absence. Upstairs, resting on a plank floor, we found a twin mattress covered by a blanket. I sat down opposite the mattress and was grateful for the near dark; for the lack of windows, the impossibility of eyes peering in at us. There was only an inverted triangle filled with horizontal slats. My own eyes soon adjusted. (Soon enough I would be grateful for that too.) As I took off my hat I was gripped by twin fears that I was supposed to be at the library or with Maria.

"What day is it?" I asked, trying to conceal my panic.

"Friday," he muttered, sounding mildly offended, as if my ability to forget the day was tied to or perhaps synonymous with my ability to forget him.

"That's right," I said, involuntarily using the voice of a library proctor who'd administered an exam he'd passed easily. At the thought of it being my day off, of Maria being at the nursery until two, I relaxed slightly.

He stood next to the dangerously low railing and looked down as if contemplating suicide. I felt a wave of concern for him, joined with a new sense of responsibility. After luring him out of school through the snowy woods and into an abandoned house, was I not ethically obligated to seduce him? His cheeks were red with what? Shame? Arousal? Some tantalizing mixture of the two? Was he too suffering from a moral crisis or was he just cold? He looked ashamed. I took off my coat and moved toward him.

"Do you want to go back?" I asked yet again, unable to shush the relentless librarian in me who felt she ought to promptly return him to his homeroom.

"No," he said quietly with the steady expression of one who does not wish to stray from the topic at hand. I touched his face, which seemed to make him happy, though the happiness was only evident in his eyes. His skin brought to mind Maria's, the downy fur of baby animals hidden from view: asleep, untouchable, now unbelievably mine.

He may as well have been shirtless so apparent were the lines of his body in his white thermal shirt. One could see he would be well suited to a varsity sports team; when he moved he moved as if in service of a greater goal. And yet there was something sketch-like about him; perhaps it was merely youth, the impression he gave of one not quite frail but also not yet finished. I stifled the urge to say something idiotic about his beauty, grateful and amazed that I had any stifling power left whatsoever.

"I'm so frightened of you," I said. "I've never been so frightened of anyone."

"Are you being serious?" he asked, that dark look of his darkening a touch.

"Of course I'm being serious," I snapped. Was it far-fetched to expect him to understand me?

"I'm not a scary person," he said. "I'm a scared person."

Was he being earnest? Or was he simply skilled at saying what needed to be said in moments of impatience? He hadn't been laughing or even smiling as he said it. Perhaps I'd become suspicious in middle age.

"Who are you?" I asked.

"I don't know," he answered, laughing a little of that gravelly laugh, the sound of which pressed a button somewhere within me. I was satisfied with his answer and resolved not to confuse him with anyone I had known before, to approach him with an open mind, as a book I had yet to read. Though the very thought, pathetically, reminded me of Var. I had to wonder if all our problems were in fact my problems, if I would carry them from bed to bed like a lady's purse: the same tissues, the same compact, the same small bills. The matter of the stuck window asserted itself but I turned with even greater assertiveness away from it.

The house, which had seemed warm when we entered, now felt cold as a barn. I wished I could put my coat back on without sending the wrong message. We would have to touch soon, if only to keep our teeth from chattering. I didn't want to hear his teeth chatter, nor did I want him to hear mine.

"Shall we get under?" I asked, eyeing the blanket, afraid he would decline. Surely a power differential exists between a highly attractive young man and a moderately attractive middle-aged woman. I felt frightfully unsure of myself.

As he nodded and bent down to remove his boots, I avoided seeing his feet. Even dressed in socks, feet are disconcertingly intimate. Though now there are moments at the library or in the apartment just before I drift off to sleep when I close my eyes and picture them—his feet, his teeth, any part of him, as clearly as I can just for the pleasure of it. My ability to do so, evidence of our intimacy. But then I had never seen him read a book or drink a glass of water or eat a piece of bread; only twice had I seen him sit in a chair. How could I possibly have seen his feet? I felt then the extreme disorder of things; I felt a compassion for us having gone about everything in such an unnatural sequence. I made my way to the mattress, (as if I could escape him there).

To cope with my mounting fear I examined the loft. Even as he lay down next to me, I was studying the rafters, the crude wooden pegs that had been used in place of nails, the stainless steel hook upon which I had neglected to hang my coat. There was a deep silence yet no sound of air in or out. It appeared that, like me, he was holding his breath. He kept his body at a polite distance, close enough so that I did not feel rejected but not close enough to touch mine. The blanket, which he had pulled up to his neck and whose olive green I could just make out, was, I realized with delight, virgin wool, incongruous with the ascetic's house and perfectly suited to us. Perhaps the owner received it as a gift from someone with slightly more luxurious tastes than her own. Or perhaps her skin was very sensitive, someone like Var or Maria who suffered from psoriasis and could not wear common wool next to their skin. These were my quotidian thoughts as my young lover lay next to me for the first time. Despite my romantic notions about the two of us inhabiting an island separate from the main, in our first moments together we were two islands, near but not touching, each of us surrounded by perilous depths.

I was studying the zigzag stitch at the edge of the blanket when the young man cleared his throat. Had he intended to remind me of his existence or had a particle of the trespassed air caught in his throat? I turned toward him to find his head already turned toward mine. His eyes looked well-rested, expectant, like those of a second-string athlete waiting his turn. How long had I left him looking and waiting (his girlishly soft neck perhaps being scratched by the wool)?

Moving toward him was like stepping into a very cold pond. My first reaction was fear, was retraction. I had to speak silently to myself. I had to inhale a large amount of oxygen and then hold it in, in order to proceed, to stun myself into being, into a shivering state of ecstatic cold until the water felt warmer.

When we had kissed for a time that in its duration and intensity can only be compared to an unchaperoned high school encounter (the toffee scent of his tobacco now a taste in my mouth), I paused and began to undress. He glanced at my body, then at the mattress.

"It's all right to look," I said, then wondered if I had been foolish to assume he would be aroused by the sight of me (and unaware that he had perfect vision). I prayed he would undress himself as I did not feel prepared to take on such a grave responsibility. He did so but rather slowly and with trembling fingers, as if he were having second thoughts. First he removed his white thermal shirt, which was remarkably clean, then his jeans, the fly of which was a challenge to unzip as he himself was now in the way of it. I admit I intervened the way a mother is wont to do when she sees her child struggling.

"Thank you," he said and cleared his throat. I found his old-fashioned politeness quite touching.

I confess I'd deliberated about whether or not to remove my glasses but when faced with the spectacle of his unclothed body, its sword so gallantly raised, all deliberations ceased. One did not want to be blind but to feast one's eyes upon beauty.

It was I who carefully replaced the blanket but then, suddenly boiling (and annoyed by the obstruction of my view), I surprised myself by roughly throwing it off. Without thinking, I knelt on all fours and dispensed a brief instruction with which he quickly complied. "I hope you won't mind," I said. "I don't think I can look at you." Glasses indeed.

"You don't have to explain." He moved skillfully toward me as he spoke and I felt once more the fear I had felt on the footbridge, the fear of violence, the fear of him being, well, a rapist. (An unfair inversion to be sure.) But once he had knelt down behind me, he froze like an icon. It was not entirely evident whether he had encountered such an offering before.

"Well, go on."

These seemed to be the words he was waiting for. I considered warning him about the stuck window but before I could formulate a sentence, the window opened. It was marvelous. The view of the lake, the jasmine, the breeze, everything was as it had been, and then some.

I looked back over my shoulder, indeed I had never been happier to be wearing corrective lenses. I wanted to see him after all, though I only glanced for the act itself began to require my full attention. As if diving into water, I closed my eyes and lowered my head. I saw him in my mind, the fleeting image of his face, his dark lashes framing his closed eyes, his brow furrowed, his chin tucked defensively, his mouth clenched like one in need of a leather strap, his expression of pleasure ultimately one of pain.

I shall never forget the way in which he afterward very quietly lowered himself down upon the borrowed mattress to rest behind me. Thoroughly exerted, freshly released, and yet he did so with such care. Another man might have collapsed like a dead animal atop me or draped himself like a cloth upon my face but he did not so much as graze me with a fingernail as he moved off and away. And then, just when I thought I would go mad from not touching him anymore, from not being touched by him, he crept closer—I was on my side with my back to him—and encircled me in the way a small child guards her most treasured belonging. She conceals the beloved object from view, she hunches down over it, bends her face close to it, disappears into it, her hair falls upon it like a curtain. It matters little if other children desire the object. The love the child has for it is secret, it comes from her internal culture; no one else need understand it. She has invented its meaning and by extension her love.

Later he would encircle me like that and I would want to shake him and shout, "Don't you see?! No one else wants me!" I didn't feel worthy of his encircling. I was more than twice his age! A liar! A cheat! But on that day I welcomed it. I was in need of reassurance, it was too early then for me to truly think of him. I thought only of myself.

My eyes had not lied. Though slight without clothes, he had a man's body. It absolved me of a portion of my guilt. Compared to Maria, he felt brawny, enormous, though I suppose a ten-year-old body might have felt the same. My tactile perspective was distorted, estranged as I had been for some time from the body of a grown man. I was accustomed to holding a four-year-old girl in my arms. (And yet I had easily accommodated him! I felt triumphant and not a little relieved, as if I'd just received a clean bill of health from a doctor.) I wondered how I'd become this way, able to betray my husband, more promiscuous than either of my parents.

It was only after we had merged and separated that we seemed to dwell at last on the same island. The house was empty, the woods quiet. I felt the distant presence of the sea.

"It's so quiet," he said, speaking the words at precisely the same moment I had thought them.

"Yes, it feels as if no one can reach us."

He nodded. He did not seem frightened to be thus stranded with me. I too felt perfectly content to exist in his company apart from the rest of the world.

We lay in this silence for a time and then from somewhere beyond the woods we heard the sound of a car in motion and were reminded that we were not alone, that ours was not a deserted island, but one inhabited by mothers driving on roads to pick children up from school, farmers who moved sheep by the truckload, children who waited to be taken to safe places, sheep who waited to be transported to fresh fields. What did the sheep do in deep winter I wondered, when the fields were covered in snow?

"Where were you all that time?" I asked. It was on that morning, after the fleet whirl of the first, that I began at last to administer my long queue of questions.

"When?" he murmured, as if he'd been dreaming and I'd woken him.

"All of December and most of January. I thought you'd never come back."

"I totaled my car," he muttered, his eyes still closed.

"What?!" I sat up on my elbows in alarm. "Were you hurt?" Rather ridiculously, I began palpating him, in search of what? Broken bones? Tender joints? Sore muscles? He opened his eyes. "No, not really," he lifted the palm of his right hand and turned it toward me to display a deep fuchsia gash. "The windshield," he said.

"God, it looks horrible, just horrible! And the car was ruined?"

"It was a shitbox," he said and then immediately amended, "sorry, I mean it wasn't a great car anyway."

I raked his leafy curls with my fingers and admired his pouting lips, their efforts at politeness.

"Here I was thinking about your absence in terms of myself. How small-minded of me! You could have been killed!" I meant this sincerely though my concern for his well-being was undeniably selfish, for the death of the young man would have meant the death of my pleasure. "So what do you do now? Did you buy another car? Do you ride a bicycle?" Relentlessly single-minded, I was thinking of his mobility in terms of my desire. I wondered how difficult it had been for him to meet me. I felt a pain at the thought of him wandering the island on foot, though this was precisely what I did most days.

"I borrow Mom's car." I reveled in the intimacy of the phrase "Mom's car" until it occurred to me that Mom was also Violet. Lying on a stranger's mattress next to him, I felt incapable of assimilating her. At least she didn't drive him to school. "Sometimes," he mumbled, "I take the bus."

"Taking the school bus is nothing to be ashamed of," I said. "I rather like the thought of you passing by my apartment twice a day. A bit of gold through the trees flashing red. It's titillating don't you think?"

"It's hard to get too excited about riding a school bus."

"I suppose I'm not the one who has to ride it. So tell me, what caused the accident?" I was thinking of the double take. Perhaps I was nothing special, perhaps he drove all over town doing double takes, meeting middle-aged women at waterfalls at myriad, secret locations.

"I was driving down Old County and a woman turned in front of me."

"A woman?"

"Someone I knew." He scratched his head as if revving an engine. "Prudy Flanders. She and Mom used to study French together when I was a kid. She felt pretty bad. But we were both fine."

I gasped. Prudy Flanders was a habitual reader of paperback romance who regularly checked out ten at a time and returned them late, stained with coffee, peppered with grit, smelling of cigarettes. "You could have died together!"

"Not really, Mrs. Flanders was in her car and I was in mine. We would have died separately without ever talking to each other. I only knew it was her because I got out of my car and walked over to hers."

"How frighteningly intimate, you could have died together," I repeated, and for a perverse moment I wished I had been behind the wheel of the car that had hit him. I resisted the image of Mrs. Flanders fussing over his bloody hand with a clean cloth in the backseat of her white Ford Explorer.

"I'd like to avoid that kind of intimacy if possible," he said and closed his eyes, presumably to rest from the topic. Though it was just as probable that, like a boy in a hide-and-seek game, he was lying quietly hoping to be found.

I pressed his fuchsia scar against my cheek. His hand smelled faintly of tobacco, like the hand of a beloved uncle. I felt at once a surge of well-being and a dimming of confidence. Unsure about whether he'd enjoyed it enough to want seconds, I closed my eyes too. I thought about our day, beginning with the waterfall and ending with the questions. All of his answers pleased me. I felt a sense of accomplishment when he answered a question in a way I had predicted and a rush of pleasure when he surprised me.

Satisfied by our own treachery, we drifted in and out of

sleep. I spent some of this time watching him. Once I dared to run my hand along the length of his body. When he seemed to have fallen genuinely asleep, I grew bolder. I woke him with my hand and then took the liberty of having him again. He cooperated so fully that I reproached myself for not having done so earlier.

After much cooperation we managed to rise, to dress in the near dark and descend into daylight the unfinished stairs that were only more treacherous on the way down. The third and fourth steps cried out under the weight of my boots and I could not help but think of having him again, his seat on step four, my hands clutching step seven. I laughed aloud at the thought. I would fall to my death as I climaxed. What bliss! I glanced at my watch as if considering it, but it was nearly two o'clock.

We reentered the world's time zone grudgingly, each of us pausing on the last rung before stepping down. On the main floor, the house was bright with sunlight and snow. The outside world was brighter still, as when one exits a movie theater during the day. Everything was beautifully, blindingly real. We agreed to meet the following Friday.

"How will I get through the week?" I asked.

"You'll be busy," he said, oblivious to my inability to think of anything else regardless of what I was "busy" doing, a condition that I could sense would only worsen now that we had made love. I wanted to say that it didn't matter how busy I was, that I would think of him constantly, but all at once I felt self-conscious, my body riddled with doubt as with a spontaneous and embarrassing rash.

"How will *you* get through the week?" I ventured. Would he confide in his mother about this?

"I don't know."

"Will it be hard for you?" I had half a mind to tell her myself.

"I'll tell you when the week's over."

"I might not want to know."

"Yes you will."

"Touché," I said, then immediately wondered if I'd misinterpreted him as he had several times misinterpreted me, if he'd indeed been making reference to my inquisitive nature or if he meant that he would surely have something reassuring if not suggestive to report. Or something else entirely.

As I pulled him closer to say goodbye, I was surprised to find him aroused. "When did this happen?" I asked.

"I don't think it ever stopped happening." His face reddened and he looked down at the snowy ground.

"Good. Constant desire is good."

I touched one of the snowflakes on his hat and then ran through the woods, already late to pick up Maria.

The nursery was a fifteen-minute walk, an eight-minute jog from the state road. I had chosen the school expressly for its close proximity to the apartment, not, by any stretch of my former Conscientious Librarian's imagination, in anticipation of the purpose this short distance would serve that Friday or on the Fridays that followed. I arrived ten minutes late, panting like a wild animal that has just outdistanced a predator in order to protect her young. I had never been late before; I had been early on occasion but never late. Maria, hanging from the crossing bars, glanced with indifference at me as I called out her name too loudly. There were other children in the yard. The scene was not nearly as desolate as my sprinting animal self had imagined. Maria was not sobbing in a corner under the impression that I had abandoned her, nor did she show any sign of relief at my appearance. Her teacher was on the far side of the grass replenishing the caged rabbit's food and water supply and seemed to have noticed neither my absence nor my arrival.

I sat down on the damp wooden steps next to the tidy line of lunch sacks, as much to cool my trembling skin (upon every inch of which droplets of sweat were now beginning to form) as to devour the remainder of my child's lunch, something I had seen other mothers do before but had never been hungry enough to do myself. In most cases, had I been, I would have been out of luck, for Maria was not a child who left her lunch uneaten. Today, naturally, was my lucky day. She had left half a tuna sandwich and two carrots to boot. I could have eaten five times that. Such a savage appetite was not in keeping with my sedentary routine. This was the hunger of runners and beasts, the pleasant aftermath of exertion! The sensation was so satisfying I knew there must be those who exert themselves as much for the pleasure of satisfying the hunger that follows exertion as for the pleasure of exertion itself. I had a glimpse of the addictive potential of meeting one's body's demands.

"It was Sophia's birthday!" Maria announced as we set off. The name Sophia, once more in vogue, with its ultrafeminine and youthful connotations, rang a bell of alarm in me. I remembered that not far from us, large groups of teenage girls, several of whom were likely named Sophia, were also being released from school and that any one of them might be entering the young man's number into her mobile phone as I stood in the cold shade of the nursery. One Sophia in particular might be pedaling her bicycle in the direction of his house whose location was still unknown to me. This was to say nothing of the actions and intentions of those girls whose names were not Sophia.

"Sophia?!" I said hoarsely, repressing my painful thoughts. "That's wonderful, you love Sophia!"

"The cake wasn't wonderful. It was vanilla! It's always vanilla. Vanilla, vanilla, vanilla. Why isn't it ever chocolate?!"

Why indeed, I thought, as Maria ran ahead to the pond's edge and began studying dead leaves.

As we neared the general store she asked, "Can I get a treat?"

"No. You've already had cake today."

"But I didn't even like it!"

"That *is* unfair. Next time say no thank you."

I bought her two chocolate kisses. She went wild. At the edge of the grass that surrounded the house, Maria began to run. I ran after her, happy to exert myself. She ran into the garden behind the house and stopped as she often did at the base of the oak tree. She was well-suited to climbing trees; she was a compact, agile, quizzical little girl with big hands that gripped like a monkey's and wide eyes that like, to peer down from high places and survey.

"Will you put me in the tree?" she asked, jumping to reach for a branch. It was as it had been on the day of the forgotten book. She correctly sensed that I would do almost anything she asked. Once more I quelled the urge to tell her my news. I placed her on a high branch and she gave a squeal, lifted up her arms, threw them around the trunk of the tree, and, in one chimplike movement, kicked her boots down to the ground. In that primitive moment, I loved her endlessly. I felt my desire for the young man and my love for her mingling. The cup marked *pleasure* and the cup marked *love* were spilling over. I didn't have to tell her. She knew. Not the particulars of course, but I think she understood the essential meaning. Who could have been better equipped to recognize my joy than the one who had most often been the cause of it?

We stayed out in the garden—she sitting high in the tree chattering, I lying on the grass with my eyes closed listening—until we could stand the cold no longer.

"Let's go in," I said lightly, expecting resistance.

"Oh yes! Let's go in now, the monkeys are cold!" To my surprise, she quickly agreed and ran up the stairs ahead of me. I followed her at a leisurely pace and then washed my hands in the filthy bathroom which now looked to my lecherous eye abandoned and sexy. I could easily imagine that lovers had lain furtively upon its cracked tiles or perhaps sat double astride the loose, squeaking seat of the toilet. Indeed I was aroused by the sight of it.

* * *

I approached the library on Sunday with equal parts titillation and dread, like one who has just sinned and feels, upon returning to church, both a shameless thrill and a longing to confess. Most Sundays I was on the schedule with Kitty, the director, and Nella, but today Siobhan would be subbing for the director and I could not help but think cheerfully of this fact as I took my last few steps toward the door. Though I had sworn myself (to myself) to secrecy, I felt my resolve vanishing like incense into the wintry air and I had not yet crossed the threshold into the warm library.

"How's Baby?" Nella's familiar interview startled me as I entered. She was lugging the metal bin from beneath the mouth of the book drop back to the front counter. Worried she would throw out her back (as she had several times done over the years), I pushed the bin forward with my foot then reached back and latched the mouth shut.

"Oh, Baby is divine," I coughed, trying unsuccessfully this time to calm myself with the humor of the secret meaning. "How's your bright shiny penny?" I asked. Suddenly I would have liked to talk of nothing more than the simple joy of cocker spaniels for the duration of our shift together. I needed something soft and undiscerning to nuzzle up against. I was a jumpy wreck.

"Well, aside from her midnight encounter with a skunk, Penny's great. I got the tomato juice, everything's fine!"

"Is Siobhan here?" I asked, for in truth I only wished I could endure the innocence of more canine chitchat. In truth, I was guilty and the guilty want to be unburdened; talk of innocence only weighs us down.

"Mmmm hmmm," Nella nodded, softly grunting as she heaved a large stack of art books from the bin and set them on the counter. "She's putting out the newspapers. All the news that's fit to print."

I stowed my belongings and carefully attached my magnetic name tag to the rather close-fitting black sweater I had purchased a month prior but had never worn. Nella began checking the art books in, lifting each one with both hands then placing the barcode under the scanner's red light. Without varying her cadence, she added, "Someone was here to see you the other day."

"Who?"

"I don't remember her name. Lily something or other. It was the mother of that boy."

I suppressed the urge to ask "Which boy?" for I feared Nella's reproach: *You know very well which boy.*

Besieged by pleasure in the company of the young man I had managed to blot Violet from my consciousness but now it was difficult to forget her. It seemed inevitable that we should encounter one another.

Siobhan returned from the bathroom, where every librarian promptly goes after putting out papers in order to wash the newsprint off her hands. I took refuge in the sight of her. Her hair too looked freshly washed and I saw her for an instant as she must have looked at eighteen, with a toss of her clean hair, winking a solitary green eye at whomever pleased her.

"Hey there, sexy librarian lady!"

"Very funny," I said a bit glumly, for though I was eager to move on from Nella's softly accusatory comment, I felt once more the awful sensation of being on an island unfathomably far from Siobhan, leagues of ocean separating us and neither of us well-equipped to swim. I lurched forward to receive her embrace (Siobhan was such a lover, I certainly could have fallen for her in another life.) and ventured to change, if only in my own brain, the subject.

"Do you mind if I work in the children's room today?" I asked. The two of them looked at me patiently as members of an audience.

"What's goin' on?" Siobhan asked.

"Just tired," I said and scuffled away. In truth, I was frightened by the possibility that Mother or Son or both would whirl through the library like moral hurricanes and derange my well-ordered world.

I sat at the desk of the children's librarian and gazed in wonder and dismay at the juvenile collection. It troubled me to recall that when I applied for the position I was asked to fill out a CORI form (whose name I always horribly imagined was the name of a dead child whose violation had not been prevented) which was then used to verify that I had never been convicted of molesting a child. I had told the truth when I described myself as innocent of such a crime. It was only years after the form was filed and made legal, only two days prior, that, unbeknownst to my employers, I had committed one of the crimes that might have barred me from being offered the position. I was not troubled by what in retrospect seemed a lack of self-knowledge—this I found heartening if anything, heartening with a teaspoon of excitement thrown in, nor was I (though perhaps I should have been) troubled by the fact that according to the law I had committed a crime. What troubled me was that in some roundabout, retroactive way, I had lied or was lying as I continued to work with the clean CORI on file. You see, despite everything, I am an honest person with a conscience, a detail-oriented person (as opposed to a detail-oriented librarian) troubled by such discrepancies.

I picked up an illustrated copy of *The Mysterious Island* from the cart and walked slowly toward the V's. It occurred to me that the young man had likely read more children's books than adult books. Which books did he love? Did he adore Jules Verne as I had? Was he a Hardy Boys boy? Had he too loved Paddington? Had he read so-called girls' classics like *The Little Princess* and *The Secret Garden?* Did he prefer fiction or non? Did he read when he was sad or happy or both? The questions still came to me like mantras I intoned to myself, beads I touched repeatedly in a circular fashion. I would have to submit to him my evergrowing list. Astonishing that I could now ask him anything.

While meditating upon our new proximity, it dawned on me that his phone number was in the library database. How could I have forgotten? I had entered the numbers myself. I turned away from the cart and glanced nervously at the monitor. Why shouldn't I have his phone number? God knew I had little else. Yet phone numbers seemed the provenance of honest people, those who loved the people they had promised they would love and who had therefore earned the right to contact them directly. There was, after all, something public about a phone number. Most appeared in the phone book and all existed in digital form in some ethereal library and could be, if only by public machines, easily recognized. *Shelve the bloody cart already.*

When I had placed the last book in its proper place, I promptly rewarded myself with a visit to the library database. I swiftly typed in his name, clicked on "Patron" then "Information" then "Phone." Voilà. Though there were neither children nor adults in the juvenile room to witness my breach of privacy (so minor in comparison to the breach I'd committed in the woods), I trembled as I wrote his number down, my heart racing as I stuffed the scrap of paper into my blazer pocket. You ought to be frightened! I scolded myself as I remembered his number was also Violet's—I had learned this the first day and forgotten. I searched for *The Days of Abandonment.* AVAILABLE. One of them had returned the book in my absence. I felt a tinge of sadness and an odd sense of reprieve. Untoward as it may sound, I'd been looking forward to chatting with Violet about it. I didn't know whether to thank God for relieving me of what was becoming a rather complicated duty or to begin pining at once for her return.

At closing time, as was often the case, Kitty slipped out without any of us noticing, followed by Siobhan, myself (for though I moved at a leisurely pace, I hated to be last, to be responsible for locking the door), and finally Nella who had to be informed that the library was now closing, so involved she was in the cutting of gingerbread men out of brown construction paper. As I stood holding the locked door open for her I could not help but pat my pocket for the phone number. It was an unconscious gesture, made as if the hidden scrap were a passport or a large bill, something I was terrified of losing. Nella shoved her cheese puffs into a sailcloth tote and swiped her hands against her cream-colored cords. There was a moment when, with the exception of Kitty, all of us were standing in the door together like a cozy and promising coterie that, as we stepped into the anonymous night, then dispersed like a group of strangers to become part of it. We called our goodbyes over our shoulders.

As my co-workers drifted in separate directions toward their cars, I walked slowly toward the opening in the trees. I had always been the librarian who lingered, the one in no particular hurry to leave. Tonight I felt acutely the need to stay and talk. I pretended to rearrange the contents of my tote and watched them go: willowy, wisecracking, well-brushed Siobhan; woolly-haired Nella with her soft, sheeplike shoulders and opaque blue eyes; and hurried, preoccupied, gum-chewing Kitty in her tattered leopard-skin coat, already entering a number into her mobile phone, a lit cigarillo trembling between her first two fingers.

"I'm in love!" I wanted to shout at them! "We made love in the woods!" I would announce it with glee in the spirit of camaraderie, as if the making of love was, like the making of cookies, something librarians regularly announced to one another. "It was fantastic! He's seventeen!" I screamed the words in silence at their backs. One by one in quick succession their car doors slammed above the asphalt. I may as well have been standing on the Crimean coast looking out at the Black Sea at three infinitesimal skiffs on the horizon. "It's true," I whispered as I turned to go, as much to the snow-touched trees as to the librarians.

* * *

The young man and I met Friday mornings. If a librarian asked me to sub a Friday, I refused without deliberation; they were refusals for which I felt no guilt, only a flash of terror at the possibility that I would be detained. Meeting once weekly required that we withstand six-day intervals of separation. My fear that he would one day fail to appear was so strong that those intervals were agonizing. I think now it was the perfect schedule for two people such as ourselves, though at the time I felt it was never enough. Not once did I tire of him, not once did he impinge upon my daily routine. Fleeting as our pulse-quickening encounters may have been, they were, I see now, dependable as an old Burberry.

During our intervals of separation, I thought of nothing else. I wanted more of him but couldn't figure out how to get it. Alternately I tried to stop wanting him but couldn't figure that out either. From Friday to Friday I dreamed of him—long, rapturous, yet unimaginative dreams in which I was highly aroused and in impossibly complex, drawn-out pursuit of him. Always, our lovemaking—sometimes pleasantly, sometimes maddeningly—was being deferred. And always, I would wake with a sunny, floaty feeling of euphoria that was then darkened by the thunderclap complaint: *Why can't I at least dream of having him?!* I was, as much as a married librarian could be, utterly wedded to the idea of loving him.

Walking to work on other mornings, when I approached Music Street, it took all my remaining willpower not to turn left and at night I fell asleep to thoughts of how I might scale the attic wall and run, wearing camouflage, like a hunter to the dark woods. Morning or night, he wouldn't have been there, yet I felt vexed to go, as if somewhere beneath the foundation of the gray house lay a volcanic stone that was exerting a magnetic influence upon me, upon us, our very own Hanging Rock. Indeed I had to imagine that he was feeling the pull too, though most of the time, I didn't dare ask. When, on occasion, I posed some question regarding his feelings about me, he grew so quiet I felt I had trespassed upon his most fundamental right to privacy and in so doing silenced him.

He seemed to have found another way in through the woods, a route more compatible with his mysterious starting point. I never asked him to show me the path; I assumed it was one of the ancient ways. That each of us should travel separately and alone to converge upon the house pleased me. The illicit nature of our affair made it impossible for me to walk with him in public or in the woods with its secret maze of paths, for on a small island, such paths are akin to backstreets and to be seen with him there would have been scandalous. I was accustomed to walking alone in nature; it had a ravishing effect on me whereas in the presence of others the natural world made me jumpy. To this day I hardly know how I withstood the pleasure of those Fridays—first the walk alone in the woods, then my tryst with the young man—week after week that swift and double ravishment.

He was a quick study. Quiet. Modest. Watchful. Though he never took the liberty of making eye contact for the duration, the way some lovers unnervingly do, plucking that easy intensity like an unripe fruit for the fun of it, simply to feel the force of nature, or perhaps to see minute images of themselves in the eyes of another. He paid close attention to my responses, to my eyelids and fingernails, to the pulse in the skin of my neck, the bridge of my back arching over the rough mattress as he held it, his trembling hands impressive as any truss. He paid the sort of attention a child devotes to an instrument he intends to master; he touched me as if I were an expensive and breakable instrument. After a few lessons, he was able to produce the desired effect. I became, as instruments often do in the hands of children, an extension of his own body. I imagine he knew how to please me as well as he knew how to please himself.

Once he overcame his initial shyness, he did everything I asked with unsettling degrees of intelligence and athleticism. At times that potent mix in such a young man frightened me. I felt it was inevitable that he should surpass me. I was a mother who imparted everything I knew about how to love, believing that in the end her child would use his carefully learned skills to love the World and not the Original, not the Mother, that First in a sequence who, like the match that lights the fire, soon reaches the end of her short stick. And why not? Not even the thought of death could stop me from loving him, from wanting to impart to him all that existed within me pertaining to love. Aren't all mother-child relationships made with that same bittersweet substance: the old earth mixed with the new, held together by that necessary, heartbreaking element of send-off? Ultimately, I wanted him to love the World, to start fires with the others, to burn brightly in the distance long after I was cold ash. Those who think one takes a young lover to escape thoughts of death are mistaken.

His lips were shaped like Maria's. Yes, rather ironically, they too were reminiscent of the Gerber baby of yesteryear: their slight pucker, their slight pout, the open mouth, irresistible to feed. How intently he would drag them across my stomach, then up to the sternum that covered, but could not conceal, my beating heart. I imagine his youthful ears were acute enough to hear its perilous pounding. He would rest his lips there lightly, as if speaking to me through a closed door, before rushing to my breasts, to my dark nipples that had by that time long since risen up to meet him, his lips, his teeth, his tongue. It was another joy of winter, the desire—so persistent and actual—to be devoured by warmth. Two hands, a body, a mouth. The sudden warmth of human touch was so surprising. That it was in winter, that the touch was his, only increased my delight.

At risk of sounding crude as a white-haired empress with her black-haired houseboy, I could hardly believe my luck. And I was luckier still, for I had no riches to offer him and he no orders to obey my commands. I had not bought him off the auction block with a sack of gold or inherited him at last from the ancestors; there had been no contract between warring nations condemning him to my company. He had come to me of his own accord. He had been given to me—he had given himself to me—and I did not know why.

Never before had I gazed so raptly at a lover's beauty. Being the woman, I had always been gazed at. I was never so admiring of men as they were of me. But perhaps it was more than that. If I had perceived beauty would I not have gazed at it or at least wanted to? I have no memory of either. Had age made youth more beautiful to me, the way one's childhood acquires a brighter light as the mind dims, or was the young man simply the most beautiful specimen I had ever encountered?

His stomach was flat as a new school desk and as bare. No scribbles, no scars, only the faintest line of black hair that began at the base of his concave belly button then disappeared into his trousers as if into a hidden future. A great scar from the past nestled just below the belt, as if everything of significance—past, present, and future—lay concealed beneath his American jeans.

He smelled deliciously of freshly laundered clothes and the English toffee that was in fact his chewing tobacco. His skin took on the scent of clean cotton and the vanilla scent of one who bakes cakes often; the smell of woodsmoke was always in his hair. His gentle manner and his shyness gave him the appearance of being docile though I soon found that he also possessed within himself, like the delicate but certain stone within some fruits, an obdurate core. I rather loved that stone of his, the way I loved all pits I had extracted from fruit with my tongue. At his core he was obdurate yet shaggy with sweetness. One could pry the hardness open and find within it unexpected fragrances and pleasing shapes, the way one discovers the scent of almond inside a plum's heart. The stone inside him protected us. It prevented him from disappearing into nothingness and it prevented me from devouring him whole.

So the voluptuous pouring of pleasure continued. What was absurdly quenching and satisfying that first morning became a natural state of affairs on the Friday mornings that followed. It was as I had sensed it would be: like some lavishly ornate fountain, my cup was overflowing. My blindness was complete, my attention span Proustian, the taste of said madeleine endlessly delicious. I wanted nothing more than to return to it, go over it, taste it, and remember.

* * *

And then one afternoon, as if she'd had a glass of good wine before leaving the house (her face warm, her eyes tranquil), as she dropped her books in, Violet said hello to me. For a moment all my sins were forgotten. I stared in disbelief at my tooth-sized nugget. *Hello.* It fairly gleamed in the pan. Greedy for more, I plunged my pan back into the river.

"Hello," I said, "how are you?" She did not reply but nodded at me in Japanese fashion before turning toward the stairs.

I pounced at once upon her returned items. It was a grim selection. One was the Dostoevsky on CD that the young man had borrowed for her. They must have renewed it several times with another librarian—each renewal, to my fanatical mind, a brute infidelity. The item was terrifying and titillating at once, an object each of us had held in turn, a material witness to the current that ran between the three of us. The other was a cloth edition of *The House of Mirth* whose somewhat flaky gold title produced in me a pang of concern for Violet's (and by extension the young man's) financial standing. Lily Bart's sad story would have been sadder still if she'd had a child.

My mind turned to Violet in the basement below. What would she borrow? What, if anything, did she know? Being alone at the desk made it more difficult to endure the brief wait for her return. There were no other patrons to distract me. I could have used a good glass myself. In a most biddy-ish manner, I began to fidget. I sharpened several pencils, cut squares of scrap paper with the metal paper cutter, affixed stickers to a cart of new cookbooks. (The director never ceased to impress me with her ongoing ability to anticipate what was to come, whether it was a great influx of summer patrons or a surge of interest in cookbooks in the dead of winter. If I could have seen the future that clearly and without flinching, I too might have been in a position of power.)

"Hello, Angel," I said, extremely grateful to Alberta Angelone, for I had run out of cookbooks and she was a favorite. She drove public buses for a living, I was a bus rider, and we had both been raised Catholic—that was enough for us. She let me call her Angel. "How are you?"

"Hi, honey. I couldn't be happier. She's got a new one out," she said, grinning at the Danielle Steel she had placed on the counter.

Violet stepped up behind her like a girl alone, waiting in line for a film, the young man there in her eyes, watching me.

As Angel turned to leave, I reddened. Violet breasted her book. There was an awkward pause in which she stepped forward but did not place it on the counter.

"Would you like to have tea sometime?" she asked.

Once more I felt sharply my inability to predict the future. Thinking I couldn't possibly have heard her correctly I answered breezily, "Oh yes. I drink tea all day in fact. It reminds me of," and here I nearly said "home" but that wasn't true so I revised, "it reminds me of days gone by."

Her cheeks looked as though someone in the basement had been pinching them. Perhaps she *had* had a glass before coming. She looked on the verge of laughter, her eyes swimming in a new wash of impishness. I was baffled, happy, and not a little concerned.

"Oh! Do you mean we would drink the tea together?" I asked. What an imbecile! Why was this happening to me now? Why not the year previous? Our timing couldn't have been more wrong.

"I thought we might, some people do you know. But if tea is a solitary act for you I understand."

"No! I mean it is (I couldn't lie) and yet I'd like nothing more than to share it with you." Idiot! Tea with the Mother of One's Seventeen-Year-Old Lover was ideally suited for a nightmare. Tea?! Oh God, better make it wine.

"Good," she said, still embracing her book. It was not until we had agreed to meet at Plum Island Provisions at 8:30 on the following Wednesday that she placed it on the counter.

It was *Ethan Frome*. Why was it every book she checked out provoked pity or concern in me?

"This is a marvelous book," I said too loudly, feeling a bit flushed, yes, a bit warm and tipsy myself now.

"I've been reading a lot more now that we've closed up shop. (The *we* of her sentence lodged in my throat and nearly asphyxiated me.) I'd love to talk with you about books over tea if you don't mind. I don't mean to assume that you read just because you're a..."

"Oh but I do! I'm ashamed to say it's nearly all I do in my

spare time. It would be a great adventure for me to talk about books instead of just reading them." And yet I'd already embarked on one great adventure, did I really have room in my life for two? Despite the flashing red lights I saw up ahead, the sirens I heard in the distance, I was eager to go forth.

"To adventure," she said, holding *Ethan Frome* up in a toast.

* * *

Once I had taken my friend's son as a lover, I had to cope with the problem of secrecy. As long as I did not become pregnant (perhaps I deluded myself about such an outcome, thinking I was still fertile, going at once to the doctor for pills), it was the kind of behavior one could in theory conceal for a lifetime, a secret someone less effusive than myself could easily have taken to the grave, and yet I saw immediately that I might not be up to the task. I was skilled at keeping secrets but what I had previously kept so well were the secrets of others. I didn't know how to keep my own secrets and it seemed paramount that I should learn.

Various techniques presented themselves to me, the primary being verbal sublimation, which I had already begun to experiment with and which I now set out to perfect. When I felt the need to speak about him at the library, I spoke of his mother or of her shop or of teenage boys in general, casting as wide a net as possible with the hope that when a co-worker or patron opened her mouth to speak, a minnow (if not a marlin) of pertinent information would swim out toward me as I lay in wait.

Alternately, I toyed with the notion that I might safely satisfy this need by selecting one trustworthy person to hear my confession. Siobhan would have been the most natural choice (with the exception of Violet, who would have been perfect had not her son been the one regularly manhandling me) but before I could prime myself for such a release, Siobhan beat me to the confessional punch with an admission of her own: She had *fallen in love* with her husband again.

"Is that humanly possible?" I asked skeptically.

"Yes!" she shouted with tears in her eyes.

Like a butterfly who sheds her wings and returns to her chrysalis, Siobhan became pupal in her viewpoint, ravenous as a larva for opportunities to fix my marriage. I feared one day I would come to work to find she had returned to an egg state, unable to think or speak, much less advise me. Between composing e-mails to other libraries requesting interlibrary loans and filling out her green cards (most librarian tasks present little challenge even to a pupa), she piped in with romantic suggestions of things that had worked for her and Nick that might possibly work for Var and me, everything from taking a couples' yoga class to exchanging positive anecdotes before bedtime to books on tantric sex to spending the night in a B & B.

Var despised B & Bs for their lack of privacy, I despised yoga as I despised most (not all, mind you) forms of exercise, and one would be hard pressed to choose between us who had a less positive outlook especially at bedtime. Indeed, tantric sex is of little use to those who have no sex at all. For the sake of my friendship with Siobhan I sometimes wished I could conform to her suggestions, the way I had once acceded, at her urging, to visiting Var's room late one night. But my attempt to seduce Var had been a dismal failure and my affair with the young man was a smashing success so I had little motivation.

The director, busy as she was, was likewise unavailable for comment. This may have been all for the best, considering CORI forms and whatnot, not to mention the matter of the Friday shift which she had recently suggested I work on a regular basis and which I naturally refused.

Now that Siobhan had gone the way of the happy wife, Nella was the only one who might have cast her fonts and cheese puffs aside in favor of hearing a sister librarian's true confession, but she continued to wrangle by drawing parallels between the young man and Var. She barraged me with questions like "He has kind of a Var vibe don't you think?" and "They have a similar look right?" which I received as rhetorical. She continued as well, inexplicably, to take longer and more frequent lunch breaks. More and more she seemed to be abandoning us but for what I wasn't certain.

When I felt the need to be counseled, which was often, I gently interrogated the librarians about their high school exploits and listened with care for nostalgic bits of adolescent lore that might enlighten me. Daily my co-workers confessed to me while I confessed to no one. These interviews did little to help my situation; nonetheless, I enjoyed them. My co-workers spoke of things they had never spoken of to me before; their faces became animated, seeming to indicate the capacity of love to alter reality long after a love affair is over. Even scurrying, unreachable Kitty abandoned for a full two minutes the DVD cleaner in order to gaze at the Elsewhere of Love, a sight both poignant and distressing to behold. It was all too easy for me to fling myself twenty years into the future, to the moment when this day too would be part of such a captivating elsewhere.

* * *

On the eve of my first date with Violet—for it was a date, a meeting in a public place, something the young man and I would never have—I picked up the phone and considered calling the number on the scrap. My desires had exhausted me. I would let Mother and Son decide. If the young man answered I would hang up, if Violet answered, I would cancel. Either scenario afforded a like anxiety. I had gone so far as to retrieve the scrap from my blazer when I thought of English classes at Hatfield and of Siobhan, who would have made an ideal classmate. Had we been students whose only obligations were writing essays about the books we had discussed, we'd have had such lively discussions! Though perhaps lonely herself, Siobhan was too busy administering to her husband and teens to meet me in my loneliness, something for which I could not properly blame her. You see, the Hatfield girl won out in the end, she surpassed or ignored the transgressor. *Grant me this! Don't rob me of this!* she begged. She reduced me to ruefulness and I, though not without anxiety, gave in.

Prior to my rustic little episodes with her son, I'd thought tea with Violet would be like winning the lottery. I could ask anything! My prize would be knowledge! I never dreamed I'd already be swimming in it. As it was, I went to bed frightened. The minute Maria had fallen asleep I took on the attitude of a fortune-teller whose only crystal ball is the dazzling opal of her own brain. What would we talk about? What would she say? The subject of men, or women for that matter, the subject of other people, seemed inevitable and terrifying. As we scaled that small pyramid, the stone of Var would lead to the stone of Maria would lead to the stone of her lover if such a person existed, would lead to the stone of the father/ex etc. No matter where on the pyramid we began our ascent, no matter how slowly we climbed, we would never be far from its apex—her son—and that all-knowing eye, able to see into the squalor of my heart and condemn it. Contrary to what I'd thought at the start, I was in no hurry to reach it.

I was at a loss as to what to bring. (I had corked my urge to bring a bottle of wine—it was a morning encounter after all. Just a few Fridays ago it might have been champagne but now it was wine, a good strong red one.) There were no flowers in the garden; the blue hydrangeas had been the color of parchment for weeks, the unidentifiable late-blooming indigo blossoms had vanished. I resolved to retrieve my Japan box from the attic, which required me to gain entry to Var's room. I didn't bother to knock for I knew he wouldn't hear me. I padded softly through in socks, averting my eyes at the sight of the carcasslike lump beneath his bedclothes.

In a hurry or not, it was always unwise to sift through my Japan box and that morning I was cutting it very fine. On any given day, I ran the risk of falling into the box, its foreign objects like so many pages of a book I never grew tired of reading. To guard against such perilous sentimentality, I repeated to myself: *Be quick about it, May, your friend Violet is waiting. Yes, be quick about it, May, your friend Violet is…* and so on. It's a wonder the incantation did not paralyze me. Twice I sifted through the box, twice I decided against going. It was a mark of my loneliness that I allowed myself to proceed. For no matter how often I berated myself for my greed (*Why isn't the son enough?! Why must you also have the mother?!*) there was something the mother possessed that her son couldn't possibly offer me and that, I suppose, was adult friendship, something I scarcely knew I needed before Violet extended her invitation. I settled on a tea set that was painted a deep green with a white wave motif, and a gold canister of green tea. Somehow I knew they would please her.

While I was riding my bicycle, a peculiar Hatfieldian sensation came over me. I felt as though I were pedaling across campus on that blustery morning in the direction of another girl's dormitory, the white gift box in my front basket a package of snacks we would soon devour together over schoolwork. What a gale fate was at my back! How sadistically it whipped at my face then sent me rolling in Violet's direction! Perhaps I should have been filled with dread but when I caught sight of the shop's handmade sign I stood up and began pedaling faster.

I leaned my bicycle against a wooden fence that looked as if it might soon topple over. In the absence of summer crowds, the shop looked smaller and in need of a good wash. Items in the yard—the rusty bicycles, the splintered Adirondacks, the antique cider press—that lent the shop a quaint, old-fashioned feel during the high season looked a bit like junk now.

I felt rather conspicuous standing in broad daylight during the off-season on property belonging to the mother of the teenager with whom I'd been having vigorous sex on Fridays. A stack of Scharffen Berger crates blocked the front steps to the shop, forcing me to scrabble onto the porch like a weasel. I'm certain my face wore the expression of a thief: greedy in the eyes and mouth, guilty. There was a brass padlock on the door, a page of dust upon the window. I knocked but received no answer. My watch, an expensive and reliable Omega given to me by my father, read 8:30. Perhaps I had dreamed everything prior to this moment. Perhaps I was dreaming now.

"I'm here," a voice called.

I followed it to a double gate, one half of which stood open. Violet was standing in the garden pulling mud-stained gloves from her hands, wearing the brown cowl-neck sweater, her hair tied away from her face. She smiled as if she were having her picture taken against her will.

"You look terribly underdressed," I said.

"No, I don't get cold. You're one to talk, your face is red as wine!"

I did feel on the verge of drunkenness. Fear, excitement, a bout of frantic winter cycling—red was entirely possible.

She led me into a room made of cloudy windows that was attached to the rear of the shop. The air was humid as a jungle and smelled miraculously of blossoms and fruit, at once slightly bitter and deliciously sweet.

"Oh Violet," I breathed, embarrassed at having said her name aloud, ashamed of the strength of my own feelings.

Everywhere I looked there were young orange and lemon trees heavy with fruit and camellia trees in full bloom. I inhaled deeply.

"What an Eden you've made!"

"It needs a lot of work. I keep meaning to wash the windows and sweep the floor." She pressed her lips together and I began to think her closemouthed smile was designed to conceal the gap I had glimpsed in the basement.

We sat at a tiny wooden table whose legs looked like they had spent many years in the rain and sun, with muddy little animal claws for feet. The trees were all around us, the orange and yellow fruits, the red and pink blooms festive as lanterns, scented, near enough to touch. Violet had covered the table with a red cloth (which brought to my lascivious mind the bedsheets of Rimbaud's newlyweds, hung out for all the town to see) and upon that a jar of pale pink camellias. There was tea in mugs and a pale orange loaf that I imagined Violet had made from garden squash stored in a root cellar, a cloth-lined basket filled with cheddar cheese biscuits.

I handed her the white box and she shook her head vehemently. "You shouldn't be giving me anything!" Like a woman hiding her handbag at a city café, she slipped it discreetly under the table.

"I feel as if I'm in another season, another world, *une autre vie*!" I exclaimed, delighted.

"*Oui*," she said, nodding ever so slightly in her Aunt Tomokoian way, "*c'est ma vie.*"

We sat for a few minutes in the fragrant silence. If she was happy it was difficult to tell.

"Mayumi," she began, "are you hiding something?" And when I didn't answer at once (thinking, here is the moment, the moment has come) she amended, "or are you hiding *from* something?"

"I beg your pardon?"

"Most people who come to this island are hiding on some level." I must have had a pained look on my face for she added hurriedly, "I didn't mean it as a criticism. I'm as guilty as the next."

"Oh? What exactly do you mean?"

"If I'd been living a nice life on the mainland I wouldn't have needed to come back."

I was at once alarmed to imagine what her not so nice life might have been and relieved that we seemed not to be, as I had originally feared, in the realm of personal secrets, at least not those of an on-island nature. "I'm sorry," she went on, "I didn't mean to pry. I just wonder about washashores and why they come here."

"You needn't apologize. Our reasons were fairly mundane. My husband..." I trembled at my own mention of him, "inherited a patch of land and we thought it would be a better place to raise our child. And yourself?" We had arrived at the pyramid.

"Like I said, I didn't have a nice life."

"I see." I braced myself for our ascent but she didn't pose a single question pertaining to husband or child. Quite handily, she didn't seem interested in the subject of other people unless they were characters in a book.

"I finished it," she said.

"*Ethan Frome*?"

"Yes." Personal secrets seemed to be a theme to which we would forever return.

"And would you still raise it in a toast to adventure?"

Violet blushed and thought. "I think so. Wouldn't you?"

"No." I helped myself to a biscuit. "Well, yes and no. I wouldn't want to be any of those people but I would be lying if I said I've never been drunk on tragedy." The biscuit was superb, my God, the woman could cook.

"I wouldn't mind being Mattie."

"You've got to be joking! Her life was such drudgery!"

"No! Housework is something we all have, it's not that terrible. She's so in love, maybe her love feels even better because of the drudgery. And she dies in bliss!"

"I'm a greedier person than you," I said. "I don't want love to end in a crash at the bottom of the hill. I want to sled on forever."

"It's not greedy to want that. It may be a lot of things but it's not greedy."

"What is it then?"

"Hope, naïveté, optimism, ambition? I don't know. You tell me."

Violet reached back and touched her bun in one swift librarian movement. How easily we might have changed places, she with a pencil through her loose knot, gossiping with patrons about Wharton characters; I bound in a canvas apron, cutting camellias from the greenhouse, zinnias from the garden, wrapping them in white paper for people to bring to dinner parties. The image of a boy playing in the garden cast an incestuous pall upon my vision.

Through a nearby glass door I saw into the shop and suppressed panic at the thought that he might be lurking within.

"Are you okay?"

"I thought I heard a rustling in the shop."

"It's probably just Fyodor."

"Fyodor?" I saw a sallow bearded Russian, tormented, humane, her lover perhaps, solemnly repairing a shelf.

"Our Siamese. Don't worry. There's no one else here. We won't have any workers until spring and my son's at school."

I smiled faintly at the thought of her son on the other side of the island, carrying books from class to class, sitting down to write sentences on lined paper, running through crowded halls to catch up with friends. Being with his mother made him more real to me. It was difficult to distinguish between the happiness of this discovery and the happiness of being in her company.

We chatted the hour away easily, though I dare say I did more of the chatting. Like Aunt Tomoko, Violet was prone to asking long questions and giving short answers (except when it came to literary discussions, during which she rather unleashed) and I was determined to find out all that we had in common aside from the obvious. I began by expressing every thought that was on my mind except for the crime that was at the front of it. But it wasn't long before the crime drifted like a sail out of sight and if I felt a periodic twinge of discomfort at keeping my secret from her, it was fleeting. I soon forgot whose mother she was.

* * *

Alone with my secret, I indicted and rehabilitated, analyzed and haggled. I accused myself of rape, molestation, and willful negligence. Alternately, I defended my right to feel pleasure and love, my right to refuse loneliness. The accusing self and the accused self, though not identical, were like two images seen through binoculars. My vision was double. As I strained to make sense of the world I saw, to make sense of my own vision, the two selves moved closer to one another. They touched hands, their hips overlapped, their hearts lay astride one another like the folded wings of a red butterfly until at last the two merged into a single image, the single self that became the self I saw myself as.

In the end, I didn't mind being a rapist so much as I expected. Transgression is less of an affront when it is draped in love and beauty. I had always felt an abstract sympathy for those whose lives had amounted to little more than a series of transgressions, those who had committed acts viewed by most as unacceptable. I did not begrudge Emma Bovary her childish fantasies and fruitless interludes. If I could have, I would have saved Anna Karenina from the wheels of the train. I had always reserved for others some measure of moral leeway but I had never myself been stripped of any honor. Now my own virtue was in tatters and I found it weirdly fascinating. It was not entirely clear how much sympathy one ought to extend to oneself.

My transgression revealed to me a few surprising facts of which I had previously been ignorant. One must sometimes commit an act against one's own goodness in order to see clearly its existence though by then it is a tarnished vision. That is, I had never known how very good I was until I became very bad. When one transgresses one does not so much inhabit a different body as wear a different coat. One remains oneself for the duration—the conscientious, law-abiding librarian slips into the criminal's leather coat and the two magically coexist. And yet one cannot remove the coat without implications. It is no ordinary coat. One is changed by wearing it, even if, in the end, one takes it off.

Transgression has a scent. One wears it like a perfume and there are those who smell it immediately. During the course of my affair with the young man, countless patrons confessed to me their crimes. Thierry Lambert's wife was the nanny for whom he had left his first wife, Joe Fischer had been banished from the priesthood for his love affair with an altar boy, and Linda Cardo continued to meet with her childhood sweetheart in an off-island hotel where they drank Chianti and floated in the indoor pool. Why tell me? Why not any of the other librarians? I'm convinced I wore the perfume of transgression and that transgressors were drawn to it, perhaps even comforted by it. I was their kind.

I kept my secret well; there was no one but Maria to notice my change of mood, no one to question me but Violet and she had thus far remained silent on the subject. I exerted an inordinate amount of effort to conceal from every person I encountered the reason for my joy. Perhaps if someone had asked me, my cork would have flown skyward and I would have bubbled over in a celebratory confession, but no one did.

There were days when I could not stand having nothing to show for our efforts. A secret has the power to nullify its own reality. But the opposite is true as well. A secret reality can override all other realities; indeed there were days when secrecy was its own reward, days it became its own vital organ of pleasure.

As for the one person with whom I could have spoken freely—the young man—I imagine his experience of secrecy was quite different from mine, that the stifling of his joy—if in fact he too felt joy—came naturally and caused in him no inner conflict. I rather think he enjoyed harboring our erotic secret, not only because he was taciturn by nature but because the presence of regular and abundant sex with a stranger means something quite different for a seventeen-year-old boy than for a forty-one-year-old married librarian. Then too, secrecy breeds secrecy. That we shared a secret perhaps inspired us to keep other secrets from one another. Had he told his friends indiscriminately about us, I don't think I could have borne knowing and perhaps he would not have been able to bear the fact that I told no one. He might have mistook my secrecy for a lack of passion or commitment and I his lack of secrecy for the very same.

My silence on the subject of the young man was a nunlike feat of discipline which may seem to run counter to my otherwise undisciplined choice to love him; it is true that every coin has two sides. Before her housekeeping days, my mother was of the Cistercian order, but once released she spoke effusively as a priest in a pulpit to absolutely anyone who came her way: bus drivers, petrol station attendants, people in waiting rooms or on tube platforms, whether they listened or not did not seem to concern her. In its ceaselessness, her chatter was a kind of silence, just as my secret turned inward was an expression of information—utterances; his voice, continuous, tympanic; his face at certain moments; his dark eyes biding their time; his soft mouth crushing itself against mine—that never ceased within me. My silence became one with my ability to remember; each one made the other possible.

* * *

It was the young man who began our tradition of bringing books to the gray house. One Friday he asked, "What did you used to do on your day off?" It touched me that he should have the slightest concept of my Fridays having been different before, the notion that there was perhaps something I had given up in order to see him. A man twice his age might not have grasped this and if he had, he might not have cared.

"Read," I answered. And the following Friday he brought with him two book lights and two books, a cloth edition of *Moby-Dick* for himself (show-off!), and a British paperback edition of *For Esmé—With Love and Squalor and Other Stories* for me, which, despite my years of library experience and my British roots, I did not know was the title in most countries of J.D. Salinger's *Nine Stories.* Oh, my pubescent professor, my juvenile reader, my paternal, patronal joy!

"I thought you might like the title story," he said, easy as you please. Indeed! Was I Esmé or the soldier and who was he? I could have asked, but I only placed the foreign copy on the mattress and began to read. He lay on his back next to me and followed suit, holding *Moby-Dick* directly above his face like a hand mirror.

I read *For Esmé* as if it were the young man's own collection of nine significant dreams he had recorded and then entrusted to me for a few hours. I, with my thirsty cup, began with the first story and drank deeply of the details. An amateur Jungian, I inserted him in the place of each character and then analyzed the implications. When I had exhausted these possibilities I did the same for myself and for the two of us together.

What if, contrary to all appearances, the young man was Seymour and I was the girl in the water? What if he was the jaded self-hater and I was innocence personified? Or was I Seymour and he, Muriel? Did he too spend hours chatting with his mother about my shortcomings? Or was he the voice on the phone outside the story, listening in, while I was naked in the hole and trapped there? Was he the mother and I the bananafish, etc.? I read entirely too much into everything and wondered obsessively about the rest.

Did he love the double meaning of "see more glass" or had he found it too heavy-handed? Had he noticed? If he were to invent a creature that summed up his condition, what would it be? Did he love the sea? (I could not help thinking also of the story that was being held in the air next to me.) Did he love fish and whales? Did he, as Maria did, as most children do, love animals?

Midway through "Uncle Wiggily in Connecticut," my frenzy of Jungian suppositions abated and I became keenly aware of my reading companion. Distracted, I switched off my book light. I turned onto my side and observed him under his tiny spray of light. His eyebrows touched as he frowned. The intensity with which he read was one of his most adult qualities. When I thought, with trepidation, of our respective ages, I would remember this and feel reassured. He appeared to be nearly three-quarters of the way through his thick book, a heavyweight next to my feather. Surely his arms were getting tired of holding it up. Then again, he was an athlete and very young; what little I knew of exertion I had learned from him.

"Where are you?" I asked. My question reverberated out of context in the dim loft. He understood it.

In that slow and jagged voice that both aroused and terrified me, he read, "But far beneath this wondrous world upon the surface, another still stranger world met our eyes as we gazed over the side. For, suspended in those watery vaults, floated the forms of the nursing mothers of whales, and those that by their enormous girth seemed shortly to become mothers. The lake as I have hinted, was to a considerable depth exceedingly transparent, and as human infants will calmly and fixedly gaze away from the breast, as if leading two different lives at the time; and while yet drawing mortal nourishment, be still spiritually feasting upon some unearthly reminiscence; — even so did the young of these whales seem looking up towards us, but not at us, as if we were a bit of Gulfweed in their newborn sight."

We were quiet. One could feel the enormous mammalian presence of the whales and their young in the loft with us, the knotty, coarse-grained rafters, now ship-like.

"Do you remember nursing?" I asked, not intending to insinuate his relative proximity to infancy but doing so nonetheless.

He confessed with a scarlet, Hawthornian face, "No. Mom only nursed me for three months. Her friend Chuck read somewhere that nursing makes kids stupid so…"

"He was concerned about your intelligence?"

"Yeah," he said. "How long did you nurse Maria?"

"She's four."

He paused thoughtfully for a few moments, he waited politely for me to finish, and when I said nothing more he started. "You still nurse her?!" He turned to face me, his eyes incredulous, innocent, a little thirsty perhaps.

"I thought you knew."

"How would I know? I've never even met her!"

"Well," I said gesturing. "Did you think all breasts looked and felt like this?!" I laughed, a bit incredulous myself now.

Certainly mine had never been this large, their nipples never so dark and obvious.

"That's not funny," he said. I was quick to repair the damage.

"Darling, did you know you're perfect? Honestly. All this time I've felt self-conscious about them and now I can feel at ease."

He got up and sat astride me. I thought perhaps all this talk of swollen breasts had aroused him, but he only bent forward and laid his cheek on my chest the way Maria did when she had finished drinking. *I can hear your heart*, she would say. *I used to live there.* My heart a familiar bell whose sound she had heard on her small island across the sea of me. Though the young man felt heavy, I lay still, sipping in air when I could, allowing him to crush me, letting him listen to the bell of my heart as it rang out.

* * *

Despite (or perhaps because of) feeling burdened by my knowledge of Violet, I would have happily pretended to be his mother if he had made such a desire known to me. As it was, we were not the kind of lovers who indulged in such games. He was not plagued by the unrequited longing for the mother so common in such game players though he liked to play father on occasion. Perhaps it would be more accurate to say he liked to play mother—for he knew very little firsthand about what fathers did, having been raised by his mother alone. He would not have wanted me to count Chuck (Was he still in the picture? Violet had never mentioned him) as a father, calling Charles as he did by that name for a low cut of meat. He would pack a lunch for us and arrange it on the floor atop a red and white cloth he had no doubt taken from Violet's linen closet (which I imagined was full of Florentine napkins, imported tablecloths, thick bath towels, and rose-print sheets), the phrase "Picnic at Hanging Rock," at once lovely and sinister, never far from my mind.

After we had eaten he would put everything away and sweep the floor with a broom that looked as if it had, years ago, been made by hand of sorghum, and which gave him the look of an early American settler, the sort one sees in library books—white blouse, shaggy brown hair, gentle yet adventurous eyes, never any acne.

Through another's eyes, his gestures might have looked like those of a child caring for his mother. I admit there were times when I felt I was the arbitrary recipient of a deep, untrammeled affection the expression of which his mother's temperament perhaps wouldn't allow. And I confess his brown leather belt with its steel buckle and tooth bore an erotic resemblance to my father's. In its plain functionality and potential for violence, it was a father's belt, and the sight of him removing it aroused me. I often thought that if we'd been granted more time, we might have veered into that forbidden territory, a father younger than oneself perhaps easy and thrilling to submit to. But we were remarkably naturalistic in our dealings with one another for our actual roles provided more than enough excitement without any need for us to pretend. Had we both been seventeen or both forty-one we might have played at other roles. As it was we were busy enough being ourselves. We were like foreigners in Japan so consumed by learning Japanese, there was, for us, no possibility of learning other languages.

I can tell you very little about what was happening on the mainland that winter, much less in the world at large. News came to me via the insular British expatriates patron network that a red neon sign had been installed in Number 10 Downing Street by some artist or other (a middle-aged woman no less) that glowed: *More Passion.* There was a miraculous, island-wide proliferation of red bumper stickers that bore the message: *The Real Revolution Will Be Love*. Kay Ryan won the Pulitzer Prize for poetry; it was the year of the woman who loves whom she pleases. A new translation of *Doctor Zhivago*—one of my father's favorites—was released and read avidly by the public, further evidence that love transcended generation. Finally, there was a flurry of then newly popular, still mind-boggling oxymoronic "raw food cookbooks" which I read as an indicator that people had little time to spare for activities as unnecessary as the cooking of food, so occupied were they by endeavors such as the making of love. I, for one, had lost almost all patience with cooking (It was so time-consuming! How had I ever found a way?), though I suspect the young man had never cooked more.

Every Friday we were ravenous and it was he who tended to our appetites. Sometimes he brought cold chicken legs (cut from a chicken he had slaughtered and plucked himself before roasting it in butter and herbs) or one-half of a chocolate root beer bundt cake he had baked using skills likely taught to him by his talented mother or by a teacher at school, always a cake that was better than anything I had ever baked and I was not a shabby baker. It was the young man who taught me about the affectionate relationship between root beer and chocolate as well as the power of root beer to help rise a cake. Though I could follow a recipe precisely without difficulty, I knew little about food pairings, especially sweet ones, and less still about fizzy water and chemistry. Mostly he brought soups, which, after sweet things, were his specialty; sometimes one-half of a spinach quiche, sometimes a small chicken pot pie or a round of bread accompanied by a wedge of pale cheese or a jar of pickles. Once he brought a tall green thermos full of pork ramen made from scratch, and I laughed and then cried as I gulped it down. It had been one of the many dishes my mother had learned to cook for my father and the taste of it—both the savory flavor of the broth and the familiar feel of the curly noodles on my tongue—sent me floating back to that first island.

From the same worn blue backpack that held his homework and schoolbooks, he brought out his weekly offerings. There were tins full of the English nutritive biscuits I had eaten as a child, solemn letters engraved on their smooth faces like epigraphs that said nothing of consequence, and paper-wrapped cookies with crushed almonds for hearts, the blue floral cursive printed in Italian, the familiar letters strung together in a foreign way, so that eating them in his presence I felt at once a sweet sense of at-homeness that I rarely felt anywhere and the delicious terror of inhabiting a country without knowing its food or its language, daily confronted with delicacies I did not understand.

There were bars of German chocolate that must have cost as much as tickets to the cinema, their outer wrappers painted with delicate landscapes of places I had never been, their inner gold foil concealing dark twin bars lying side by side within. He was like a traveler bringing me souvenirs in that backpack of his, hoping with a taste of sugar or salt to transport me to a world he had known, even if he too had known it only secondhand. I could not help but feel Violet's presence when he made his offerings. She had almost certainly purchased the items and with other purposes in mind. I felt some measure of guilt for inadvertently depleting her inventory and at the same time I felt happy to be cared for, not only by him but also in some unintentional, meandering way by her.

During these afternoon teas—with my impassive, ticking wristwatch as our constant companion—we talked about nearly everything, but never about the fact that I had made a vow to love someone else, and never about the future. I told him odd bits about my housekeeper mother and my economist father—her funny habit of sleeping with a pillow over her face, his tendency to treat every surface as if it were a mahogany podium before which he had been invited to stand and deliver an important lecture. I explained my love of the British Library in winter, in particular its collection of illuminated manuscripts, my longstanding affection for the cherry blossom's many developmental phases.

He brought an MP3 player and two sets of headphones (including the alarmingly plush black leather set from his early days at the library) and we listened to his favorite songs. He confessed that he dreaded sleep, that when he lay next to me with his eyes closed he was not sleeping but composing music. For him, the words *nightmare* and *dream* were interchangeable. Once, after I'd described a dream of mine to him, he said: *I like the place of your dreams. I think I could live there.*

He told me his mother had studied English literature for a year at Oxford, that she had left university to study cheese making in France and had shortly after bought land in South America. She had given birth to him at home; there was a small orchard of Liberty apples beside the two-hundred-year-old house that contained the enormous library that she had inherited from her father who had inherited it from his. The young man bore a whale-tooth-shaped appendix scar eerily identical to my father's. His mother had taught him to swim in a pond called Ice House whose waters were not always as cold as its name. During the high season he worked for her at P.I.P. (both his nickname for the shop and the name of his favorite literary character). *I have a good Mom,* he said. *Not everyone has that.*

During the off-season he earned money babysitting a neighbor's child. He dreamed of traveling to California, Antigua, the Riviera, places that were seaside and warm. He had left the island only twice, once to visit relatives in upstate New York and once to attend a Celtics game in Boston. He listened religiously to reggae on Sundays. He was learning to play the guitar, a fact that had the rare effect of bridging momentarily our difference in age. (As a teenager, I had known boys who had done the very same!) All of this was news to me, every bit of it breaking. The more he reported, the more I wanted to know.

Despite the fact that we never ventured beyond the gray house, his kindness was everywhere evident. I could see it in his eyes and mouth when he spoke of others, in the way he bit his nails when I spoke of anything even mildly difficult. Though I had never seen him bend down to hand money to a beggar or carry an elderly woman's bags or guide a blind man to safety, I was convinced such acts would be second nature to him. There were times when, in my conviction, I wished I could protect him from the future, from the wider world whose endless suffering would one day assault him. He was unusually attuned to the suffering of others, so much so that I could not help but wonder if his interest in me had been driven by pity, by some pathological impulse to repair suffering and fulfill needs. My needs after all were fairly plain and when my needs were fulfilled I ceased to suffer. Perhaps he sensed the simplicity of my case, how easy I would be to accomplish.

Not far beneath the grassy slope of his gentle, well-mannered exterior lived a well of pure rage. Its origins were unknown to me; whether they were present in him at birth or had found and surrounded him as he grew, a gang of external forces that wouldn't relent, I didn't know. Had he been older, I might have been frightened by it. As it was, I felt only compassion and, at times, a twinkle of amusement. I liked his rage, it excited me. It lived in his eyes, and helped equalize us. His humor was very tied up with it. Like his eyes, his rage was cutting and dark. I would not have wanted to be on the wrong side of it. I pitied the poor person who was, if there was such a person. Likely he was his own primary target. He was not a malicious person but I'm convinced that someone, at least one, had wronged him and that he expected to be wronged again at any moment. I had never known anyone more defensive than myself so I had a special sympathy for him. His bitterness was like black tea. It didn't deter me. On the contrary I wanted to pour into it heaps of milk and sugar and then drink.

Our confessions, our picnics, everything took place in the loft. It was a place of suspension and yet time always intervened. Time resided in the silver face of my Omega which was the size and color of ten pence and which I set under my half of the pillow while we made love. I muffled time's voice with linen, I gagged it with down, I hushed time with the plush black hairs on my head, the weight of my encyclopedic brain, until the sunlight snowing upon the floorboards downstairs told me that it was time to let the ticking be heard and the numbered face seen. But before then, while we loved, I rid myself of all thoughts of it. For what could I possibly gain by remembering the face on which the future was so clearly drawn, the voice whose insistent sameness was both eternal and forever threatening to cease? I wanted only to remember the face of the young man and glimpse for a moment the double reflection of my own panting visage in the dark inlets of his eyes.

The loft was a place of surrender, abandonment. The only struggle there was moral. We laid our bodies down the way some lay down arms or ideas. In the physical act our only struggle was the struggle to repeat. The slats of the inverted triangle were ingeniously designed to allow a small amount of light to enter without allowing our eyes to see out. We were blind to the woods, blinder still to the world outside them. Our nearest audible neighbor was a male cardinal whose bright red body we glimpsed outside now and then, a fist of fire burning in the air as we came and went. I loved to see him alight, apple-like, on a tree that was covered in snow. He was like us: his heartbeat swift, his visits fleeting, his face flushed and festive in the cold. Although there were human indicators (car motors, the smell of wood smoke, the blast of a shotgun, the buzz of a chainsaw, the faint and solemn dong of the distant town clock) not once from our suspended isle did we hear the sound of another human voice.

By midwinter we had begun fearlessly lighting the woodstove downstairs. The young man arrived early to chop wood and I, upon arriving, immediately set about building the fire. As a child he had played alone in the orchard next to his house and the woods, in which he had spent countless solitary hours, were home to him. Any labor that brought him outside he seemed to view as a respite from confinement, a chance to commune with beauty, and so he was perfectly content to chop the firewood though it was physically demanding.

I, with my kindling and moxie, was somewhere between a Wampanoag sending celebratory smoke signals to an uncomprehending world and the kind of small-time criminal who neglects to wear gloves when opening a safe. But in truth I thought none of this until much later. I confess that the obvious fact of stoves leading to chimneys that transport and then expel smoke visible to the human eye virtually escaped me. Gone was Miss Marple checking for footprints in the snow, gone the discreet librarian who lived in fear of being found out.

Here were ill-sorted lovers for whom time was a sensitive matter and for whom pleasure had become an urgent priority. Here was an adventuresome boy who would soon finish high school and a celibate mother who had marked five years of estrangement from the same lacquered, moustachioed man. We, who had once been so tentative when expressing our desires, so shy about nudity, so willing to suffer for the sake of discretion, now refused the physical discomfort that had thus far been a hallmark of our lovemaking. We surrendered to warmth, to comfort, to imagination, to the satisfaction of building our own fire in our own stove in our own home. By which I mean we began to pretend that the house and everything in it belonged to us.

We took possession of the house gradually; we began by adding our own small objects to it. The young man brought a blue ceramic bird whose back was a receptacle and he set it like a family heirloom on the windowsill next to the table downstairs. I brought a secondhand, leaf green tablecloth, cross-stitched with pink and red roses, trimmed with white lace, and smoothed it over the table. He set an orange and white canister of amaretti upon the tablecloth. I filled it with Flower's Kiss candy. For our slim pillow, I sewed a case out of the gray linen that I had bought in Japan and had been saving for more than a decade for a "special occasion." He laid down a flax-colored flannel sheet that I covered with a white down comforter.

Every Friday, toward 2:00, by some feat of intuition or fear, I would feel compelled to unmuffle the watch, as if it would otherwise suffocate. Then the ticking would become audible again, like a bomb recently discovered, and I would strap it to myself once more and prepare to meet the world without him. Though in truth, the unwanted face of the watch became an emblem of him that accompanied me, so that even in my most morbid states—thinking of death, thinking of separation—he was part of the fabric of this thinking and so thinking such thoughts was a strange pleasure. I was, as it were, duly wrapped in them as I walked the snowy streets of the town.

* * *

Meanwhile (even now I despise the notion of a *meanwhile* in the context of the young man; it is with a sadness that I compel myself to utter it), in the actual apartment whose walls were uninsulated and many of whose windows were cracked and let winter air in even when we closed them, Maria and I bundled ourselves in freshly laundered quilts (painstakingly made and relinquished only in death by my mother) and watched Charlie Chaplin films while Var kept himself in his room. He sat whittling away before his desk of apple crates, the portable heater hissing just centimeters away so that I could not relax and watch a film without at least once imagining his entire menagerie, along with the desk, going up in flames, bringing an end to us all.

Maria and I could not agree on a favorite so we alternated between her favorite, *The Kid* and my favorite, *City Lights*. When it came to *The Kid*, we both identified with Chaplin, the lone person who comes upon a baby and feels obligated to care for it, the any person who quite absurdly falls into parenthood. When it came to *City Lights*, our identifications diverged. She wanted to be the blind flower seller and I could not help but be the tramp who woos her without being seen; I use her blindness to my advantage for I fear that if she were to see me she could never love me as I really am.

In my relationship with the young man, he too was the flower seller and I, again, was the tramp. His blindness was youth and I feared that when the day came that he was no longer young, he would see me as I really was and turn away. Like the flower seller he wouldn't recognize me at first, like the flower seller he would be kind. But he would see me as through a plate glass window from inside a heated, well-lit shop that looked out onto a cold, gloomy street where I would be lumbering along on my way to the bus stop, a book in translation in my gloved, arthritic hand.

Then again, I too was blind. He could have been a murderer and I might not have seen. He could have easily pulled the wool over my eyes if he'd wished. These fears coursed through me as I held Maria and laughed at the films. We laughed together as I thought of him. It was as close as I came to confiding in someone, as close as I came to sharing with another my fear of and love for the young man.

We made popcorn and hot chocolate, gingerbread and oatcakes, all the quickest and most satisfying things. Thursday evenings, I reserved a small portion of whatever we had made and discreetly tucked it into my cloth bag while Maria was brushing her teeth, though my baked goods were never as good as his. Our oven was unreliable and I was less patient. These were my excuses in any case. Perhaps he had simply surpassed me. I sometimes felt I had another child hidden away to whom I brought food in secret. Other times the young man was more akin to the child who lives in the closet so that the town can have its happiness. Our happiness—mine, Maria's, and even Var's—now depended on him.

It was his love that allowed me to tolerate living in the apartment and my contentment with him that prevented me from leaving. There was, in that wintry apartment, a deadlock between us, one it seemed only I could break, for Var was not the sort to break things. I was the sort who did though I tired of it, I was tired of being the one taking an axe to the frozen sea of our love. The axe was heavy and the sea endless. I was tired and sometimes, I confess, I wanted him to suffer. I didn't care if I did too. I turned my back on our frozen sea and let it grow colder still.

With the British edition of *For Esmé—With Love and Squalor* on my dresser, the room looked different, the frameless bed, the bruised walls bandaged by Maria's drawings, the windows that gave out onto the silent, snow-covered garden. The American island upon which I had felt such desolation, such resignation, became the place where locked windows were opened and lost vistas found. I was an enviable woman, a bewildered, perimenopausal, libido-high librarian suddenly in love with my life.

* * *

Thursdays I invariably found myself in a heightened state of agitation, brooding upon my future. If Fridays were the grand vista, the bright expanse of the sea in every direction, and Saturdays were the hard push down the rocky backside of the mountain, then Thursdays were the final ascent. I felt the exhaustion and light-headed anticipation that results from a week of strenuous climbing.

One such morning, warming myself in the cold, tomb-like basement with thoughts of the young man, I looked up from the old British novel I was weeding to find Violet standing before me. Much (too much) had happened since our tea date. Chances were, either her son had confessed or she'd pieced things together herself. Convinced she knew my secret, I prepared myself for reprisal.

Although she was about my height, she seemed to be looking down at me, her suffering, rifle brown eyes cocked, accusing. She was wearing the same rifle brown sweater whose cowl neck crept close to her mouth. It was a thin-lipped and delicate, reddish-colored mouth, very different from her son's. His pale and sensual pouting lips must have come from the drifting father. The skin of her face was lighter than my own mother's and smooth as a fresh oval of chèvre. The young man's dark beauty mark was missing from it.

Perhaps I should have been startled to see her. I suppose my physiological response—my quickening pulse, a rapid yet thudding heartbeat, the vertical lines of sweat that were traveling at an alarming rate from each of my armpits down my sides (yes I was literally sweating with fear)—matched that of one who is having a startling encounter. But my thinking self, the one that read books and composed questions, drew clever analogies and made dire predictions, that self was not at all surprised to see her at last stalking me in the basement. I was surprised she had not come sooner. I expected punishment of some kind, possibly violence.

I picked up the book—it was Evelyn Waugh's *A Handful of Dust*—and held it to my chest, protecting my most vital organ. I felt incapable of arguing with her. She had every right to feel betrayed. There was a cold silence that could easily be perceived even in the library.

"Hello, Violet."

"Hi. You okay?"

"Yes. May I help you with something?" At last resorting to the language of servitude, my inner housekeeper meekly took charge.

"Yes, thanks. I was hoping you might have another recommendation. I loved those books you gave me." She hadn't come to hunt me, she had come to hunt books. I could hear it in her voice.

"I'm so glad." I was safe. "What did you love about them?" I dived into Conscientious Librarian protocol.

"They were intense. Bold and transgressive and strange. I read them in one sitting."

"Me too! Oh, Violet, I have the perfect book for you." Following CL protocol tended to empower me. No sooner had I passed through the first circle of suffering than I felt primed to enter another.

I walked guilelessly to the N's, pulled down a book, and handed it to her. What was it about Mother and Son that made me want to leap wildly in their direction?! High upon my lonely cliff, staring down at the lazuline blue of them, I was suicidal.

"Have you read *Lolita*?" I asked.

"No, I've always avoided it." Her eyelashes fluttered every so slightly. She was internal, understated, yet curiously expressive, with the silent potency of a church altar. "Isn't it about a pedophile who kills someone?"

"Well, technically yes, though I think of it more as a story about forbidden love." Sinking rapidly into a sea of my own making, I cast about for a viable defense of Nabokov's masterpiece. The famous *Vanity Fair* line (which leapt into my brain like a man trying and failing to save me from drowning) "the only convincing love story of the 20th century," seemed, in Violet's presence, phony and inappropriate.

"Why do you like it?"

"It's queer. It tells the story from the queer person's point of view."

"Are you saying that being queer and being a pedophile are somehow similar?"

"No! Of course not. I just mean he captures what it's like to be in the queer person's position, the person whose desires are criminalized."

She stepped closer to me and whispered, "You're not gay, are you?" If only I could have answered honestly in the affirmative my problems would have been solved (only to be instantly replaced by a barrelful of others).

"No! What I mean to say is..."

"May, you don't have to explain. If you think it's a good book, I'll read it. I trust you."

Violet hugged *Lolita* to her chest, she buried the sulky nymphette in her sweater. "Do you have time for tea next week?" she asked cozily.

"Of course. Which day would be best?"

"How about Friday? We can discuss forbidden love over Earl Grey." She gave me a sultry Rachel Ward half smile.

"Oh," I said. "Actually Fridays are difficult." Actually Fridays were easy, actually Fridays were the best thing about my life because actually every Friday if I wasn't reading a book in translation I was bedding her son.

I hesitated.

"Here." She scribbled her number redundantly on a piece

of scrap paper and handed it to me. "Give me a call if you have time. I'd love to catch up."

* * *

I have always been someone for whom winter never lasts long enough and that winter was far from an exception. Cold has never bothered me, it is darkness I hate. Winter is a season that improves with every passing day; it is when it is at its best that it ends. Far worse than winter's cold or fall's darkness is spring's incessant buzz of activity, its sense—even on the quietest days—of fanfare and commotion, which one feels more acutely on an island known to travelers for its beauty. Meanwhile, there are those around me who rely on the idea of spring's inevitable return to carry them through the cold months. Conversations turn to the natural world: birds being seen and heard for the first time in months, bulbs rising from their dark beds, the smell of blossoms. *Don't worry, spring's almost here!* patrons and co-workers alike say with smiles that, like light clothing, they had almost forgotten they had. Their happiness is as palpable as my dread.

That winter, more than any other, I was snowbound. I was Eskimo. Love was an igloo built with the most obscure blocks of blue-tinted ice; it existed in a polar region invisible to the rest of the world. The same cold that made it necessary was also what sustained it. When at times the harsh winds of Reality threatened to blow me in a more practical direction, I threw on a bearskin rug and dove back into the igloo, determined to spend my winter with the young man, lighting our love from within. I no longer feared being discovered, I only feared the proliferation of water droplets running down the inner walls of the pleasure dome, I feared the very heat of us would melt the house down.

Indeed, I felt a terrible sense of urgency when I thought of the coming of spring. The slow drumbeat that would lead us closer to the onslaught of summer, the blossoms, all those exotic emblems of youth and sexuality that would alter the very air we breathed, and worst of all—I had once been an academic, I knew the spring calendar well—the many acceptance letters typed on university letterhead that would arrive in the mailboxes of high school students everywhere, notifying them of their fate and by extension the fates of those close to them. The young man had not mentioned applying to schools but I remembered clearly the time he had spent typing at the library computer and was sure that this had been the task that he had so swiftly and steadily accomplished, sure that I had aided him in moving closer to that which would bring him further away from me.

But while it lasted, when one boiled it down, winter was everything. I say *boiled*, for in no other season will you find such extreme heat: gas, electricity, wood fires, the steam of hot soup and tea, the electric neon green of the moss underfoot after a heavy rain. The white sea of winter surrounded us with a silence I had waited months to hear. The gray sky of it cast a shadow I never wanted to get out from under. Winter lasted three months and winter was endless. Every winter to follow—every season—was touched by it. Winter announced the heat of every living being: the tiny red hearts of birds who had not yet flown north, pumping triumphantly their fluttering eyedroppers of blood; the hands of children, busy and dumb in their mittens: the sweaty groins of gardeners under their stiff, muddy layers; the clean hands of chefs as they sliced and stirred; even within the decaying mouths of the oldest islanders, their pink tongues were warm in comparison. And if the others were warm, we in our loft were tropical, our isle afloat, on fire, ephemeral, and yet, an absurdly sensible destination in a world so cold.

Spring

And so the winter melted away. Try as I may, I could not stop it. Yellow-green buds, those bright eyes of youth, appeared in the trees, in the bushes, on the ground—I could not look anywhere without meeting their gaze. Maria mastered the alphabet, she was fond of taking dictation letter by letter, Var ceased carving animals and began carving gnomes. I had never been happier and lived in fear of losing my happiness; it seemed to be made of a substance similar to winter itself, one that chilled and dazzled but, in accordance with the laws of nature, would not last. I recalled with increasing frequency the time the young man had spent quietly striking the keys of the public computer, the then-unfamiliar headphones touching him, bringing him music or messages I could not hear. I could have asked him about that day directly and perhaps put my fears to rest, but knowledge of the future often aggravates me, so I didn't dare. If he was going to leave I wanted his leaving to come upon me suddenly, without warning, in the way of a natural disaster; I wanted a blow dealt to me not by him but by fate.

Spring is always a bit of a miser's bargain—apple blossoms rain down from the trees even as lilacs open, falling to bits beneath irises fast on their way to becoming desiccated scrolls. That spring I had the sense of the bargain being a losing one, the young man nothing more than a loan that I would soon have to make good on.

As the weather grew milder, the high school girls, instead of walking from the bus to the library, returned to their places at the long wooden bench on the porch of the general store. Maria and I sat on the glider and watched them as they strode off the bus, threw their bags roughly down on the bench, and disappeared into the store. When they returned a few minutes later with their Starbursts and their miniature Reese's, their salt and vinegar potato chips and their Almond Joys, we studied them, each with her own purpose in mind. Maria eyed their junk food and their gestures as she eyed everything in the world, as things she might possibly try, and I, how closely I studied them now, his potential suitors; my left eye a loving mother's, admiring their long, tumbling hair, their fresh cheeks, my right eye a watchful rival's, assessing various sorts of compatibility.

As these and countless blossoms continued thoughtlessly to display themselves, the apartment grew cozily warm then unbearably hot. Not even I could be persuaded that the attic inferno was preferable to the heavenly outdoors. Despite my professed dread of the season, like the Sophias and the Rosamonds of the world, I too felt compelled to go out and join with the soft, fragrant air.

The thought of a girl his own age one day materializing never frightened me as much as the thought of the world at large—the mainland, other countries, other continents, other languages and customs—possessing him. I could live with, perhaps even learn to love, watching him grow into a man alongside a Sophia or a Rosamond, glimpsing them in shops on occasion, issuing library cards to their young children with my liver-spotted hands, but I could not abide the idea of his total disappearance. And when I turned to my own steadfastness for comfort, my longstanding ability to work and to wait years for something I wanted (it was a well-known fact that a large percentage of islanders who left eventually returned) it only accentuated my problem. Time was becoming a currency I could no longer deal in. In twenty years he would be middle-aged, but I would be in my sixties—the phrase "my sixties" already frighteningly intimate. Indeed in fifty years he would be almost seventy and I would likely be mingling with the sandy loam of an island cemetery.

The young man—if he can be called a man—was closer to Maria's age than my own. At the time she was four and I was forty-one. On those rare occasions when I doubted his capacity to meet me as an equal, or when I doubted my choice to commune with a mind so young, I thought of Keats. I would open *The Poems*, read a line or two, and then, unable to focus long enough to read a poem in its entirety, I would turn to the timeline at the front. On a piece of scrap paper I had taken from the library, I would solve the equation 1821 minus 1795, taking into account the month of his birth and the month of his death. *Twenty-five*, I would say to myself. *See what youth can accomplish. See how capable the young.*

While I made my useless calculations, he was learning to make Portuguese kale and sausage soup alongside sushi and cheese-stuffed canapés for parties of ten or more in the catering unit of his twelfth-grade cooking class. He was beating other boys at Frolf, yes Frolf, which he'd taught me was an energetic, pastoral hybrid of golf and Frisbee. He was learning to tie a tie, he had gone with Violet (whose phone number lay like an ember next to its twin in my wooden letter drawer, the pair of them threatening to set Var and his trim moustache ablaze) to a mall in Rhode Island and had driven on a highway for the first time. She must have marveled at his latest increase in size when she bought him the new high-tops and black jeans; she must have feared for his life at the sight of him, man-like, steering the wheel of her car.

How I envied Violet's natural right to watch him grow all the rest of her days, her right to grow old before him. I had no natural right to him except that afforded one in love, and such a right was not typically granted to one in my degraded position. As for my love, there was no earthly proof of it. My right, if I had a right, was ethereal. Compared to that of a mothers (concrete as breast milk or large, dark eyes) mine was vapor or fog. Then again, surely I romanticized Violet's position; surely she too lived in fear of the day he would leave. When one departs an island one departs a world, one puts a sea between oneself and one's loved ones. Those who are left (and those who are leaving) feel it more acutely. She must have shared some of my dread and when the day came—somehow I knew it would—perhaps it wouldn't be easy for him either.

Since the young man was ten and had read *Treasure Island*, he had wanted to "get off the rock." His vision of the world was a touching embroidery of scenes from Stevenson, Melville, and celebrity cooking shows, and a Mother Earth at once pregnant with beauty and at risk of being destroyed. He wanted to discover all that was alluring about the world and repair all that was broken about her. He wanted to save trees from being cut down, animals from impending extinction, he wanted to save the very air from the fumes of factories and cars.

I too had once been young, I too had found reasons to leave my first island, but my reasons, like those of my parents before me, had not been so noble. My mother left Stockingford in search of work and my father emigrated from Tokyo to study at Oxford. He hired her to clean his modest apartment when he was an assistant professor; she moved with him from apartment to house to manor until at last, when he was no longer required to teach, he married her, mop and all. In every way, she was his housekeeper and he her employer. It was a dynamic that persisted throughout their marriage and followed them to their graves.

My father's being an economist was not analogous to my being a librarian. He was in love with numbers and systems, addicted to the solving of equations and the isolating of patterns and perfectly suited to it. (While I was in love with books and forbidden to read on the job. Indeed I spent my days abstaining from books so that others might more easily read them.) His blue-black eyes sparked like lightning when he was on the verge of a solution or had just been struck by a new idea. His thinking process was totalizing. The sky of his being changed completely when he was deep in thought; customary modes of communication ceased to function between us. He was his own weather system, a storm moving about the room.

How I envied the natural forces that shone from within him and what seemed to be his natural right (yet another natural right I had not been endowed with) to succumb to them—my mother like a Red Cross worker forever at the ready with a tray of food for him to hurriedly devour or a pressed suit and a polished pair of shoes for him to absently put on while reviewing aloud his forthcoming lecture. When I was old enough I too was expected to carry the tray and deliver the clothes and shoes but I was never allowed in the kitchen, not even to learn to cook. (This I taught myself later using library books.) It was as if my mother was cooking for a god and would not—even if I pleaded—relinquish her sacred duty.

As one outside their natural disaster, there was little left for me to do but praise her efforts and so I left, as soon as I was able. My parents, in their aversion to all things American, were, as in most other matters, a united front and I, in my decision to study here, was a deserting rebel. I never quite knew whether I was the child of the employer or the child of the help or schizophrenically both. This was another reason why I ventured to America for my education. I imagined it to be a place where equality was functioning at its height, a place where I might be less of a walking contradiction. Imagine my confusion when I was called a chink while on special scholarship for Japanese Americans.

During my second year at university, my parents died in quick succession. First my father, setting the schedule until the end, and then my mother, eternally happy to comply with his itinerary. Once they had gone off together without me for good, I was left alone in America and resolved to stay. How selfish my choices seemed when I considered them against the young man's desire to leave an island of happiness to tend a sea of despair. He wished to make others happy whereas I wished only to avoid despair.

* * *

It was an unusually mild spring. This made summer seem nearer still and caused one to wonder if the rapidly warming globe was not yet another bomb busy ticking. Maria celebrated her fifth birthday in the back garden with four friends. In years past it had always been too chilly. I sat at the round glass table with its white cloth, its chocolate cake and pink candles, watching the children as each one in turn, in a manner reflecting her temperament, swung the bamboo stick at the rabbit-shaped piñata. Charlotte fairly stroked the rabbit's hindquarter while Sophia (my heart quickening each time a child shouted her name) clutched the stick in terror and did not so much as tap it. Ella swung happily but ineffectively at it several times. Josie, in her zeal, let go of the stick and it went flying into the air behind her and had to be chased down by the party's hostess. It was Maria who gored the rabbit's neck; then its stomach burst open and all the peppermints gushed out onto the grass. The little girls looked like rabbits scampering to retrieve them.

After her fifth birthday, I began to suffer from the fear that not only would I die before Maria, I would die without her.

Nightly, I began to hope, more ardently than I had ever hoped for anything, that when I was on my deathbed I would be able to recall perfectly the many hours I'd spent alternating between reading a novel in translation by book light and watching her sleep. Under the minute light, I studied her—the way she turned her right wrist in sleep, the way her lips pursed to a point and her eyebrows lifted slightly as if in amazement—for proof that she was the same child who'd been brought to me five years prior in the narrow hospital room whose only lit feature was a steel stink, the same child who'd known me in the dark, without features, and without a name.

Only the prospect of memory relieved my fear of dying without her. If not Maria, then the memory of Maria. Nothing and no one were equal to that. If one's beloved can't be at one's side, it must be easier to die in the presence of a benevolent stranger, easier to weaken in the face of one who has never known your strength, to relinquish while pressing the palm of one whom you've never held onto. To accept someone as they die requires either deep love or immense distance.

Conversely, I felt an aversion to the thought of the young man attending my death, which caused me to further doubt my already dubious motivations. Perhaps I was no different than the filthy old men of the world who chased after young girls as after fountains of youth, that red-cheeked nubility so incompatible with deathbeds. Being reminded that he was not my child nor could he take her place disturbed me. I did not like staring into the chasm that stood between my affection for them; it diminished him, which diminished me, and at a time when I had thought I could not be further diminished. She was she and he was he and if I were dying it would be Maria who I'd want in the bed with me. And if somehow if she were terrifyingly missing from the scene, better a kind nurse or a lonely passerby than my seventeen-year-old lover watching raptly my flame extinguish. Yes, let him remember me as flame, as fire, as the heat that kept him warm in the un-winterized house.

* * *

"If you were going to be stranded on a desert island and could only bring one book, what would it be?" he posed the question one day over an irresistibly *wabi* lunch of rosemary beans and olive bread, accompanied by a wedge of Manchego. I had never tasted anything so delicious in my life.

I burst out laughing, astonished that he should care to know the slightest thing about me.

"What's so funny?" he demanded softly.

"You," I said and looked at him while trying to imagine what he would look like when he was a grown man. It was a dangerous habit of mine. "I like knowing in advance that I'll be stranded. There's something funny about that. I mean the whole notion of being stranded typically implies something unforeseen. I've always thought your question was designed for one not already stranded on an island. Your use of the conditional is funny."

"But you're not stranded, you have a library. And you have your collection at home and you can go to the bookstore and buy new books anytime. I'm talking about one book for life. That's it. One."

"Like 'One Book, One Island'," I said, referring to the island-wide community reading program of which neither of us was a member, "except it's till death."

"You *would* look at it like that," he said cuttingly but not, I thought, without affection.

"Is it because you're young that you don't consider yourself to be already stranded on an island?"

"No. Neither of us is stranded. No one is."

"No one?"

"Well, almost no one. Maybe there are a few people who are physically incapable of moving but they would be stranded anywhere." He was cocksure as he said it, his logic fairly overwhelmed me.

"You're going to be such a handsome man," I said, slipping my hand under his curls to stroke the fine hairs on the back of his neck.

He looked away, as if insulted, and in the process disengaged my hand. I had indirectly violated our unspoken agreement never to speak of the future and implied as well that he was not yet a man.

He ran the calloused tips of his fingers along the blue ticking of the mattress and turned toward me again. "If you don't choose a book in the next five minutes, you won't be allowed to bring one."

"A difficult question for anyone," I said, "but especially for me."

"Why? Because you work at a library?" With that bewildered, immigrant gaze of his, he seemed intent on mastering my world, its customs and mannerisms, its ethics and currency.

"No, I should think that would make it easier—so many titles fresh in my mind all the time. It's because I've recently and rather drastically changed. I'm not the person I was before I met you. Before I might have said *Wings of the Dove* or *Ethan Frome* or some such nonsense but now the thought of reading those books for eternity is a nightmare." I too had traveled a great distance.

"Why?" he asked, perhaps not understanding the literary references or perhaps not wanting to assume anything about them or about me, yes, likely more open to others and to the world than I ever was even when young.

"It's one thing to read about tragic love affairs when one is happily living outside such circumstances, it's another thing entirely to..."

"Three more minutes," he said. "Choose a book now or you'll be doomed to live the rest of your days without one."

I paged nimbly through my inner card catalog. None of my old favorites made sense anymore. After what seemed like more than three minutes (time must have passed more quickly for me than it did for him), I announced my choice, "Saint-Saëns Concerto in G minor for the piano."

"No musical instruments allowed on the island."

"God, I really will be stranded."

"Yep, thirty seconds," he said and began raising the palm of one hand to meet the fingertips of the other.

"Keats's *Collected*!" I fired just as his two hands touched to make a T.

"I thought you'd had your fill of tragedy," he said, surprising me with the insinuation that he had read Keats. I replaced my hands upon his neck.

"Poetry is different," I said at once. But he was right. I was not ready to give tragedy up just yet. I clasped his neck more tightly. I studied his face until I saw the man I thought he would someday become and felt him rise to meet me.

Ritual accomplished, candles snuffed, chalice generously filled, I lay on the ascetic's slim mattress content as a nun (save for the young man lying next to me) who has said her prayers and can now rest. I began dreaming of us renting the little gray house, painting the inside walls a pale yellow, sewing eyelet curtains, baking cakes, roasting chickens, adding a window to the loft and a real bed, lying together under a red coverlet watching the cardinal fly and the snow fall and the sun rise until the young man rolled off the mattress and put on his jeans.

"I have to leave early today." I watched him pull on his socks. He had never left early; he had never left first. "I have to take a test."

"What sort of test?" I imagined, absurdly, a test of character in which he would be faced with a series of ethical dilemmas.

"Advanced Math."

"How very advanced of you," I said, genuinely impressed. "I only got as far as Algebra II. You've already surpassed me! How terrifying!" The inevitable began innocently enough with high school mathematics.

"Assuming I pass the class," he said darkly, alluding to the possibility that his previously pristine record was under threat.

"Is there a girl at school you like a lot?" I had begun to want a girl his own age to love him, and even for him to love her, though I also dreaded such an outcome.

"No, not really." This was not the correct answer. Though I suppose the "not really" appended to the "no" might be taken less as a warning than a sign of one intent on honesty.

"Surely there has to be a Sophia or a Rosamond who's caught your eye, someone with long hair and a pretty name?"

He looked at me, all at once very quiet and handsome and irritated, then said in a soft, punishing voice, "Why don't you visit the school if you're so curious? Take a look for yourself. Meet all the girls. Meet the guys while you're at it. I'm sure you'd like a lot of them. You could meet my friends. We could all go out for pizza afterward." His voice grew quieter and quieter.

"Will you think of me while you take your exam?" I asked contritely.

"Of course," he crackled as he laced his boots. "I always think of you when trying to solve difficult problems."

"Won't you stay a bit longer?" I tried to sound cavalier, but cavalier and contrite were a difficult pairing.

"Okay," he said.

"Never mind, I shouldn't have asked."

"It's okay."

"No, it isn't. Go on, ace your exam."

"Okay." That word again, I thought, and reached for his singlet. How was I ever to know if he was consenting to me or if he felt cowed by my adult requests? He put his arms through the holes and I tugged on the neck until it had passed over him. I took his face in my hands. His cheeks were faintly toffee-scented.

"Don't ever listen to me," I warned. "I'll only corrupt you." There was still not the slightest hint of any facial hair upon him, just the nearly invisible down that covers the faces of children. "Quick!" I said, "Before I change my mind and decide to hold you hostage for eternity."

He laughed but was looking down at the floor as if at the room below; it was a Violetine moment. He turned to go. "Don't you think I'm capable of it?" I persisted, at last feeling cast-off and impotent.

"Of course you're capable," he said as he lowered himself down the ladder. But you wouldn't," he said. "You're too nice."

"Is that good?" I called down after a minute or so. But he had already very quietly gone, if only because I had instructed him to.

* * *

With or without the threat of a husband nearby, the young man was not the sort who would ever conceive of taking me away. Even if he had somehow managed to formulate such a plan, he would not have carried it out. Herein lay, like two strands of wire twisted endlessly together, both the deeply appealing safety of the relationship and its dangerously strict limits. The onus, if there was to be an onus, was upon me and I preferred it that way. I did not want a man with money and power and ideas who might threaten to wrest me away from my present circumstances. This would only have caused problems for me. I was trapped in an age-old paradox, like the woman who falls in love with a "family man" precisely because of his devotion to family. She remakes him. The moment he begins to love her he ceases to be her original object of desire. The very inexperience I loved in him I unwittingly proceeded to destroy. My logic was terribly flawed. I went searching for innocence using corrupt means.

As soon as I began to love him I began to see our love as a prison and myself as the warden. I could not love him without wanting also to set him free. I wanted him to ace his math test. I wanted him at the top of his class! Meanwhile, the more regularly and intensely he related to me as a source of love and pleasure, the more devoted he became, the more at home he became in said prison. The prison of our love was not unlike the Alcatraz of my childhood, an island whose shores no outsiders tread upon. We were alone there, consigned to one another's company insofar as we had agreed to protect our secret. The prescriptive remoteness of our relationship was at once a prison requirement and a feature of most beautiful places in the world. We had never been seen walking hand in hand along the road by our fellow citizens (in fact we had never walked hand in hand anywhere), we had never sat at a table in a restaurant or asked for food from anyone other than ourselves, he had never studied more because of me, when he passed a test it was despite us.

And yet I could no longer drink from the cups of complacency and disappointment nor could I fathom a return to the empty pleasure cup. In the end, my objective was not to be good in the way that nuns are good, but to make something useful of the remainder of my life. That was how I rationalized my choice to love. Of what use would a miserable mother be to a child? Of what use would an unhappy librarian be to a library, an unhappy woman to her friends? (Here I included Violet if not placed her at the top of my list.) I had to believe that my happiness counted for something beyond my own personal satisfaction.

Perhaps in an attempt to normalize my questionable undertaking, I developed an appetite for stories of deviant love: *Lolita, The Price of Salt, The Cement Garden, King Kong, Beauty and the Beast*, even *The Thorn Birds*, which was, though not particularly well-written, with its blasphemy and incest, doubly satisfying. That spring I read more queer novels than I had read in my entire adult life. (Queer was a term I was borrowing with increasing looseness and frequency. Indeed if this was queer society, I too was a member.) I both relished their transgressive hotness and tortured myself with the fact that many a homosexual would find me morally repulsive. Heavily peppered with scenes of socially unacceptable sex, descriptions of guilt, fear, and forced secrecy, fascination with beauty and frustration with an uncomprehending world, such novels were like compact mirrors that I carried in my cloth bag. One could always pop one open, look in, and see oneself reflected there.

And yet I could no longer read deviant novels without also thinking of Violet. Which would be her favorites? How much tolerance did she have? Would she find lesbian sex gruesome? Incest a crime? Could she find it in her heart to love a predator? Humbert Humbert, Father de Bricassart, I, the worst of all? If she knew the truth about what I had done, would she still want me?

One evening, in the heart-racing aftermath of a *Lolita* reread, terrified and yet incapable of waiting any longer, I at last brought the scraps out of the drawer. Like a Hatfield girl on a dormitory phone, I fiddled with them until they were ragged with the sweat of my palms. I could have sworn I smelled the lemon wax from that dim, wooden booth. Briskly I punched the numbers into the phone.

It did not grant me even a single ring but sent me, like a troublemaker, directly to voice mail. "Hi, you've reached Violet. If it's important call me at the shop." She had omitted P.I.P.'s number as if to point out that if one didn't already possess it there was no need to call. (I knew the number by heart, I had found it in the Island Book and memorized it.)

She was too busy to see me. If I'd had any sense I'd have received this as spring's consolation, its one bittersweet gift. But alas, I was senseless.

* * *

Only once during our time together did the young man visit the library while I was on duty. Predictably enough, seeing him in public caused in me an intense, albeit fugitive, moral confusion. When at first my secret was brought out of the woods and placed in full view of the town, I was paralyzed.

It was a Friday. Maria had gone home with a friend and I had come directly from the gray house to work the afternoon shift for the director. I was seated at her desk, rather hypocritically hand-addressing envelopes to delinquent patrons and then stuffing the envelopes with warning letters when I heard the slow, unmistakable crackling of his throat being very politely cleared. Instantly the button within me was pressed, which alarmed me, for it had already been urgently, repeatedly pressed earlier that morning. His politeness had a particularly indelible effect on me that day. There he stood, the way he had the first day, an anonymous patron quietly waiting to be acknowledged.

His unentitled attitude toward me made me want to bestow upon him any and all titles he might have wished for, but it also frightened me. A young man with such a strict sense of propriety, I thought, would certainly grow into a man who disapproved of our current relationship. The very respectability that attracted me to him seemed a constant threat to our unrespectable arrangement. Perhaps he had come to end things. These thoughts assailed me even before I had time to raise my head and meet his eye. Knowing he would not speak first, I paused. I bought time. I tried to imagine the precise words he would use and how I would feel afterward. Then I tried to speak but could not, my throat had closed. It was only as a librarian, a public servant, a paid town employee that I was able to recover myself.

"May I help you?" I asked coldly though I was hot as a pyre of burning books.

"Uh, no," he started to chuckle. "Sorry to bother you," he managed and then backed away. He seemed aggrieved by my professional treatment of him.

"Don't be silly," I whispered, half-expecting Violet to appear beside him with a knife or a revolver. "What are you doing here?" I demanded with some irritation, for it was impossible not to recall the slow, proficient way in which he had, just two hours prior, set his fist like a key inside me and turned it.

"I'm looking for a book," he said. (What a relief to hear that he had a legitimate reason for visiting the library and had not come to deliver my death sentence.)

"So there are books you don't have after all," I said. I was beginning to warm to the sudden appearance of beauty there in the otherwise chilly, forgotten basement.

"It's for school," he admitted and I was forced once more to recall our respective places in the world's chronology.

"Do you need help finding it?" I asked, feeling a bit teacherly, if not like a children's librarian.

"No, no thanks," he shook his head and then smiled briefly. "I just thought I'd stop by before I looked."

I wanted nothing more than to stand up, walk round to the front of the desk, and kiss him hard on the mouth as I had so many times imagined I would if given the opportunity. Instead I sat like a prisoner during visiting hours, one ankle shackled to the director's desk.

He browsed the fiction section while I longed to touch him. A more reckless woman would have approached him without hesitation, but I felt incapable of rising. And yet once I had renounced all thoughts of disengaging from the desk, I was able to thoroughly enjoy observing him. To watch him walk, to watch him stand impatiently in front of a book shelf and take down a book, leaf rapidly through its pages with his nail-bitten fingers, these were rare pleasures for me. I was, I realized, starved for such ordinary moments. He moved through the stacks with a confidence I was not accustomed to seeing in him. Greedily, I took in his buoyant, absurdly youthful stride. What a thrill it was to see him encounter another patron, to see the way in which he sensed her approach and then moved politely to the left to allow her to pass. For a moment I saw him as she might have—a polite, studious seventeen-year-old—and then I allowed the memory of our morning together to overtake that. On his way out he glanced at me and I glanced back—indeed I never once allowed my eyes to leave him—but I played, with some gratification, the role of lady stranger and he understood. He brought the book (the title of which I strained and failed to see, hidden as it was by the navy blue crook of his arm) upstairs to be checked out by another librarian.

As soon as he had disappeared into the stairwell, I rolled my chair to the wall and climbed upon it, nearly toppling over in the process, so that I might look out through the high window and watch him leave. From my unsteady perch I saw him striding across the parking lot with the book in his hand. There was something perpetually preoccupied about him, even from the back this was evident. I was never able to determine whether he was hurrying toward something that held him or away from something that did not, whether he pulled a leash behind him or was pulled by one.

Once, when we had gone dangerously over the time allotted us by the nursery, I had ridden with him in a car, which, the shitbox having been totaled, was not his but Violet's toffee-colored minivan and which I could see was now parked in the library lot. As I watched him climb into it, I remembered how sweet it was to be driven by him, his thin hands a younger, more masculine version of hers, his lost-father eyes scanning the road as furiously as if the remainder of our time together depended on it. I had been overtaken at once by the thought of a crash in which one or both of us died a gruesome death or deaths, ultimately resulting in what somehow seemed a fate worse than death: the exposure of our relationship. The young man did not find this amusing nor did he seem frightened by my suggestion of the possibility; he simply attempted unsuccessfully to reassure me. "Don't worry. I'm a good driver. I've been practicing a lot."

I watched him set his book on the dash and put the van in gear. He checked the mirror and then turned his head to look over his shoulder before backing out. From where I stood on tiptoe, peering through the powerful yet foggy lenses of my glasses (I was, not surprisingly, overheating, as much from the fact of his nearness as from my awkward ascent of the office chair), he looked to be an excellent driver but then I was a fine one to judge. When he and his skillful maneuvering had disappeared from sight, I went immediately upstairs and informed Nella of my need to refresh myself. I left her paging, amused yet captivated, through the current issue of *People* while I escaped to the lavatory, ostensibly to relieve my bladder but in fact to satisfy an even baser need.

The most remarkable feature of the staff restroom is its sorry lack of reading material. One more easily understands such a situation in a public facility. No one, least of all me, wants to encourage any undue loitering on the part of our patron population. But an absence of books and even periodicals in a *librarians' restroom* seems an affront to the phrase. Granted, it is not often that I relieve myself in any significant way during my shift. I do not mean to imply that I should like to read a chapter by Tolstoy whilst otherwise engaged but there is something to be said for *The New Yorker* or *The New York Review of Books* (actually I would have preferred the *London Review of Books* but alas, it was not part of our distinctly American collection) within the confines of a restroom. Such periodicals are sufficiently distracting and would keep one's eyes from wandering nervously to the often open window which, though high enough to shield one from a small to average-height Peeping Tom, seemed low enough to easily accommodate a tall one.

One's only chance at rest in such a room is to read the labels of the many office and toilet supplies that are stored there. Indeed a floor to ceiling shelf chock-full of toilet paper, paper towels, copy paper, reserve/request cards, scotch tape, book tape, and number two pencils is the view one commands, which in the end prevents one from forgetting about work entirely. Though on this visit I confess none of this mattered. I brazenly closed my eyes for the duration. I washed my hands most thoroughly afterward, spritzed myself jauntily with the all-natural hand sanitizer and noted the undeniable flush of pleasure on my cheeks reflected on the communal mirror as I exited.

* * *

Soon after her marriage to my father, at his urging, my mother took up Japanese. For years she attended night classes and my father home-schooled her. One of her favorite phrases was *shikata ga nai* or "it can't be helped." She employed it loosely, whenever it suited her. *You don't even know what it means, Mum!* I complained. Or she was deliberately misusing it. I suppose I would have preferred the former, better ignorance than arrogance. Although I wondered if there wasn't something profoundly similar about the two modes. To my mind, "it can't be helped" was a phrase one used sparingly in the silence that follows the sharp slap of fate—it was a phrase belonging to the *hibakusha*. It meant: *This has been done. What can we do?* It was not a phrase one used to relinquish responsibility.

My mother used it as an excuse for missing appointments or burning cakes or when she did not understand something my father or I had been trying to communicate to her. The phrase, instead of inspiring acceptance and action, induced in her complacence and passivity. It was, in many ways, her tacit motto, and, rather fittingly, borrowed and translated, its original meaning lost.

That spring I adopted my mother's usage of *shikata ga nai.* I ate my own words. I caught myself muttering the phrase, unsure of whether I was imitating her or saying it myself. It became my response to every ethical question I had thus far been unable to answer. How can you do this to your family? *Shikata ga nai.* How can you deprive him of a lover his own age? *Shikata ga nai.* How can you go on deceiving every person you know, not least of all Violet? *Shikata ga nai.* How can you refuse to work Fridays when the library is understaffed and your family needs the income? *Shikata ga nai. Shikata ga nai. Shikata ga nai.* The phrase became addictive. When I thought of where Fate had placed me in relation to the young man, at once on the very same island and yet estranged from him in years, I felt the allure of the phrase's fluidity. One day it meant our estrangement couldn't be helped, one day it meant our love.

In my highly confidential state, I turned, if only in my mind, to loved ones for support. Alive or dead, they did not respond as they truly would have, but as I imagined them to. I fancied myself a good judge of character, able to predict with startling accuracy their responses. When at last I was too enthralled to disengage from the young man, it was my father—twenty-one years in the grave—who dispensed, like a life-saving drug, the most illuminating if loosely interpreted bit of advice: *The man with the moustache is the man who will do you harm.* I took this to mean: *Don't bother with that bandit of a husband!* I took the liberty of inferring the inverse to be true as well: *The (young) man with the smooth, hairless face will bring you happiness and pleasure.* Parenthetical mine.

* * *

I looked down at the paperback copy of *The Lover* that he had placed sideways on my side of the mattress. It was the edition with young Duras's face on the cover. "I'd rather not read this," I said.

He did not retort with a sharp "why not?" as I immediately would have but waited, like a musician accustomed to collaborating, several beats for me to elaborate. I waited too, testing the endurance of his patience and passivity but being no match for him I soon explained, "I told you I've had my fill of tragedy."

"I remember you telling me you hadn't."

"Must you remember everything so precisely?"

"Yes."

"Really? And do you remember because you're young or because you're so madly in love with me that you're utterly devoted to your memories of our time together?"

"I don't know." He sat propped upon his elbows with his hair in his eyes, like a dog who can't possibly comprehend why he is being scolded. And yet he had not a single hair on his chest. I stroked it to affirm its existence. His was the clean slate of torsos, the smoothest, most untraveled of pectoral regions. And he had read Duras! A delicious combination to be sure, a bit like cold vanilla ice cream with warm chocolate cake, that manically exciting sensation from childhood.

"Do you really think stories of doomed love affairs are in order?"

"Why not?" Ah, at last the sharp retort driven by the black engine of his voice.

I felt a pronounced affection for the moments in which he finally agreed to argue.

Perhaps because my parents rarely disagreed, I found argument to be one of the most compelling forms of passion. But when I reflected on this particular assent, I was filled with doubt. Was this the flip "why not" of a noncommittal lover or the earnest "why not" of one devoted to knowing my inmost thoughts? Why not indeed? Was he not, as I was, sufficiently frightened by the constant threat of separation? Did he not care enough to be frightened by it?

"It can be a relief to read about other people's problems."

"That's true, but have you read this?"

"Yeah, it's great. You'd like it if you gave it a chance."

"I'm not averse to it based on hearsay, for God's sake, I've already read it!" I picked the book up and pointed to young Duras, feeling conspicuously like my father. "Do you know who this is?" I asked.

And when of course he didn't answer immediately, I raved on, paternally waving the book for emphasis. "This is me. I'm the one doomed to return to the place where I came from and I don't mean bloody England! Someday you'll go tromping off on some Melvillian adventure and I'll return to the island of middle-aged librarians with five-year-olds whose noses need wiping and husbands who stay up late carving gnomes. The island where books provide the only excitement.

"As for you, you're the rich Chinese guy. Your youth is your wealth. You have it to spend and no one, but no one, expects you to spend it on me. Your youth waits for you the way his money did. It's what separates us, it's what makes me ridiculous. I'm the trashy visitor. In truth you would never dream of marrying me."

"You're already married," he said softly as if afraid to upset me further but quietly determined to rein me in.

"That really isn't the point now is it?" I didn't know what to make of the fact that we were having an argument. It rather excited me. I felt as if we had left the realm of the fleeting and entered the real. Wasn't there an Old World saying, something to the effect of: "Trying to love someone without hurting them is like trying to walk in the snow without leaving marks"? We were leaving our marks in the snow.

"What *is* the point?"

"The simple point I'm trying to make is that I can't bear to read this particular book at the moment." I felt a rush of remorse for my fretful outburst. Contrary to appearances, aversion had not been my first response—that had been arousal—but I had swiftly, defensively bypassed it in favor of self-protection, a move for which I now felt ashamed. "Thank you," I said, moving closer to him, "I like very much that you've brought me this to read. It's one of my favorites, it's endlessly sexy I just..."

As I opened my mouth to explain, he kissed me, and I, at last abandoning all explanation, kissed him in return.

"Don't watch me," he muttered. I was astride him; I had a spectacular view.

"Have to," I managed. I kept my eyes trained on his face as he clenched his mouth and let out an anguished, primordial sound. "Why come here if not to witness your pleasure and trace its origins? You can't ask me to forego that. It would make our time meaningless."

"Wow, meaningless?" He spoke with his eyes closed.

"Well, not meaningless but you know what I mean." Did he?

How was I to fend off the image of his pleasure when it was just centimeters away? Why would I possibly want to turn away from it? The viewing of his fulfillment, the experience of my own, these were indistinguishable. More important still, I was storing up images for a future from which he would likely be absent.

* * *

One Saturday morning Var announced that he would be

taking Maria to the dump. Such impromptu expeditions were rare and typically lasted twenty-five minutes. I had learned to seize such opportunities. I hurried alongside them out of the apartment and immediately began walking to the woods. Saturday was the young man's busiest day at P.I.P. so there was no chance of a last-minute meeting. Still, I wanted to go to the house and sit a while. I considered staying in the apartment to phone him or to phone Violet, but I faltered. The truth was I didn't like speaking to people on their mobile phones while they were prowling around doing other things. I preferred to have conversations with people while they were seated at home. Using a landline was for me quite literally akin to being on land while using a mobile phone was like being at sea or, worse, up in an airplane. I preferred a seated, stable connection. Just the thought of the scraps of paper in my drawer made my palms sweat.

The walk to the waterfall always brought me some measure of happiness. All walking does something to lift my spirits. Striding the length of the library to retrieve a book for a patron revives me, walking in slow, wide circles in the garden puts me at ease. I walked briskly, free to travel at my own pace (Maria's legs were considerably shorter than mine and her attention drifted free as a leaf on a river). Even without the prospect of seeing him, I was happy to be released from my motherly duties and walking.

As I neared the trailhead I began to have nervous thoughts about the property owner. It seemed inevitable that I should encounter her; she must have used the trail but thus far we had never met. The white NO TRESPASSING sign gave me a sinister jolt as always, the late afternoon sun shone on it as if to point it out. I curbed my anxiety with thoughts of the young man and entered the woods.

Almost immediately I heard the rush of the waterfall and felt the Pavlovian flush of arousal that so often accompanied it, my ears the ears of a captive rat attuned to indicators of pleasure. I crossed the bridge, then scrambled lightly down the bank to the stone bench, where I sat for a few moments and watched the water. But like a stray metal filing, I felt magnetically drawn to the site of fulfillment.

Once in the tunnel I noticed how very green the trees were from the recent rain, the birds singing all around me; I recalled with unladylike satisfaction our meeting the day before (the young man's fingers extending and then twisting before curling into a fist; his fist turning, each of his knuckles touching me in slow succession as the notch of a dying Rota Fortunae touches many possibilities before entering one) until my autoerotic reverie was interrupted by the sound of uproarious laughter. I stopped walking and listened intently. It was the sound of people at play and yet the voices were male and that frightened me. I was a woman alone in the woods after all. Teasing, yelling, bellows, more laughter. Such happiness! I couldn't resist following it.

I broke into a run and nearly tripped over an enormous tree that had fallen during the storm onto the trail. For a moment I was poleaxed by the sight of it, panicked in the face of an obstacle. I knelt down before it. Gruntingly I tried to push it forward but the tree wouldn't budge; it was heavy, riddled with thorns and sharp twigs. I stood up and kicked it with the blunt toe of my boot to no avail. Finally, in the way of an unskilled hurdler who leads with her hands, I cleared it inelegantly, scratching my face in the process. The savage mark seemed a small price to pay for my freedom.

I had almost reached the gray house when I heard a male voice shouting the young man's name. My heart folded in on itself like an antique camera. Black box shut. The voices were coming from the gray house. He was being teased by another young man and then another. They were shouting suggestive things to each other and laughing. I inched nearer and crouched behind an oak tree to watch.

They had opened the windows, something we never dared to do. Puffs of smoke were coming out of the window on the left, the very window I had often looked out of while sitting at the small table eating candy. His name was shouted again. How it pained me to hear it! The name insisted upon the existence of another reality to which he belonged apart from me. Again the boy yelled it, the name that I had never so much as whispered to another. The boy stuck his head out of the left-hand window and blew several smoke rings. I feared he would yell the name again but it was the young man himself who yelled next, his gravelly voice somehow smoother and less mature at that decibel. *I told you not to smoke in here, dog!* But he was laughing, he wasn't really angry. (Did he ever really get angry? Another question for the queue.) They all appeared to be quite stoned—everything was funny to them, it was difficult for them to utter clear sentences without laughing. Var and his friends at university got this way sometimes, I recognized the behavior.

For a few minutes I listened to them yell expletives rather affectionately at one another. From what I could decipher there was Liam the ring blower who seemed to love any word or code word having to do with marijuana and Will the extremely giggly one who kept saying *shit* and *ass* when he wasn't expressing himself in preliterate whoops and finally the young man, whose fixation was sex. What issued out of his Gerber baby mouth was *horny, hot, in the mood to fuck* and a string of other sex-related obscenities for which I felt partly if not solely responsible. What had I done? And had he told them? Did they know this was our love nest they were trampling upon? A sudden fear of the law accompanied by my longstanding fear of being humiliated by young men welled up in me.

Smoke continued to rise from the left-hand window, the right-hand window flew open with a screech. A boy I assumed was Will hung himself out like a dog on a joyride and giggled. He looked ugly and wild, the extreme paleness of his skin accentuating the redness of his acne, his mouth lolling open as he laughed, his teeth covered in muzzle-ish braces. I wished, in vain, for a third window through which the young man—*my* young man, not these others—might appear. For despite the fact that soon Maria and Var would be back from the dump if they weren't already, despite the fact the young man and his friends might leave at any moment, I wanted, naively, recklessly, to catch a glimpse of him. I wanted, like some candy-eating, hand-waving groupie, to see what my rockstar was wearing! (Was it the white T-shirt, pristine and detergent-scented, or the same shirt covered in mud from the storm, saturated with the smoke of an illegal substance?) Simultaneously, contrary to my history of endless inquiries, I didn't want to see him in this other mode, this world so painfully identical to our world and yet so different from it. I felt myself stepping backward in the way of someone bidding a difficult farewell; one exits the station slowly while keeping one's eyes on the train. In the end, my fear of seeing who he was without me was stronger than my desire to see him as he was and I turned from that new world and fled.

I beat Var and Maria to the shack. I entered it the way one enters a screened confessional, not wanting to see a face, not wanting to confess but seeking absolution. I stood trembling before the sink washing dishes, praying they would not break. Like a child who has pushed open the door to her parents' bedroom at the wrong moment and cannot erase what she's seen, my former way of seeing things had been altered; I tried but could not retrieve it. Within minutes I heard the door downstairs unlatch, creak open, I heard the stampede of their feet upon the stairs.

Quickly, I slipped into the bedroom and went online. I typed the four words I had been avoiding for months: *Massachusetts statutory rape laws.* I was like a murderer vexed to read the ten commandments. I needed to be told by some higher power that what I was doing was wrong. I needed to know my punishment. Child rapist. Prison term. I was ready to hear it.

One cannot adequately convey the chilling depth of one's surprise at learning, just as Maria began pounding on the door, that the age of consent in Massachusetts is sixteen.

"Mama!! Open the door!!!" More pounding.

"Just a minute, darling!" How could that be? One could be punished for consensual sex with someone sixteen and older if and only if the prosecution could prove that the young person in question had been chaste until that point, and that, most experts agreed, was virtually impossible. On the other hand, the crime of adultery was punishable by three years in prison. (This I could hardly take seriously, it must have been an archaic law that no one ever adhered to. If such a law were truly in practice, a large portion of the population would be in prison.) My eyes lit upon the phrase *carnal knowledge.* Maria screamed again. I closed the window, cleared history, then opened the door.

Maria whirled through the room in her usual dervish-like fashion, a little goddess with multiple limbs, and I allowed her—the real child—to supplant my own childlike despair and confusion (Why didn't I feel better? Why didn't I feel reprieved?) for the remainder of the day and night until the following morning.

* * *

She woke before me. I was not eager to greet the day. "Mama!" she bellowed.

I turned onto my side to face her. The room was terribly bright. I had not slept well.

"Maria my love," I cooed cloudily. She kicked me forcefully in the stomach with both feet. "Right then," I got up.

"I want you!" she screamed.

"You have a very odd way of showing it!"

"I! Want! You!" she growled with feeling. This call and response was recurring. Every morning she kicked me away then commanded me to come back when I got up from the bed. Sometimes the back and forth ended when she managed to pull me back into the bed using her legs as pincers. Very rarely, she submitted a revised, more polite version of her request and sometimes I crept away to forage for a bit of food that like magic when placed into her mouth would change her back into the lovely Maria. This morning I crept away as quickly as I could. It was Sunday. The juvenile room with its stencils and crayons, reading rocket and chrysalises, was waiting.

* * *

When I sat down at the children's librarian's desk, I winced at the row of Harry Potter books opposite. The previous evening's research had done little to alleviate my guilt. Indeed the pot party had somehow annulled my findings. I argued with myself. *Shikata ga nai. It can't be helped.* I muttered the phrase in both languages for emphasis. *But what if it* can *be helped?!* It had been far from reassuring for me to see him with his friends, sloppily overtaking the gray house as if it were a fraternity or a jungle gym. Their adolescent bellows and smoke rings had chastened me. I could not forget his boyish voice intoning the ridiculous sentence: *I told you not to smoke in here, dog!* This was not the young man I knew. This was an ill-mannered, vulgar adolescent. I felt both repelled and sorry. It *can* be helped!

I sat trying to argue it out. Indeed I must have been very involved in sorting my arguments for I did not notice anyone had entered the room until I heard the clearing of a throat. The sound was the mother of the other sound I knew so well. It was she. Her hair was loose, a bit turbulent, worn precisely the way Siobhan had correctly imagined would suit her.

"Mayumi! The woman at the desk sent me. When she said *you* would know where the Bradbury books were I didn't know she meant *you.*" I felt like a Mexican burro upon whose back an entire family's belongings had been heaped. If one more item was added to my load, I would not make the journey.

"Bradbury?" I brayed and thought with bleak terror of my last recommendation.

"*Fahrenheit 451*, it's for my son. He's reading it at school."

"Oh yes, of course. We have multiple copies." I wobbled on the step stool, my low heels disgustingly hooflike. I reached up to the top shelf and felt faint.

"How have you been?" she asked. She looked at me closely. Had she seen the vulgar throb in my neck?

"Very well, thanks. And you? You must be busy with the shop now that spring is upon us."

"Yes. I wish I weren't so busy." She glanced out the window. "I'm ashamed to say I haven't even started *Lolita.*" Ashamed indeed.

"Oh, you'll get to it eventually," I said. I was in no hurry to begin our discussion of Nabokov.

"I hope so, I really do want to read it."

"You must be proud of your son." I stamped his book eagerly. "My daughter is just learning to read."

"I am proud. It's like a miracle when it happens. You're lucky you have that to look forward to." She wore the distracted expression of one following a long to-do list. "Well, thanks for the book, I'm sorry I have to run!"

"No apology necessary!" None indeed! By all means feel free to exit the building! By all means leave me to brood!

She turned to go and then turned impulsively back again.

"Hey! Do you want to go for a walk sometime?" The burro in me balked but she pressed on, apparently unperturbed by my beastly withholding. "I go walking every morning around 8 if you want to join me. The trailhead's right behind P.I.P."

"Sure, thanks. I love to walk in the morning, especially in the woods." The sentence sounded vile when I said it.

She picked up a summer reading brochure and tucked it into the book. "I hope you'll come."

I was like a student with too many subjects to study, a slew of examinations pending, and the wretched fact was I could only concentrate on one subject at a time.

Summer reading. Such dreaded words! They were yet another reminder that in all likelihood my youthful fountain would soon stop playing its music. Then again, summer as end date was a compelling argument. What difference did it make if one quit now or very soon? (I tended to use the language of addiction with regard to the young man.) Couldn't I indulge in one or two months more of pleasure? Couldn't I simply vow to quit when summer began?

I stood up (as I often do when at the end of my tether) and resolved to shelve the red cart. A sixth grade science class had checked out over fifty books for various special projects and had just returned them. Thank God. I was not daunted in the least by the three solid rows of 500's. I shelved ruthlessly, like a mercenary being paid to make each book disappear. My deliberations had exhausted me. All too quickly the cart was empty. I reseated myself—always a mistake at moments such as these—and immediately began to cast about for something reassuring to do.

Unthinkingly, my hand clasped the mouse the way one might clasp a handrail for support and before I had time to fully ascertain my own movements I had entered the young man's hyphenated name into Athena. I refrained from opening his account—I knew precisely what it contained. Instead I ventured to type in the second half of his surname, curious what it might yield. Perhaps he had paternal relations on the island. If so, it couldn't hurt to learn what sort of books they read. Insatiably, maniacally curious, I would have settled for the borrowing history of a fifth cousin.

What I found, contrary to his earlier claim, was that he had two accounts. The one I had generated was his second, the first, generated when he was a child in the company of his mother (the word CHILD in all-black caps shone after his name), long since forgotten, the first card long since misplaced. I sat looking at his first account as if at a holy text, the careful study of which would reveal forbidden truths and long-held secrets. First I clicked on Patron Status then Info, which informed me that his address was the same then as it was now. But of course I knew that fairly well, I knew he had been born in that house, the house of the Liberty orchard and the voluminous library. I paused before clicking on History. I was not wholly convinced that unearthing such a thing would be reassuring. But indeed I did click. I was hopelessly in thrall to the possibilities.

It was a history befitting a child. There were only three items, all of them films:

-*Snow Day*

-*Pocahontas*

-*Swiss Family Robinson*

At the sight of the list, my heart closed the way it had in the woods. Black box shut. I stared at the three items. A few tears fell from the corners of my eyes and onto the keyboard. I clicked on the X in the uppermost right corner of the screen. *Do you really want to exit Athena?* she asked. I clicked Cancel. It didn't matter that I then closed his account and didn't open it again. The titles had been placed in my inner card catalog; they had become part of my permanent collection.

For the rest of the day, I said the six words silently to myself. I said them while I was waiting for the computer to perform a function and later, while washing my hair in the shower, and later still, while reading aloud to Maria. (I confess I had mastered the art of reading aloud while engaged in my own thoughts. Had it been an official Olympic event I would have won a gold medal.) I too had watched films such as these (I too had read Ray Bradbury) but decades earlier—his close proximity to them was undeniable. *My God*, I thought to myself at last. *He's a child.*

* * *

I had the week to contemplate his short history. For the first time I felt some hesitation about seeing him the approaching Friday. As a nun who contemplates a simple prayer that both uplifts and agonizes, my best self (Was it my best self?) understood the six words as a plea and wanted to grant it. The rest of me (Or was that the best of me?) found the words, the boy, the man, whatever he was, quite fetching and wanted to bargain. Bargain I did with myself, the toughest, most compliant of customers. We came to a cheerful agreement: I would quit him when summer began whether he stayed or went. My instincts told me he would go and if he did, well, then nothing would be lost in the bargain.

The next question was, could I, with those six guileless words fluttering like kites in the sky of my mind, still make love to him? I thought it likely, but perhaps I was overestimating myself. If the boys in the woods had chastened me, the six words were belt-like, each one an iron barrier to my fulfillment. To add to the growing body of evidence against me, there was the unfortunate eavesdropping contretemps to consider and, of course, the precarious matter of Violet.

When at last Friday arrived, I brought a small bucket of cleaning supplies to the gray house. Ever the child of a housekeeper, I turned to spring cleaning as a diversion. The young man was sitting on the porch. We had plenty of wood, it would have been silly to chop more, every day was now warmer than the last. In light of my recent discovery, his habit of waiting for me before entering the house seemed slightly ridiculous, if not a bit foxy.

"You don't have to wait for me, you know," I called out.

"I want to."

"You want to wait for me or you want to sit outside?"

"Both."

As I approached he stayed sitting there with his elbows on his knees, his eyes alternately watching me and scanning the ground, which was dotted depressingly with a cheerful array of wild violets and buttercups, a double reminder of his mother and summer's golden approach.

The blue backpack whose curved flap he usually kept shut lay open as a lake on the top step. I could see, floating within it, a round tin of chewing tobacco, a pale orange and white pack of cigarette rolling papers, a red, white, and blue American history textbook, the black father-wallet I had glimpsed once at the library counter, two raspberry-flavored Tootsie pops, a red guitar pick, a well-worn composition book with the words AP English scrawled in small letters on the cover, a silver CD player adjoined to the now familiar headphones he had worn at the library, and a black mobile phone. It was a hasty glance but it made its impression.

How very real he was when we were apart, whether in solitude or in connection with others. I had never seen him use a mobile phone or heard him play guitar or observed him rolling whatever forbidden substance it was he rolled with those papers of his. He must have had so many habits that were unknown to me, ways of moving and speaking; the Saturday previous had merely been a sample.

"We don't have to go inside," I said, afraid the house would smell distastefully of smoke and perhaps prevent me from venturing further.

"Okay." He picked up a rock and threw it at the woods.

"Do you know I bloody hate that word!"

"Why? Is it not proper English?"

"I could care less about proper English. It's just so bloody agreeable."

"Would you rather I be disagreeable?"

"If I did, then would you be?"

"I don't know."

"If I asked you to drink poison would you drink poison?"

"You wouldn't do that."

"The appropriate answer is no."

"Okay."

I sighed. "You have to understand I'm in a very awkward, some might say, compromising position. When you say 'okay' I'm never sure if I'm forcing you along or if you're truly in agreement. Does that make sense?"

"Okay," he said and laughed.

"Stop!"

"What's in the bag?" He nodded at my camouflaged bucket.

"Oh! I thought we could do some spring cleaning today." God knows the place probably needed it after Saturday's shenanigans.

Absurdly, I unveiled my housekeeper's surprise. Why on earth would he want to spend his morning scrubbing a toilet? At the moment it seemed unlikely that he would consent. Though I myself had misgivings, my best self (Was it my best self?) proceeded to explain. "I thought we would spruce up the house. If it were ours we'd certainly keep it clean, wouldn't we?"

"But it isn't."

"Are you refusing to play house? I mean are you actually not saying okay?!" I felt weirdly triumphant. Free will! Agency! Freedom of choice! Equality!

"I'm not saying okay."

"Oh, good for you!" I threw my arms around him and gave him a congratulatory squeeze. I had unwittingly administered a test he'd passed easily. He'd done beautifully, nothing less than an A. We were both adults, he had confirmed it.

I opened the door and was relieved to find that the smell of smoke, like all my good intentions, had dissipated. "Let's go in," I whispered, holding the door open.

"Okay," he said and stepped in.

* * *

The following Friday we entered the gray house to find that workers had been there in our absence. White drop cloths covered the furniture and counters like shrouds, the walls had been sanded but not painted, the windows were lined with blue masking tape, the wood bin next to the stove was filled with short planks of wood that I recognized as formerly being rungs on the ladder that was now missing from the loft. The place was a complete wreck.

"Jesus," I said.

"Shit," he replied.

"How will we get our linens down from there?" I asked in a panic, though as I said it, I realized few people, if anyone, could possibly trace the linens back to us. They were not exactly monogrammed after all.

"Where should we go?" he asked rather pragmatically, impressively undeterred by the disaster at hand.

"I don't know." I was aghast. I walked over to what appeared to be the table and slowly lifted the drop cloth in search of the blue ceramic bird, the Italian cookie tin filled with Japanese candy, the green cross-stitched tablecloth, but found the table underneath denuded, our precious things gone. For the first time I took his hand and we walked around the house for a few minutes, surveying the wreck. We were like a couple at a funeral viewing, the corpse on display the battered interior of the gray house itself. "Wait, look there!" I said and ran to the kitchen to pick up the small postal box from which the bird's beak under the green cloth protruded like a diminutive Anglo-Saxon nose. I lifted the colorful homespun shroud. Our things in a heap looked unremarkable, like the belongings of a dead person waiting to be given or thrown away.

"Let's go," he said.

I took the items out of the box and handed them to him. "Could you put these in your backpack?" It seemed a question a girl would pose to her boyfriend. I was afraid he would refuse, but he submitted.

Before we closed the door behind us, I paused to look up at the ladderless loft. How lovely it had been while it lasted, I thought, with the resignation of one destined to become a senior librarian. I felt grief mixed with awe for all that had happened. Our world was truly floating now, the site of our pleasure aloft. While I looked back, he waited outside, ready in the way of the young to change course.

We walked in silence to the waterfall and sat on the stone bench. I summoned from deep within my maternal line a sad housekeeper's restraint and refrained from weeping.

"Mom has a summerhouse." The young man stared at the waterfall as he spoke. I myself was too distracted.

"Does she?" I put in politely, absently. My mind was on the lost linens, the lost hours.

"Yeah, she rents it out to year-rounders for nine months during the year and then for three months to summer people."

I was in no mood for idle chitchat about tenant shuffles. I'd always found the practice morally abhorrent, though the longer I lived on the island (not to mention the more morally abhorrent I became), the more I could imagine doing such a thing myself. It was difficult to make ends meet. The island's opportunities by definition were limited and its economy was far from booming. Though even as I had these thoughts I railed against expressing them. There were more urgent (and morally abhorrent) matters at hand that required my attention.

"Every year after the tenants move out, she hires workers to clean and paint before the summer tenants move in."

"Do you think we should go back to try and fetch the linens?" I interrupted, forgetting momentarily that the workers would likely be arriving soon if they hadn't already.

He didn't answer me but doggedly resumed his explanation.

"They only work during the day though," he said and then at last was silent.

I was trying to devise a method of accessing the loft from the outside when it occurred to me what it was he was alluding to, what it was he was making possible for me to suggest. I felt a bodily joy, the rush of feeling wanted.

"Why, you're brilliant!" I said, feigning decisiveness though in truth I was, as always, filled with fear. "Absolutely brilliant. Let's say 9:30 next Friday night. Will that work?" I added doubtfully, readying myself for the blow of his refusal.

He nodded then startled me by putting his hand on my knee. The morning, like the man, was still young! I placed my perspiring hand upon his. Where would I take him now that our house had been entombed, our loft suspended? I cast my eyes about until they alighted upon the first set of wind chimes.

But of course! I would take him to the place for lovers and children! Pleased now with my own brilliance, I tapped the chimes lightly with my fingertips as we went. I hummed while I walked. He followed. He sat on the bench and I climbed on. I found his lap to be a most comfortable seat (flanks larger and more muscular than last time I was certain). With a few minor adjustments it was superbly, surprisingly doable. Like an eager new father he endured my weight, while I rode him in full view of the Buddha.

* * *

The children's librarian, for whom I had become a paltry if not offensive substitute every Wednesday and Sunday, had a nunly aspect. She was vivacious yet remote, silver-haired and silver-spectacled, and her spectacles hung on a string of red beads reminiscent of a rosary. Despite her preference for wearing brightly colored fabrics (which somehow brought to mind the clothing of children before they brought to mind the exotic countries in which they had been painstakingly hand woven) it was easy to imagine her in a white habit, her clean flat fingers and their clean flat nails quietly turning the tissuey pages of a King James Bible in earnest search of the answers to difficult questions.

The sin for which she could never forgive herself and for which she daily did penance was a sin the staff referred to as "The $300 Mistake." She herself had rather good-naturedly coined the phrase. I'm certain we would have all forgotten about it by now if not for her habitual references to the costly escapade. I no longer remember when it occurred but one year she dutifully ordered, as she was annually expected to order, a "Corduroy" costume (which in lay terms is a life-size, stuffed yet hollow bear with detachable head) in which she was also annually expected to sweat for the duration of a thirty-minute story time. The spectacle was always well-attended. Indeed it seemed to please everyone but the one inside the bear, who inevitably spent the remainder of her day with perspiration-marked clothing and matted hair, made mysteriously more bearlike by the experience.

Perhaps it was the nuisance of such unfortunate details that distracted her from her next task: return the woolly bear to his enormous coffin-like box and arrange for a pickup. One distracting detail led to another and somehow the cardboard coffin was delivered to its destination sans its furry corpse. The cost of redelivery combined with what must have been an unreasonably stringent late fee amounted to a total of $300. Several years must have passed since the incident but I found myself thinking about it again. In light of my recent transgressions, I felt a new sympathy for the children's librarian and her expensive mistake. I too had been distracted to the point of idiocy; I too had made an unpardonable error, though I counted myself lucky that no one had yet thought to tally up the damages I had incurred.

* * *

All week I plotted precisely how I would exit the apartment undetected and arrive in the most expedient way possible at the gray house. Rather ridiculously I did a trial run the night previous and after landing upon the grass realized that I had not dressed warmly enough. This only made the trial run worthwhile, another cause for rejoicing. My plan was approaching perfection.

When finally Friday arrived, I was overcome with fear of the risks involved: What if Maria woke to find me gone and in turn woke Var with her screaming? What if I fell off the roof or was hit by a car en route? I was stricken by thoughts of all that could go wrong. A foolish, reckless plan I suddenly thought it.

At 8:00 I climbed into bed with Maria as usual. I kept my eyes closed while I waited for her to fall sleep. Once she was asleep I waited the twenty minutes it takes for a sleeper to enter deep sleep (a handy fact gleaned years ago from a parenting book). Then I dressed (I could not allow him to see me in Aunt Tomoko's lace-trimmed flannelette), raised the window (the screen of which I had discreetly removed earlier that day), placed my feet first on the dryer vent, then on the rain gutter, and finally on the frame of the downstairs window before leaping to safety onto the soft grass.

A moonlit walk was one of the many famously beautiful things about the island that I had never experienced firsthand. Once I had left the state road and was walking down Music Street, I relaxed a little and began to appreciate this stunning novelty. The birth of Maria had meant the death of (among other things) my acquaintance with the night. Granted, I had never been terribly intimate with the hours of darkness, tending as I had since childhood to rise and retire early, but I had known moonlit walks down piers and avenues, I had beheld the reflection of ships' lights on the surface of the sea, and more than once I had encountered a starry sky upon exiting a late night concert. One summer there was even a boy with whom I would lie on the grass at night, each of us reading a book by the light of our own torch.

It also happened that Maria's birth coincided with our settling into a house surrounded by tall, leafy trees. When on occasion I remembered the moon's presence and wanted to see it, I had difficulty finding a gap in the dense foliage that would allow me a glimpse. I would flit from room to room, press my face to this window and then that one, craning to see a portion of the moon's face. (I found myself in a similar predicament that year with regard to the school bus, its vanishing gold flashing red through the trees as fleeting as any fall leaf.) Indeed there were likely more trees on the island than there were books in the library.

To be out walking on a moonlit night was magnificent, seeing the nearly full moon ringed by a bluish-yellow light akin to seeing a world-famous painting whose existence I had never doubted and yet had never confirmed. It didn't bother me to be strolling in the moonlight alone. The utter darkness of an island night, even with a moon, affords one a snug feeling of anonymity and the silence of a rural town after dark is rather breathtaking. What an extremely pleasant sensation it was to feel alone in a hushed world, all the while moving closer to the young man.

When I reached the dirt road, I sprinted to the trailhead then walked the remainder of the way in order to regain my composure. The journey from apartment window to gray house doorstep took eleven minutes. He was already inside the house when I arrived. He had opened and laid upon the floor a green sleeping bag whose tan flannel lining was decorated with hunting scenes, as if we were children playing a camping game. The room was lit by a lantern and smelled of the beef jerky he was eating. He undressed me slowly, as had become his habit, beginning with my shoes and stockings then turning to my blouse and bra, saving, as always, the skirt and underwear for last. Then he kissed me until, unaware of my own cries, I felt his hand gently cover my mouth. We made love quickly. I was tired and aware of the possible peril of falling asleep.

"Do you prefer making love at night?" I asked.

He shrugged and then ever so slightly nodded. "It's better," he mumbled, shaking the hair out of his eyes, "it feels more like you're mine."

"I am," I said, at once touched and ashamed that I had ever induced him to feel otherwise.

Then, in a voice in which I heard the desire to know competing with fear of the very same, he asked, "Do you do this with your husband?"

"No," I said, relieved to be telling the truth but afraid he would not believe me.

"Why not?" he asked.

"I can't explain it. We're like two puzzle pieces that don't fit together anymore."

"But you used to?"

"Yes, we did."

"The puzzle changed?"

"Yes, I suppose we're like pieces of some ever-changing puzzle. Like all the outdated globes in the world. One can feel nostalgia, even affection, for an old globe but there's no disputing the fact that it's no longer accurate. It doesn't tell the truth, it doesn't match up with reality."

"So what do you do with two puzzle pieces that don't fit together?"

"What does one with an old globe?"

"Wait for the world to change?"

"One can wait quite a long time for the world to change or one can..."

"Go out and buy a new globe?"

"You sound as if you're sympathizing with him."

"Maybe I am."

"I'm sorry everything is so imperfect, so morally corrupt. I truly am. You deserve better."

"It's not your fault."

"Isn't it?"

"Not really."

"The part about the world changing isn't my fault but the part about buying the new globe is."

"Does it show the way things really are?"

"I don't know."

It was high time I changed the topic. I was fairly certain that if I did he would not resist. One ought to find something convenient about passivity, oughtn't one?

"What will you say to your mother when you arrive home?" I imagined them huddled at a table, murmuring over tea.

"Nothing. She'll be asleep." He made it easy for me, it was part of his endless appeal.

"What if she wakes?"

"She won't. She never wakes up. She has pills to help her

sleep and they work pretty well." The inside of my throat hurt at the thought of Violet nightly ingesting a pill.

"I better be getting back. But you know I hate to, right?"

He nodded and stayed lying on the sleeping bag while I dressed. "Goodnight," he said, stretching kittenlike before me.

"You've never said that to me before."

"I know."

"It's very appealing."

"Yeah." He rubbed his eyes.

"Don't fall asleep there, drowsy drawers."

"I won't. I'll get up soon. I'm hungry anyway." For him, the night was just beginning. There were meals yet to be prepared and eaten, roads to be driven upon, dreams still yet to be dreamed.

Yet even I, sleepy and perimenopausal, was experiencing the woods as if for the first time. The moon and the night made it new. In the distance I saw the slight silhouette of the property owner. She was walking very slowly, either mildly crippled or severely arthritic, up the hill to the pond where Maria and I had once seen a turtle. There was a large dog at her side. I noted with some concern the absence of her second dog. Perhaps the woman preferred the anonymity of an evening walk. Or perhaps being a dog owner required one to take evening walks. I knew very little about evening walks and less still about dogs. The dog barked. Both the woman and I paused. Then she continued on in her slow way up the hill and I, still flushed with pleasure and nervously panting, sprang into action, giddy with the speed and strength of my legs as they carried me.

* * *

"What's the most beautiful thing you've ever seen?" I asked. It was one of my earliest questions, something from the fall archives. Administering questions in a jumble on the floor felt a bit haphazard if not downright distressing. It was yet another reminder of the proximity of summer, that the only time left for the posing of questions might possibly be now.

"I don't know." He was lying, as he often did in the afterglow, with his eyes closed, a raspberry Tootsie Pop plugging his mouth.

"It's a difficult question isn't it? I'll revise it for you: What's *one of* the most beautiful things you've ever seen?"

He was silent for a few moments, perhaps to steal a few more sucks of that cheap candy which he obediently removed, if only briefly, to submit, "Okay, a moth."

"Where did you see it?" I kept on. At this, he removed the pop from his mouth and placed it in the wrapper. I had won. His lips wore a delicious garnet stain. I kissed him and tasted the candy's chocolate center.

"At school. Actually it was a photograph of a moth." His eyes returned to their closed position. I prefer to think he closed them for my benefit, so that I would feel free to gaze upon him.

"Where?" I asked, intent on prolonging my freedom. He bore an absurdly beautiful mark on his right cheek that looked as if it had been made by the blunt point of a sepia Derwent.

"In a science book."

"How did it look?" Like a hypnotist I pressed him.

"Red, blue, green, yellow, all different colors." His lashes were longer than Maria's, which regularly drew public comment.

"A rainbow moth?"

"Yeah." His eyes opened.

I didn't know whether to be touched by his book-related answer or disturbed by the fact that what he had found most beautiful was an image of the beautiful thing and not the thing itself. Somehow it seemed a youthful answer, a perception of beauty filtered by media.

"What about you?" he asked. He propped himself up on one Eton blue elbow. Now he would look at me and I would refrain from looking. I would allow myself instead to become obscured by the clouds of our conversation. I would go under.

"Me? Oh God, I don't know. I'd have to think about it." Never in the ecstasy of composing questions had I paused to imagine the young man turning my own questions upon me. "I honestly haven't thought about it. Embarrassing, isn't it, that I've wondered endlessly about your most beautiful thing but never once about my own."

"What's the first thing that comes into your mind?"

"The first? Well, truly the first thing that comes to mind isn't a visual—although I did see it—but rather a series of acts I watched being performed in an airport. Isn't it odd that both of our beautiful things were things we saw indoors? One so often thinks of awe-inspiring beauty as being out in the natural world."

"You're really distracted by ideas," he said.

"Am I? I suppose ideas are beautiful to me, better company than most humans."

"What did you see in the airport?" Firmly, the young man led me back.

"Oh yes. I was at Heathrow, waiting to get on a flight to Japan, and I saw a mother—she was Japanese—with three small children, making use of the layover to prepare them for the flight. First she peeled three apples in quick succession using her teeth and then handed one to each child. After they had eaten their apples, the children lined up before her and she administered what must have been herbal essences or vitamin drops to each one's open mouth, like a mother bird tending to her babies."

"What was beautiful about it?"

"Everything! The mother's absolute efficiency, her ability to create order in a chaotic environment and yet also the reverse.

In that cold and industrial setting, she and her children were like creatures obeying their natural instincts against all odds."

"Would it have been as beautiful to you if she hadn't been Japanese?"

"I don't know. Why would you ask me that?"

"Well, you're Japanese but you don't have a Japanese mother. So maybe that made her more beautiful to you. Finding a lost thing can be beautiful."

"True, but why would it be a lost thing? You don't have a German mother but I doubt you experience that as a loss."

"That's different."

"Is it?" I asked.

"I saw a mother bird feed her young once. That was pretty beautiful," he looked up, as if he could see the birds in the rafters above us.

"Were they in a nest?"

"Yeah. When I was a kid I had a tree house and their nest was up in the same tree." I ventured to look at him again. I kept prompting him, trying to prolong the trance.

"One of the apple trees?"

"Yeah." His Maria-like lashes blinked languorously as he continued his upward gaze.

"And what about now?" It had been a poor suggestion, an error on the part of the hypnotist. My eyes lingered upon his cheek's pencil mark.

"I still go up there sometimes." A look half sheepish, half fleeced crossed his face. He faltered.

"What about it was beautiful to you?" I tried once more to coax his gaze toward that twiggy, feathered place in the rafters, but it was no good. He turned to look at me again thirstily, some part of him knowing his own power was there like a well he could drink from.

"It was like the mom and kids in the airport. They were in their own world within the world. They had everything they needed. They were doing what they were meant to do and I got to see it. No one else saw it but me."

We were quiet for a spell. "What about you?" he asked. "What's the second thing that comes into your head?"

"I'd have to say the cherry blossoms in Japan. When I was at my aunt's house I lay on the lawn under an enormous *kanzan* tree during the *yae-zakura* season. Everywhere I looked there were pink blossoms and each of them with ten petals! The sky was blue as the sea in summer behind them." I sighed like an *obaasan* remembering.

"Was anyone with you?"

"No, it was after the blossom-viewing picnic, after everyone had gone home."

"That does sound beautiful. You lying there alone under the cherry tree like that. How old were you?"

"Sixteen. Let's not talk about it anymore, okay?"

"Why not? I thought you liked talking about beauty."

"I do. It's an important idea."

"You like talking about it as an idea but not as it relates to you personally?"

"No, that's not true. I don't like the topic of youth."

"Why not?"

"You're full of childish questions today, aren't you?"

"What's childish about them?"

"There you go again! Everyone knows curiosity is the mark of a child!" I was full of contradictions. The thought of losing him always had that effect on me.

"Not necessarily."

"I don't understand you."

"What's there to understand? I'm only seventeen."

"What is it you want from me?"

"I don't want anything."

It frightened me to think this might be true, that one's student in pleasure had grown tired of the lesson, would soon shove his books into his backpack and set off for the woods in search of something newer or more wild.

That night when I climbed in through the bedroom window, the rope within it snapped. The frame slammed shut. I watched stricken as Maria stirred but did not wake and then I heard the dreaded sound of Var opening the door to his room. I tore off my jumper and stuffed it into the cloth bag, I kicked off my shoes. Desperately I felt around for the book light and clicked it on just as Var was rapping softly on the door. "May?" I grabbed *Lolita* and pretended to be reading. He opened the door. "Did you hear that loud noise?"

"Oh, sorry, that was me. I was trying to get a bit of fresh air and the bloody rope snapped in two."

"That's annoying," he hissed and then sat down next to me. My hair was still cold from walking in the night air, though I suppose one can acquire a similar chill by leaning out a window. I prayed I was not giving off an odor. One would have a more difficult time explaining that.

He did not move closer, but he put the question to me nevertheless, held it out to me like a gift I didn't want, a perfectly good meal that I was too full to eat or a warm coat in a color I had tired of. But I took it anyway and in so doing gave myself to him, beaten as I was into submission by the fear that he would otherwise suspect me of infidelity and prohibit me from seeing the young man in future. The window (that other) opened easily. It was obscene. I felt sickened by my own behavior and yet I would do anything—even sleep with the husband on whom I was cheating—in order to protect my secret.

Up to now I had been faithful to the young man. Now I had cheated on him too. Through this disturbing new lens, I saw that by staying with Var I was engaging in a far worse deception—for it was one motivated not by love but by fear. In contrast, I began to view my affair with the young man as honest, if not with respect to Var, then with respect to my own desires.

* * *

Despite my perennial dread of the tourist season, which begins not in early summer but in late spring, its arrival surprised me. Why was I surprised when, instead of being first or second in a line of one or two, I found myself standing in an obnoxiously long line at the general store, if I had thought of nothing but such perils all winter? How could it be that in my endless brooding frenzy about time I had mysteriously lost track of time entirely?

My bewilderment—like the rest of it—was temporary. As I stood holding my rolls of lavatory paper and lightbulbs among the others with their crisps and ice lollies, kites and sun lotions, time once more overtook me. While awaiting my turn, I watched the second hand make its minute movements across the face of the shop's trick clock whose numbers were scrambled and whose hands were perpetually askew and knew, regardless of what time it was, that with each dizzying tick another second was passing in which I was apart from him, in which my physical body continued ever so slightly its decline. Meanwhile, like a tree he was growing taller and stronger, indeed, somewhere not far from me, he was coming to leaf.

Equally bewildering was what I can only call the mystery of fate. Every week for several years I had cycled to the grocery store on the path that ran the length of the town. It began in front of the library and continued for two miles then ended abruptly in dense foliage and grass (in the way of a wrong turn taken within a maze) just a few steps in advance of Plum Island Provisions. The shop was not visible from the path; one could easily miss it as one followed the signs instructing bicyclists to cross the road to where the path resumed, on what must have felt to most Americans like the deviant side of the road and where I naturally felt quite at ease. What did it mean, this weekly detour that I had followed and so comfortably?

Hundreds of times I had raced towards him only to veer off course at precisely the same spot each time. I hadn't overlooked the shop completely—I had eyed it many times with a panting housewife's curiosity as I pedaled past (the wild roses and the vegetable garden on its left, the antique bicycles propped against a crooked fence on its right, the prismatic bottle tree and the empty Scharffen Berger crates set in the shade of the ample porch)—but I never paused to go in. I would have had to cross the road a second time to reach it and then a third time to return to the path.

Yet despite what seemed to be our fate never to cross paths, we met. Countless times I went over our first meeting in search of a meaningful explanation. I gave myself heart palpitations reviewing the instant that I turned from the window, from the exhilarating end of the leaf-watching season and the spectacle of the ravenous birds, to see him standing at the counter. He, without a need for books (or a library card for that matter), had come to the library and I, so captivated by the world outside the window, had turned away from it. How easy it would have been for another librarian to rush to his aid behind my back or for him to give up waiting and exit the building! But the young man had waited and I had turned. He had forgotten the first card and I was all too happy to furnish a second. Indeed the existence of the two cards seemed yet another inexplicable insinuation of fate's involvement, as if we had each been assigned a first fate that we had then refused or replaced with a second. Or had we been reassigned? Is that not the meaning of fate, that which exists before us, beyond us, and yet is everywhere with us, assigning and reassigning us at every turn?

* * *

Absurdly undaunted by my late night encounter with Var

(in fact more determined than ever to evade detection), the following Friday I managed to safely exit the apartment and run my obstacle course unthwarted.

"I like it when you sweat," the young man confessed. He dabbed a droplet from my temple with his thumb.

"You're embarrassing me," I said. "You're so clean and dry."

"Come here." He drew me toward the hunters and my heart began beating more rapidly. I felt the fabric of us being slightly cut and then his fingers—could it be they were trembling a little less now?—slowly unzipped my skirt, the sound of its metallic teeth, another opening, another snip.

Afterward, we lay on a faded infinity quilt he had smuggled from Violet's closet. I was still wearing my shoes. They were ballet flats made of washed red leather, each one had a red leather rose at the toe. I looked up at the loft and pondered aloud various points and methods of access. He listened politely as was his habit but the moment I finished my speech he began one of his own.

"I'm going to California," he said. I couldn't tell from the way he said it whether there was fear or regret or happiness in his voice. I turned quickly to face him, as much in an attempt to read his expression as to see him again before he vanished. He did not turn to meet my anguished eye but kept his eyes trained on the loft, which now seemed to me an emblem of impossibility.

I answered lightly, to hide my devastation, that I had visited California as a child and that it had been very beautiful, and he, not sensing the enormous effort it had taken me to muster such a nonchalant sentence could not hide his curiosity and asked, "What was it like?" The young man failed to realize the extent of his power over me; he somehow thought me invincible.

I ignored his question. "When are you going?" I asked. He finally turned toward me though continued to avoid my eye.

"July 1st."

"But that's my birthday!"

"It is?"

"What, do you think I would lie just to make you stay?!"

He caught my eye and smiled slightly. He winced then cleared his throat. "Sorry. I didn't know that was your birthday." I felt a pain when he said it; it was a reminder of all that was unknown—of all that would remain unknown—between us.

"Of course you didn't, how could you? I've done my very best to avoid the subject."

"It doesn't have to be July 1st."

"Lovely," I said. I was at a loss and yet I feared that if I did not recover myself quickly I would stand to lose more. "Give me the gift of leaving some other day, would you?"

"Of course."

"Don't you mean 'okay'?"

"No."

He had read an article online exposing the high levels of toxicity in the Russian River while praising the work of a particular nonprofit organization devoted to the river's restoration. Within a matter of minutes, he had clicked on the organization's link and registered to volunteer. When this fateful series of clicks had occurred I had no idea. I had no desire to know; I had lost my spirit of inquiry.

He had, with this news, at last subdued me. I said nothing for some time. I felt very cold and heavy there on the floor among the drop cloths and paint cans. My skin grew clammy, chills prickled the backs of my legs. My heart—so predictable and yet so wild—beat like a hummingbird's inside me. The rest of my stolid body belied that hidden trill.

"I'm tired," I whispered. "I can't get up." He touched my forehead. The skin of his palm felt cool and smooth. Waves of nausea washed over me.

"You're sweating," he said.

"Enjoy it while you can."

"It's just for six weeks. I'll be back on August 14th."

"Okay," I said, trying out his word.

And then, despite my catatonic state, he pulled from his back pocket an exuberant color brochure promoting the environmental program that had just stolen him from me. He held it out. I saw in his eyes the look of youthful excitement, the child wanting to please, the young man wanting to impress, and I turned my head away. "Not now, darling, please. It's still June." I heard him swallow hard and I am certain he blushed then, if not from embarrassment at my refusal then from shame at his own insensitivity. "And what about you? When's *your* birthday? When will you be legal?" I withheld my newly acquired age of consent tidbit. Let him think me a criminal, let him think I've risked everything for love.

"November 4th."

"Ah, not until the fall. Well, I'm glad I never asked, I couldn't have waited that long anyway." I turned onto my back and gazed up at the beams. "So what does Mom think of all this?" I gestured limply with one hand in the direction of the gaudy brochure.

"Mom's excited for me of course."

Of course? What had happened to *okay*? Had he bequeathed it to me, left it here already as a souvenir? Amazing what Mother Earth and her promoters could do for a young man's self-confidence and speech patterns. I suddenly despised Mother Earth and her beautiful, tainted waters. They only made me feel further estranged from the young man, hopeless in fact, being as I was so far from him on both environmental and philosophical continuums. His sense of the tragic was well-developed and yet his curiosity about the world was naively shot through with hope, as if some part of him suspected that his own tragic circumstances (to which I was not privy but could sense) were defined by his island existence and that once he was on the mainland he would be free of them. *You won't!* I wanted to protest. I too was passionate about my cause!

His love of nature and his desire to leave the natural splendor of the island existed inefficiently together, they were exasperatingly contradictory, each canceling the other out. There was no way to comprehend his impulses except as part of the larger phenomena of youth, which, from where I stood, was synonymous with inaccessibility if not menace. Like a centaur, even as his human eyes gazed at the beauty that surrounded him, his horse hooves were galloping away.

In order to fend off a fit of sadness I said brightly, "Well, anyway," went outside, and began pacing the porch. When I came back inside I found him sleeping the deep, impenetrable sleep of well-exercised children. He lay on his back, still shirtless, exuding the perfection all children do when they sleep. I lay quietly on my side facing him. His dreaming eyes were racing but harmless through the smooth shutters of their lids; his usually wary eyes occupied, blind to my gaze; his nose functioning but unable to smell the transparent scent of the tears that had begun to mark my face as soon as I'd seen he was sleeping; his mouth drooping a little in its silence, no abandonment speeches, no proclamations of love on his lips. He stirred a bit as I studied him, summoning all my innate powers of memorization, my learned cataloging skills, and then he draped his arm over his eyes with a sigh as if to undermine my project.

We slept on the floor of the gray house all night. Very early the birds woke me with their warning songs. I sat numbly for a few moments watching him though I could hardly see his face for his arm remained like a rag upon it. As I hurriedly put on my clothes and gathered my things, he slept on. I did not wish to wake him. I did not wish to see that young look of his at that hour or at any hour for that matter. Indeed I feared I might not be able to bear seeing him again for fear of meeting that look.

Quietly I slipped away, afraid he would catch me in the act. I jogged through the woods, past the waterfall, through the lush tunnel of trees. Once I had crossed the land bridge, I slowed to a slouching pace. I cursed myself for being sleep-deprived and matronly, in love with a seventeen-year-old whose allegiance was to Mother Earth, not to me. I had no desire to reach the apartment except to appear in time to prevent Maria from thinking I had abandoned her. If not for her I might not have returned. I didn't care if I was caught. I cared even less about Var now. I no longer had happiness to spare; I could no longer afford to be tender. The man with the moustache be damned! What did it matter, I could crash through a window and he would never wake, sealed as his ears were with white putty, his entire being absent, deep in its shy, sativic stupor. Damn both men for being unwakeable and passive. Damn myself for always waking early and taking action.

After I left the dirt road and began plodding along Music Street it began to rain. I felt an odd sense of relief, for now it seemed nothing more could go wrong. Drops of rain began dripping from my hair down my face. I kept expecting tears to fall as well but I was as dry-eyed as one caught in a rainstorm can be. I was without feeling. It was as if the bird of my happiness and the bird of my sadness had flown off together and I was left empty-handed.

In the end my desire for him won out. Excuses for pleasure were easy enough to find and my taste for pleasure had become stronger than my fear.

I got over this *of course*—yes, I too tried on the force of those two words, the brisk syllables like consecutive slaps, shoves that kept me awake, kept me moving, but from which I never recovered. I proceeded, I kept the sting to myself and returned to him. I was in no position to abandon him. To abandon him would have been to abandon my own pleasure. Ever the immigrant, I adjusted to the new terms in order to survive. My memories of that suspended country of snow and cardinals and woodsmoke receded; they became like forbidden photographs that I would take out on occasion in secret. The same skill with which I had kept our secret from the world I now used to keep my sadness a secret from him. My only solace was the idea that after the young man left the island, I too would leave. Not to follow him of course. I wouldn't dare overshadow him; there is nothing more futile than trying to stop youth, nothing more morally repellent than squelching potential. I didn't know where I would go or what I would do but I decided that somewhere, somehow, I would put my transgressive sadness to use.

He was a tender young man. But for all his tenderness he was a young person who moved through a world inhabited not by people like myself but by other young people, that distant and ruthless race of beings for whom change and happiness are often synonymous. Such was the fact that I brooded upon as, minute by minute, spring bloomed more completely around us.

On the nights to follow his dreadful announcement, he seemed to take great pains to muffle his exuberance, an act for which I did not know whether to feel gratitude or indignation. I could not help but wonder if he had not muffled his exuberance with regard to other matters—girls his own age, the prospect of living off-island, perhaps even his feelings for me. Both my father and mother had been expert mufflers of exuberance, as was Var; it seemed I was a magnet for such personalities.

Back in the apartment I minced about sweeping—my tattered broom an echo of the one in the gray house. I could do nothing without thinking of him, not even sort the house, which was cleaner that spring than it had ever been. I did what my mother would have done. For every word of protest I might have uttered, I made myself sweep another stroke. I was no muffler of exuberance; I was a muffler of pain.

As the date of his departure grew near I became increasingly despondent, alternating between an agitated state of hyperactivity (expressed as housecleaning) and a sluggish paralysis (expressed as heavy sleep). (Yet even when I laid myself down upon the bed, it was my body whose functioning slowed to a near stop while my brain, like some frenetic bean counter locked within a vault, spent the nights counting days, tabulating outcomes, striking bargains, haggling endlessly over each and every bean.) Var's room became unendurably hot (while the rest of the apartment was only sweltering) and so he ran a loud fan the size and shape of a fraternity boy's refrigerator around the clock. Day and night the steel box roared on. It sounded as if we were aboard one of the island ferries steaming toward the mainland. In my current state, the noise was torture. If I had never had any tolerance for the thought of leaving the young man, I had less tolerance still for the thought of him leaving me. I could not hear the sound of a boat leaving without wanting to weep.

Even as I stole like a teenage girl out my window then raced through the woods to meet him, back in the apartment the X-marked days on my endangered sea life calendar began to outnumber the clear days; indeed our time together, like the manta ray, was fast becoming extinct. My only hope—which Violet must have shared—was that he would return.

* * *

"I'd like to adopt you," I proposed.

"That would be incest."

"Must you put it so crudely?" Alas, the profanity of my solution had not escaped him. He was so clever.

"There's also the matter of Mom."

"You're right. She might not allow it." I should have shuddered at the thought of Violet signing a written agreement but I laughed. He began to laugh too.

"You'd be surprised. Mom's a pretty understanding person."

"If you were my child I'd keep you with me. I'd forbid you to leave."

"I could run away."

"Would you?"

"I'm almost eighteen. That only leaves you a few months."

"A few months longer than I have now."

"Why talk about it?" he asked. He put his lips upon mine as if to shield me from their power. I felt them move to form words. "You're upsetting yourself," he whispered.

"Don't you dare."

"Look at me," he said.

I wouldn't glance. I stayed lying on my stomach; I inhaled his brought from home pillow (likely belonging to Mom).

"I'm still here." He stroked my neck as if I were ill. "I'm not gone yet."

I turned my head. The pillow was wet with my tears. He got up and placed his hands on the backs of my thighs, one hand lightly upon each thigh. He waited for me to raise myself. I didn't move. I felt something terrible might happen if he kissed me and so I lay still. He was, as always, very patient. He rested his hands there for a long time, he kept his touch light, never varying the pressure, neither going forward nor retreating but making electricity. Like a boy alone in the wild, he built his fire soundlessly, with little movement, adding branches until his part of the woods was lit. The thought of him there alone with his patience moved me. I raised my hips slightly. I could hear him lie down behind me, I could feel the warmth of his face. His mouth was near me but not touching. His patience outdistanced my resolve. I lifted myself fully now, obscenely. He touched first with his hand, slipped it in like a man reaching into his own pocket for warmth, as if I were a coat that belonged to him so that each time he withdrew his hand I had no purpose but to wait for its return. If I could wait long enough, (and I could always wait long enough) his kisses would come next.

He loved to lie before me, beside me, behind me, and kiss. In my life before him, I had always thought men did such things in service of love or kindness. The young man taught me it can be done selfishly, in service of a man's pleasure. It was like wine to him, a forbidden drink that calmed him. Once he discovered it, he liked to have a glass every morning, sometimes more. And like an errant mother I couldn't stop myself pouring it out for him. He liked the taste, he said, and the feeling of my legs pressing his cheeks.

Waiting for him made my thoughts explicit. I became aroused without touch, by my own thoughts of his touch. I grew so euphoric waiting for him that I was startled to finally feel his lips and tongue. It was like being kissed from behind by an intruder whose face I couldn't see. I felt such fervent palpations, such fear! Then he kissed me as if working—slowly, diligently, with a grave interest, as if he enjoyed and was grateful for this profession upon which he so depended. He took and he gave. He kissed and he kissed. In the end, the act's incredible calculus of generosity and greed silenced my thoughts. I felt blessed, blankened, enraptured by my own effacement. They were sensations not even the most beneficent gods could have designed. To be deprived of them would be just punishment indeed.

* * *

I was working the front desk in dreary silence, depressed in the face of Love's impending extinction, when Nella, as if hearing my pitiful thoughts and finding them funny, began to laugh uncontrollably. I turned back with the hope of seeing some amusing spectacle that might make me laugh too but the cause for her laughter seemed to come from within her. I, for one, saw no sign of it. In her hilarity, she doubled over and then lurched back so that her chair rolled away from the desk and hit the red children's cart behind her. Underneath her blue-rimmed glasses, there were tears in her eyes. "Care to let me in on the joke?" I asked.

"I think it's time for lunch," she said, blithely wiping a tear from her face.

Why, when I had come so far and the end was in sight, did I feel the abrupt urge to confess? After she'd gone, I dwelled upon with whom, if anyone, I could entrust my secret. I decided, using the bold arbitrariness of one who is soon to lose everything, that when Nella returned from her clam chowder and Milky Way, I would tell her everything. It was a suicidal idea to be sure. Not once had Nella indicated the slightest hint of interest in my situation. She might easily have guessed my secret by now and could not have cared less. I was not ignorant of such a possibility but the chance to make real my ephemeral experience, the chance to somehow anchor that floating world to this one by uttering it, outshone all other logic.

I resolved to spend the next thirty minutes pondering how best to summarize my amorous adventures thus far—which events warranted mentioning, which might better be omitted, and which might be especially funny to recount. I prioritized and censored as I worked. Indeed even as I articulated words aloud to the patrons, I was thinking inappropriate thoughts of the young man. Words like *Hi there* and *These are due in a week* and *You're welcome, have a lovely day* issued like puffs of smoke from the stovepipe of my mouth as my brain burned through image after lurid image. As I scanned each book's bar code under the red light, what I saw was his jaw clenched in pleasure.

Eventually the lunch crowd disappeared. I checked my watch for the fourth time and looked out the window. Nella was late. This was not surprising. Lately it seemed every break she took was longer than the last. It was as if she was making up for the time she'd been cheated out of by abstaining from breaks all those years. I kept looking back at her desk between transactions only to find it empty. She'd been gone for two hours. Finally I got up and walked over to her desk and saw that the tiny yellow Post-it in the middle of her screen, which I had previously assumed was a note left for Nella, was in fact a note written by Nella herself, just two words: *I quit.*

Needless to say, I was incapable of reading this announcement in any manner but a selfish one. I could not bring myself to care that all of Nella's shifts would now need to be covered, that her many full-time responsibilities would have to be swiftly transferred to the hands of another librarian, or that the rapidly approaching summer season would make all of this more pressing and difficult to accomplish. No, what I saw in those two words was a refusal to meet my need to confess. It did not occur to me to telephone her, to reschedule my imagined outpouring. I was in need of a confession that was face-to-face and immediate. I read the two words, like the ladderless loft, as yet another emblem of impossibility, their cutting message foreshadowing to my own impending abandonment. What did I do with my need to confess? I did what I had done so expertly for years prior to the young man's arrival, what I would soon have to do quite regularly with my desire: I crushed it.

* * *

The next morning—it was just after 8:00, I couldn't take

leave of Maria any earlier—I ran like a dog to P.I.P., my ears listening to footfalls miles away, my nose sniffing for a familiar scent. Violet's favorite trail was an ancient way, one of the many that had existed, unbeknownst to me, for hundreds of years. When I set off, my animal self sought companionship, I wanted only to confess. I wanted to sit on my haunches before her and howl. But as I reached the crest of the first rise and began to tumble toward the next, I saw her walking ahead of me, light-footed, alone, wearing a pair of sand-colored shorts, a white T-shirt, a braid in her hair. At the sight of her delicate, Hatfieldian shape I bounded forward with concern. I wanted to be her friend, doglike, loyal in the face of any threat. Who better than Violet to remind me that there were others in the world whose troubles were worse than my own? While we would both soon be without the young man, every night of our separation I would sleep with Maria in my arms.

When I reached her she stopped to kiss my cheek and then we resumed walking together. We said very little. As we paused at a marker under a canopy of trees, the trail empty, the woods alive, perfumed, she said, "My son's leaving in two weeks."

My first thought was sadness, Violet's face streaked with tears, but when I stole a glance I saw she was smiling, letting the gap show. It was a charming gap, like an actress's scar. Each time she let me see it I loved her more. "Is he?" I said, caught between wanting to be a polite listener and not wanting to lie.

"Yes. Unlike his mother he prefers his adventures off the page. I think it's healthy. I think it's a good thing."

"Yes. That makes sense."

"I always thought it would break my heart when he left the island. But I'm ready."

How on earth had she prepared herself? I could hardly bear the thought of *her* child leaving the island much less my own. "You're very brave," I said.

"No. It doesn't take much to stay home and do what I always do."

"Won't you miss him?" I dared.

"I'll miss him. But I'll also be free. We both will."

"Yes, of course."

"And it's only for a few weeks. He'll be back mid-August. We'll still have some summer left to spend together."

I said nothing. What was I to say? How was I to act? I already knew all of this.

"I suppose you'll be quite busy as well. Summer will be in full swing."

"Yes," she gave me another gap smile and sat down on a stump. I sat down too. We were both a little out of breath.

The thought of his six-week adventure was unendurable; it was a calamity. I wished I felt even a portion of Violet's excitement on his behalf but I had yet to be emancipated from my orgy of wanting and regret.

"If I were a character in a book, would you like her?" I asked.

"It's a funny thing to ask."

"It is and it isn't." Had I been asking as the woman she knew firsthand, it would have been an odd question but in truth I was asking as myself, the one who had committed ordinary yet unspeakable crimes and repeatedly. If the real me, the one who just yesterday had crouched like a dog before her son and then growled with pleasure as he entered, were a character in a book, would she like her? This was the impossible question I was trying to ask.

"I would definitely keep reading," she said.

"Would you?"

"Yep."

"But why?"

"Oh, lots of reasons." I wondered for the first time if our friendship had been a way of safeguarding her son, knowing the enemy, so to speak, a way to know intimately the company he kept, a mother's education.

"Any you care to share?"

She paused as if considering and then said, "I would keep reading to find out what happens to you in the end."

"Oh dear. It's a bit frightening when you put it like that."

"It is, isn't it?" she said and laughed a rowdy little laugh I'd never heard before.

* * *

My penultimate meeting with the young man was dominated by talk of his imminent journey, one of the few topics of conversation that, rather handily, had a murderous effect on my desire. He lost hold of his ability to muffle exuberance; he became unusually chatty and I, painfully disinterested. At the sound of his enthusiastic sentences, at the thought of the impact their meaning would have upon my daily existence, I nearly brought my hands to my ears. I was incapable of listening. I fell asleep during his monologue though he seemed not to notice. When I woke a few minutes later he was recounting his mother's good deeds. I waited impassively for him to finish.

In her preparations for the departure of her son, Violet had surpassed herself. Had I been in her position I would have done the very same. (And yet I *was* in a very similar position insofar as I too loved him and would soon be without him and I had done nothing to prepare either of us. Not a whit. I had not even managed to check out a book in his honor, lacking as I did the generosity and acceptance to grant him an extended due date. Devastation was the fine one would have to pay, one had dimly known all along but denied it.)

For every leg of his journey, down to the briefest of airplane layovers and the most fleeting of afternoons spent in the company of relatives, she provided him with the most splendid supplies a traveler could hope for. There were abundantly-sized clothes for all weather and occasions (one could well imagine her following him in her mind from one climate zone to the next, growing as he went), nonperishable provisions including several bars of the now familiar chocolate wrapped in painted landscapes, a tin of her own toasted granola, an assortment of dehydrated fruits and spiced nuts, a smartphone that also functioned as a camera, a compass and a light canteen (visions of him getting lost no doubt accosting her), three maps (one of the Boston subway system, one of the United States, and one of the large state of California), and, as if to confirm that there was nothing I could possibly offer the young man that he did not already possess, the book *Siddhartha*. I was not the only reader in his life after all, not the only middle-aged woman with access to a library. Though I would never have chosen *Siddhartha* (I did not care for the West's version of Buddhism nor did I care for the religious writing of Hermann Hesse), I confess it may have been an apt choice for the young man, being as he was on the brink of so many transformations and on his way to rescuing a river.

Loquacity did not suit him. I didn't want to hear another word. When at last he paused to take a breath, I cut across him, "You know, you've ruined me. And I don't mean that from a moral standpoint." I was feeling sorry for myself. What else could I possibly do?

"What standpoint do you mean it from?"

"What do you think?"

"I have no idea."

"None whatsoever?"

"Well, I could list possibilities. Or you could just tell me what you meant, since you're the one who used those words to begin with."

"From the standpoint of pleasure, obviously."

"Why do you sound so annoyed?"

"Do I?"

"Yeah."

"I suppose I'm annoyed because I'm ruined. One rather hopes to avoid being ruined but then again I'm so old it doesn't matter. But if I were younger it would be easier to bear."

"Easier how?"

"I would have a better chance of replacing you."

"And that would have been easier?"

"I think I'd rather you judge me than quiz me."

"But how would being younger have bettered your chances? I'm interested in your honest answer, not in changing your mind about anything."

"You actually want me to spell it out?"

"Yes."

"I haven't been crude enough?"

"No. I don't pick up on things quickly. If I were older, I might have understood you. Maybe you're forgetting. I'm only seventeen." He was toying with, if not patronizing, me. Glimmers of manhood, perverse glimmers of a future together.

"If only my memory was as much of a failure as the rest of me. Of course I haven't forgotten you're seventeen. My father was seventeen when he left Japan. I was seventeen when I left England. And you will be seventeen when you leave this island."

"You haven't answered my question."

"If you have to ask, I shouldn't bother. You shall find out when you're forty-one. I won't spoil it for you." I went on. I couldn't stop myself saying crude things. Being faced with the prospect of relinquishing him to a river brought out the Hyde in me. "You know I didn't come here to mix with your sort. If anything I came here to escape such excitements."

What had in it the seed of a compliment came off sounding like a snub. He drew back slightly as if I had just hit him. "What I meant to say," I persisted, determined to salvage the moment and bolster his confidence, "is that this is a highly unusual circumstance. I've lived a very sheltered life, sheltered from good as much as from bad. I've minded my own business. I never sought thrills. I've been content to avoid the company of youth and beauty. Before you, I had no desire."

"With all due respect, May, I find it hard to believe," he finished in iambic pentameter, "that a woman with your brain and your appetite came halfway across the world in search of nothing."

He was well-mannered yet restless; his eyes studied me as though I were a page in a book. I had the sense of being one among many, of being read intensely but fleetingly by a reader who would soon turn the page.

* * *

Our last evening together he wore sunglasses and a red T-shirt, both of which I asked him to remove. I had never seen him wear red and silently disapproved. I observed changes in his body since the previous Friday (broader in the shoulders, thicker in the flanks, more pronounced cheekbones, an olive cast to his skin) the way I had upon seeing him at the library after his long absence. Sometimes a similar phenomena occurred literally overnight with Maria; swift change is one of the many confounding symptoms of childhood.

It was really quite a pleasant evening considering. I arrived determined to make the best of it. He undressed me slowly beginning with my shoes, as had once been his habit. We made love several times in silence on the floor, revisiting various Fridays in our private history. He seemed to be commemorating the other times, remembering them as I was. When he wiped the sweat on my temples away with his thumbs, it felt as if he were pressing the memories in place. I was touched by his impulse to revisit the past when the future was so close at hand, no doubt glittering and beckoning. Every doubt I had ever had, of his sincerity, of his capacity to match my depth of feeling, was erased, if only for the evening.

After about an hour he produced a red and blue striped climbing rope that he had recently purchased for the purpose of learning to rock climb in California (Was there no end to the bloody adventures?!) and which I mistakenly assumed he had brought for adventurously adult purposes. Instead he showed me several rather clever knots with clever names then tossed one end of the rope up into the loft. I watched while miraculously the loop he had just tied landed precisely on the steel wall hook upon which we had so often hung our clothes. When he tugged swiftly on the rope, the loop closed like a little noose around the hook's neck. He was very adept at handling it. It gave me an uncanny feeling. I was at once aroused by his agility and cheered by the thought of him gaining a new skill. Unbidden, the words *snow, day, Pocahontas, Swiss, family*, and *Robinson* returned to me. How it pained me to hear my inner voice pronounce them in his presence, each one an emblem of his future life.

"But how will I ever climb that?" I asked, understanding at last his intended purpose.

With the rope in his hands, he stepped backward away from the loft and then in one motion swung and began to climb. When he had reached the halfway mark he paused. "Push me." Echoes of Maria at the playground. I touched his back with both hands and then pushed. He swung. "Harder," he said. I obeyed and then watched as he swung near and far, down and up, and then I understood the physics of his plan. The higher he swung, the closer he came to the loft. After a few swings he let go and landed.

"You've done a magnificent job but you can't possibly expect me to follow you. I know it's not exactly Mount Everest but I'm not a rock climber, for God's sake, I'm a librarian. I can't possibly do that."

He threw down the rope. "Take it," he said. "You don't have to do anything. I'll bring you up."

"You sound like my father," I said, wondering how I could withstand the pleasure of this contradiction.

There was a glint of something—happiness? pleasure? arousal?—in his eyes and then it faded. He said it again more gently, "Take it."

"Okay." I took the rope in my hands and thanked God I was not yet arthritic. My mother had been and her mother before her; I was part of a long arthritic line.

"Hold on," he said.

"Okay," I said yet again. "But I don't think I can do this. It's not exactly doing nothing you know."

"Make a foot loop," he said. "Tie a knot and make a loop to put your foot in. That'll make it easier."

"What kind of knot?" I asked, overwhelmed by my recent introduction to several.

"It doesn't matter," he said.

"Really?"

"Yeah. It only has to hold for a minute or so,"

"And then it will unravel?"

"No. Just tie one. Tie an easy one and step in."

He was frightfully assertive and I, for my part, unnervingly compliant. I tied a saucer-size noose for my foot and stepped in. I looked up at him the way children glance at their parents before undertaking some new challenge, and, without missing a beat, he winked at me fatherlike. I was disarmed by this Swiss Family Robinson moment. He, Mr. Robinson (if not Rousseau himself), and I, Jenny the English orphan.

"Are you ready?" he asked.

"Of course," I lied, the words becoming easier to use the more I used them.

He began deftly to hoist me up. My fear of the rope unraveling or slipping through the young man's hands vanished in the face of his swift show of athleticism and strength. Never before had I been besieged by such masculine wiles! My desire to arrive at my destination receded and was replaced by a desire to remain there suspended, looking at him, being held by him as he brought me closer. If I could have chosen to make those moments my eternity I would have. To be forever moving closer to him, floating without effort, without fear.

"Wasn't that easy?" he asked and pulled me up over the edge of the loft. As he let go of the rope, I crumpled like a sheepdog at his feet. Masterfully, he reeled the rope in and wound it into a figure eight.

The mattress was there where we had left it, the workers had done nothing but destroy our means to ascend. I wondered uselessly whether, if we could have continued to visit the gray house, we might have eventually found the ladder restored, the loft beautifully refurbished. Just as likely we would have found someone in it. Still I was happy to see the slim mattress. I was certain it was thinner than when we first began, which made me feel at once guilty and truly pleased. For the first time, he led me to it. I took this as a sign that he was ready to leave me, that it would not have done for me to keep him here at the gray house on future Fridays.

We lay there quietly marveling over the dark chocolate Violet had recently imported from South America and that he had pulled for the last time like a Boy Scout from his blue backpack. It was infused with orange—a concept I'd always put down—but it was weirdly good, heavenly, like eating sunshine and chocolate at once while surrounded by the fragrance of Valencia oranges. It melted in our hands as we ate it, it made our mouths delicious. I couldn't get enough of those Valencian kisses. I dabbed my fingers against his face so that it was streaked with chocolate but it did nothing to diminish his late paternal aspect. Finally I succumbed to telling him my wish to pretend—just for this first and final time—that he was mine.

Not only did he indulge me, he confessed to being aroused by the idea and so together we pretended possession. We discussed our upcoming travel plans, where we would stay and with whom, which sites we intended to see when we arrived.

And then, when I felt I could bear the game no longer, when instead of cheering me the pretending made me sad, I asked, "How will we ever get down from here?"

"Have you ever rappelled before?" he asked in that shamelessly cheerful tone reserved for fathers teaching their children new things, things typically more exciting to the fathers than to the children. I had no idea what he was talking about. "You'll have to practice," he said, handing me the rope. "You'll be doing this a lot in California. You may as well start now."

Summer

On the morning of his departure I lay with Maria in my arms, waiting for her to wake. I thought of him at some near yet unknown location, inside his grandfather's house, I thought of Violet, perhaps in bed as well, distraught as I was. Then again, perhaps she had been up for hours, wearing some approximation of the green apron with yellow ties that I had imagined for her in the beginning, stepping softly in slippers from counter to counter and drawer to drawer, preparing, with her usual care, the last of his provisions.

When Maria woke she asked, "What does pathetic mean?" And I thought of the way children taunt one another: "In the dictionary the word pathetic has your picture next to it!" I could see the photographic entry clearly in my mind—I'm wearing Aunt Tomoko's flannelette nightgown and a pair of square, unfashionable glasses—as I answered her, "A pitiful person, a person one feels sorry for. Someone or something woefully inadequate." One of my many faults as a parent was delivering encyclopedic answers to simple questions. *Someone like me*, I wanted to add but restrained myself. Why point out in advance that which she would someday figure out herself?

She had gone to the window and was looking out. "We're going to the boat," I said cheerfully.

"Why?" she whirled around. "Where are we going?"

"Nowhere, we're just going to take a look."

She returned her gaze to the window and slumped forward.

"That sounds boring." Perhaps, but boredom beat the void of not seeing him.

"We'll go to the beach and you can build a sand castle, all right? Quick like a bunny! We don't want to miss the bus."

Yet as soon as we'd taken our seats, I wondered if I had made a mistake. I did not have to reread *The Lover* to know that the scene of the ferry's departure was bound to be very Duras, pathetically Duras in fact, with a few ridiculous revisions. Exchange the randy, prepubescent nymphet for a perimenopausal librarian; replace the black limousine with a public bus; insert a restless five-year-old; replace the South China Sea with the Atlantic; remove the land that attaches the peninsula; make it an island.

We arrived early in part due to my longstanding compulsion, in part due to the bus, whose service, even at the height of the summer season, was not frequent. Maria asked intuitively for an ice cream and I, fragile, without resolve, complied. We spent about ten of the twenty minutes remaining strolling the shore. I avoided looking at the water, yes, I turned from that blue emblem of separation and concentrated instead on what lay in the sand at my feet: little orange shells, smooth white stones, indigo mussel shells, bits of abalone, seaweed labyrinths, the usual seaside rubble. I was attentive to my watch and undecided as to whether or not I should make my presence known, assuming of course that I could find him. I had never had to pick him out of a crowd.

Nine minutes before his departure time I heard the boat arrive. I could not help but turn.

"Let's make a sand castle!" Maria cheered.

"Sure," I said, trying to sound unhurried. It seemed perfectly feasible that we could spend the next five minutes building the castle as I contemplated my dilemma. I sat facing the ferry and began digging with my hands. While Maria made a moat, I erected a tower, monitoring the ferry's progress all the while. Cars and people disembarked for a few minutes and then the flow reversed. My heart tightened; if I was to make my presence known I would need to do it soon, if not immediately. I scanned the perimeter of the terminal, the walkways and parking lots. I watched the ramp for a dark-haired figure wearing a blue backpack, though Violet may very well have bought him a larger pack in a different color. There were very few solitary figures. I had the passing thought that I had made an error in timing but that was impossible—I had followed the calendar far too closely for such a confusion to arise. It was the last day of June, the day of the Mediterranean monk seal, there were fewer than six hundred of them left in the world. I picked up a piece of seaweed and pressed it into the top of my tower. "Voilà!" I proclaimed. "We'd better run along now."

And only then it occurred to me—I don't know how I had overlooked it—that in all likelihood Violet would be with him (my inability to picture them together had become a troubling coping mechanism). Squinting at the sun, I looked again, this time for the two of them. "I'm burning up, love!" I complained, wiping my brow for emphasis. "Let's go see the boat."

"But I'm not done with my castle!" Maria protested. "I want to finish my castle!"

I got up and began to walk toward the dock then glanced back at Maria. She was digging her hands into the sand. "Come on, love."

"I'm busy," she said firmly, shrewdly borrowing the words I so often used with her when she interrupted my reading. I kept walking, gambling upon the fact that once I established enough distance between us she would panic and follow. I shouted over my shoulder as I walked, "You can't stay by yourself, love. It's not safe!" I quickened my pace, determined not to look back, determined to spot him. Perhaps she saw me accelerate or heard the white thread of surrender in the red flag of my voice as I shouted, for just as I saw Violet's head of curls, and next to it, waves of the same color, Maria screamed bloody murder.

"Maaaaamaaaaa!" I made the mistake of turning to look at her. She didn't move, only kept screaming, increasing her volume all the while.

Mother and Son were standing awkwardly across from one another, talking quietly, shuffling, deferring the moment they would embrace and then have to part. It was their moment; I didn't dare intrude. Had she been a stranger I still wouldn't have dared. Across the parking lot, across the shore, the intimacy between them was palpable. Meanwhile, Maria's screams were drawing attention, I strode towards her; she had called my bluff. I prayed he would not embark while my back was turned.

"Ave Maria!" I sighed and then sat on the sand next to her. She was crying but her hands continued their work, vexed in the way of the young to build, to learn, to go forth. I wrapped her in my arms. At last her crying ceased. She wriggled away and began a new tower. When I looked up, they were gone. I may have seen him disappear into the boat's side entrance but I wasn't certain and she, emancipated, against sentiment, had likely driven away.

A few moments later I saw a dark-haired figure leaning Duras-like against the rails of the top deck. He would have had to sprint up the stairs to reach it so quickly. I was too faraway to be sure it was him. Still I kept my eyes fixed on the figure. Though he seemed to be gazing elsewhere, I held up my stricken hand in the event that it was him and that he too was watching. If I had been the sort of woman who carries a mobile phone, we might have confirmed our proximity to one another but alas, I was of another century.

Mercifully, the boat did not give three desolate Durasian blasts but one proud bellow. I survived it. There were no tugboats of course, it was a new ferry complete with modern conveniences and the best of engines. Its withdrawal from the dock looked effortless, smooth as that of a toy's pulling away from the edge of a bathtub. I watched the dark-haired figure until I couldn't see it anymore and then I watched the moon-ish crescent of the boat move across the blue sky of the water until the crescent became a sliver and then the blue was all.

"There!" Maria clawed roughly at my silk blouse and beamed. I turned very slowly toward her to observe her handiwork, trying as best I could, for the duration of that inevitable gesture, to restore myself. She had lined the moat with tiny orange shells and placed a white pebble at the top of each tower. In my highly susceptible state, I was nearly moved to tears by the care with which she had executed her project.

"Bravo, darling! You've done a lovely job of building your castle," I said, trembling from the effort it took to dismiss all thoughts of him in favor of Maria.

"I know!" she shrieked. And then, with chubby energetic fists, she smashed the towers down. I looked at her lips pursed with triumph, at her exultant, imperious eyes, and felt acutely that our days of symbiosis, of shared happiness over milk well drunk and a nap well slept, were gone.

With that, I had had enough. I dragged her, kicking and slapping in a fit of rage, to the bus stop. She had wanted to build a replacement castle (if not thousands of replacement castles) but I could no longer withstand the beach charade. The perplexing truth was, despite my tendency to inhabit islands, I loathed beaches. The continuous motion of the sea nauseated me and I had an aversion to the many grains of sand that always found their way into our food, our bed, my books. I preferred the shelter of the woods, now more than ever.

* * *

The next day, quite miserably, was my birthday. There was nothing to celebrate. Of course I had brought such desolation upon myself by idiotically requesting from the young man the "gift of some other day" which, I realize now, did nothing but prevent me from seeing him on my actual birthday. Seeing him, even from a distance, would have been a gift, albeit a tortuous one. It was another unfathomable miscalculation on my part.

Maria woke early and immediately began kicking me. "I want you on your back! Put your glasses on!!!" I had grown accustomed to such commands and was at a loss as to how to curb her tyrannical impulses. My primary concern was keeping her quiet so that Var would not wake. Hauntingly, overnight, I had been rematronized. How quickly the terms came back to me. When one marries one arrives with another on an island whose size, shape, flora, fauna, climate etc., one's marriage defines. One may abandon the island, though in many cases this is quite difficult. Often there is no boat, nor materials with which to fashion one. Often there is a boat but no paddles, or paddles but no boat. More often still, both boat and paddles await at the shore but one has no life jacket, swimming ability, or provisions. My only respite was to be the hours during which my husband slept.

When at last Var woke, he went to the restroom directly and I heard his torrential stream of urine spilling into the bowl. He came out, put his well-washed hands (he always washed well, one could always smell the soap) on my cheeks and kissed me. "Happy Birthday!" he said and smiled. I'm fairly certain he hadn't smiled at me since my last birthday. Birthdays brought out some tender strain in him. This too I had forgotten. I was an amnesiac with no interest in being cured whose memory was all too quickly returning. Before Maria was born Var had pampered me like a child on my birthday. After she took her rightful place on the little girl throne, he maintained his yearly expression of tenderness though now it was more like that of a son towards his mother, the sort of tenderness one has for any old person on her birthday. Our slight difference in age seemed to grow more pronounced over time. Now when he smiled I felt him pitying me; when he held my cheeks I imagined he palpated my aging skin out of curiosity, my body always one year closer to death than his own.

That evening he made his customary announcement. "I want to take you out to dinner."

"But how will you pay for it?" I asked as gently as I could. He had not worked in months (unless one counted his Etsy site and I, perhaps heartless, perhaps unforgiving, did not), there was no possibility of there being any money in his account.

"Credit card," he said emphatically, sounding sure of himself as always, my cautious question an insult to his intelligence.

"Great!" I assented at once to increasing our credit card debt.

"Where do you want to go?" he asked and our debate, annual and tedious, ensued. Var disliked my favorite restaurant (freshly baked muffins and cakes, locally grown produce and meat just down the road) and I was averse to his (BBQ joint down-island) and so, despite it being my birthday and not Maria's, we settled on her favorite (Brazilian cafeteria near the post office) which Var and I both felt tepid toward but not opposed to.

There was no menu to inspect so we were at least spared the tedium of that ritual. *What are you getting? What should we get for her? She won't eat that. She never eats that. Yes, she does. Yes, she will. She ate it with me last time*, et cetera, et cetera. We stood speechless in a line with our sickly, yellow trays and shoveled food onto our own plates and onto the plate of our child with the public spoons. I took the rice and beans and some pickled cucumbers. There was no cooked vegetable that evening. It was not, I was reminded, my lucky day. The food was tasty enough, not fresh but tasty. I quite like Brazilian food but could do without cafeterias on my birthday.

As fate would have it, in the rear of the restaurant, there

was a little girl in a red dress having a birthday party. From where I sat I could see a bouquet of balloons and her impressive heap of presents. Our meal was accompanied by children's shrieks of laughter and adults praising the children and clapping. At the end of the meal a yellow frosted cake ablaze with hot pink candles was brought out and the whole restaurant, even Var, sang "Happy Birthday." Maria was thrilled by the coincidence and kept saying, "Mama! When are they going to bring your cake?!"

The happy scene reminded me of the young man's impending birthday. What would he look like on the 4th of November? Would he have cut his hair or would he have let it grow? Would he be tan? Would he have facial hair? If so, would he have shaved? And what of his voice? Would it have grown deeper still? And what about today? Where on this earth was my seventeen-year-old lover on the day that I turned forty-two?

I did not know how long I could endure the sensation of being once more married to Var. Certainly nothing had changed with regard to his schedule; he was in the apartment day and night as he had always been. But my eyes, which had been turned elsewhere, swiveled back to our life in the apartment and were sharply in focus. I saw bits of his moustache caught in the bathroom faucet fixtures, his bottle of dandruff shampoo in the shower stall bubbling over with blue shampoo, coffee grounds on the counter, used filters in the sink, dribbles of the black liquid in a trail from the sink to the garbage pail, a snow-like dusting of dandruff on the black hills of the sofa, wood shavings upon the floor, knives lying about like toys on the coffee table within Maria's reach. Everywhere I looked I saw Var.

And then, like the view through the enormous metal machine at the optometrist's office, what I saw changed. Not quickly of course; alas, there was no kindly man in a white coat to press the lever that would make the view immediately more pleasant for me, but soon enough, quite magically really, Var's presence receded once more to a tolerable level. Indeed I found ways to occupy myself.

* * *

Once I had faced squarely the fact that the young man had crossed the sea and would not, even if I were to plead, turn back, I resorted to following his course on the large noncirculating maps kept in thin wooden drawers in the Reading Room. For the first week of our separation I spent my lunch breaks poring over various physical, political, and road maps which I took the liberty of spreading out on one end of the long table despite the continual presence of patrons working quietly at their laptops. The maps crackled loudly when I set them down and I had to take my glasses off to read them but I didn't care. It became a compulsion, something I both looked anxiously forward to and deeply dreaded. Always, when the maps cracked like lightning I was filled with anticipation, as if, when I put my index finger on the place where he now was, rain would fall from the ceiling, thunder would sound, and, like a god, the young man would materialize. And always, after I had placed the maps in their proper drawers and shut them, I felt a sharp sense of disappointment at my own failure to conjure him. Each of these sessions was marked by a vague sense of idiocy and hopelessness for I knew how very old the maps were and had to wonder if the many streets and highways I studied so closely even existed any longer.

What saved me from complete cartographic insanity was that the young man arrived in California and called as promised. We were eating dinner when the phone rang. I leapt to answer it and brought the receiver like a lover to my bedroom. It was, not surprisingly, a bad connection; the new mobile phone had poor reception there where he was on the river. His voice came and went the way songs do on car radios when one is driving (or in my case being driven) in a remote area.

"Hey," he said. Then the connection seemed to die. After a few moments, I heard him say, "I made it." I thought I heard the sound of the river (or was it interference?) which was a comfort to me. He was there. Somewhere.

"Good. I'm glad you're safe."

"Thanks," he said and somehow this time, his politeness wounded me. He said he was standing next to the river, he said it was beautiful. His voice sounded deeper. I didn't know if this was due to the poor connection or whether during the time it had taken him to travel from coast to coast, he had matured a great deal. It was certainly possible. If a child could change overnight, I hardly dared to think what ten consecutive days and nights could accomplish. He sounded older, twenty at least. I was afraid if we spoke again he would sound older still, that by month's end he would have surpassed me, his voice in early August that of an old man. I did not receive the comfort of hearing "his voice" for his voice had changed, it was no longer the voice I had known.

"I miss you," I said, feeling trite, craving convention.

"Me too." We stayed in silence for a few minutes. I lay on the bed pressing the phone to my ear. I heard the sound of the river again, sure this time that it was not static but something beyond it. It sounded like he was walking, crunching on gravel or rocks. "I have to go," he said.

"Okay," the word was mine now. "Thank you for calling."

"Of course," he said, the words his utterly. "I'll think about you later," he mumbled.

"Me too," I said, having no idea how very true this would be, how very deep into the future this *later* would extend.

When I went to the kitchen to replace the phone Var asked, "Who was it?"

"No one," I answered and felt I was being truthful. For all

practical purposes the young man was no one now; I was certain of this. Perhaps Var sensed my certainty because he did not press further. He returned to carving his *kokeshi*, which I, being a sentimentalist at heart, could not help but wish he was making for me and which he later gave to Maria.

* * *

My first foray into a Violet-style emancipation—unexpected, overdue—began the next day. Helmetless, in a red sundress, I rode my bicycle to P.I.P. under the auspices of buying a pie. It seemed a shame to deprive myself of such a luxury in the absence of any reason not to. There was no crime in shopping there, no longer any need to hide myself from view. How deliciously ordinary I felt! Never mind that the small parking lot was swarming with expensive cars, the tiny aisles jammed with respectable people. Any one of them could see I was doing absolutely nothing wrong. I was a middle-aged woman come to buy a pie from a friend.

A bell tinkled as I opened the door, an elderly man on my left was carefully weighing white peaches, two girls laughed together at something on a can, the telephone rang and Violet—cordoned off behind the counter in the way of a celebrity—picked it up and said in a cheery public voice, "Plum Island Provisions!" The narrow produce corner was packed tightly as a pint of figs, the glass door of the cheese case fogged from being opened so often. There was no way to access the foreign section due to the line that now curved in front of it. It felt more like a Manhattan deli than a country farm stand, an island within an island.

I joined the line and waited. I watched Violet. I studied the lines in the wood floor. When I reached the display of foreign goods I bypassed the South American chocolate infused with Valencia orange in favor of a Scharffen Berger milk. This was not the time or place in which to experience uncontrollable fits of desire. As it was, I was out of my element, there was not one book on the shelves.

Slowly, I neared the front counter. Violet wore a white apron with the bodice folded down, its straps wound back and tied in front. Through the bakery glass I could see her retrieving a familiar-looking biscuit. She didn't see me.

She stood up again, her face flushing a bit, and asked, "May I help you?" and then she saw who I was and we laughed. "May! What are you doing here?" she asked, as if her establishment were one of ill repute.

"I've come to buy a pie."

"Really?! Which one?"

"Strawberry rhubarb, please, if you have that."

"Yes, one left. We saved it for you."

"Oh, good. I've been wanting to buy this pie for about ten years." I fumbled with my money, feeling not unlike her son, awkwardly and with trembling hands, paying overdue fines, as if it were she, the one invisibly connected to him, that I'd been destined for.

"Let's hope it's fresher than that."

She took my money and handed me the pie. "Come swimming with me!" she said loudly. I couldn't help but feel pleased and a little proud at the front of that long line. She had declared me to everyone: the chosen one, her swimming partner, recipient of the last strawberry rhubarb pie.

"I'd love to."

"Tomorrow morning earlyish?"

"Sure."

"Meet me here and we'll drive over."

"Okay!" I found myself in constant agreement.

***

And so it was Violet who introduced me to Ice House, the pond deep in the woods where she had taught her son how to swim. They were not the woods of my transgression but another woods very near P.I.P. We strolled the broad, shaded trail like Hatfielders on holiday, I could see a watery glint in the distance where the sun shone on the pond. There was no beach, only a wooden staircase that led out of the woods and then an iron dock that jutted out into the water. The pond was pristine, glacial in origin, now spring-fed. Two striped towels hung upon the black rails; I looked out with some dismay to see two swimmers already in the water. Violet hung her towel alongside theirs and I followed suit. We swam without stopping to the other side. I struggled to keep up. Her strength surprised me.

Once on the other side, we draped ourselves like washed clothes upon a large rock. We murmured as the sun dried us. Across the pond the two swimmers arrived at the shore and vanished into the trees with their towels. We were alone in summer's kingdom. It was a small, oval-shaped world like the inside of a locket, one side the mirror of the pond, the other the sky.

"Our little glass lake," Violet sighed.

"Not a grain of sand to trouble us."

"No, not even one."

"Are you happy?" I asked.

"Yes."

"Even though your son's away?" I couldn't imagine Maria off-island much less forget her son.

"Yes. I like to be alone."

I felt buoyed by her certainty. She seemed very wise to me lying there in her white maillot like an *Amaterasu* under the sun. We were not without him, we carried his image in our locket as he journeyed west walking barefoot, eating avocados, seeing orange trees growing outside for the first time. Perhaps he too was swimming, in a river, in the sea, it didn't matter. I felt the kind of happiness one feels in the presence of a friend when one's child is in the next room—nearby but requiring none of one's attention.

"He arrived in Mendocino last night."

"I hear it's beautiful there."

"I think he'll like it."

I opened my eyes and turned to see her smiling through closed eyes, drops of pond water dotting her face like dew. I studied it for signs of danger but she looked completely at peace.

"I'm proud of him. He's more adventurous than I was."

"But you're very brave. What about Europe?"

"It's not the same. I went with a girlfriend and we always had creature comforts."

"Oh," I said dumbly, nearly blurting out, "He never told me that," but I caught myself, pretending our many conversations had never occurred. In a way it was easy, for I had begun to doubt that they had. My memories of our time together seemed sadly delusional if not completely insane. I half wanted to ask Violet for verification. As with a small boat in the wind I struggled with thoughts of him. In my effort to steer myself to safety, I grew tired of rowing, my arms were as weak as my will, and in the end I lay down and let the boat drift.

"Will you freckle?" I asked, thinking of his skin, the way he could take on an olive cast in a single day.

"Yes. That's another difference. My son tans beautifully and all I get is spots."

"I don't see any spots." Her skin was pale and clear.

"SPF 50," she said.

The mention of her son's beauty had a predictable effect. I bent my legs and wondered about the missing father. Romani? Wampanoag? Italian?

"When he comes back, I want you to meet him."

"All right."

"You'd like him."

"Why's that?"

"He reminds me of you a little."

"Of me? How so?"

"I don't know, he just does. Or maybe you remind me of him, I'm not sure which. You both have strong feelings about things and you're both smart."

"Well, if he's anything like you, I'm sure he's lovely."

"It's funny, I sometimes forget you've never met. It's as if you know each other."

"Yes, I feel that too," I said, my heart throbbing obscenely beneath my suit, my pulse flashing like a diamond at my neck.

"When he comes back, we'll all have lunch."

"Okay," I agreed. I closed my eyes less to feel the sun upon them than to cover their expression.

When the sun had dried us we rose without speaking, like nomads whose movements are ruled by the stars. We looked out across the water. Violet glanced at me in a kind yet cursory way and I gave her my best Aunt Tomoko nod. She dove in first, a a shimmering whitefish entering the dark water. I scrambled awkwardly down from the rock and waded in, my elbows flying up when the cold water touched my warm chest. Clumsily, I splashed in after her.

We swam near each other, Violet slightly ahead. Her strokes were strong; it would have been an effort for her to remain beside me. Somewhere near the middle of the pond we heard geese overhead. Within moments the birds had descended and joined us, some of them flapping and splashing the surface, others gliding like small ships alongside us. Violet turned cleanly to swim on her back and flashed me a sleeky gap smile. It was as if together we had entered a room where two people were making love. One felt simultaneously a sense of trespass and sensuality, nearness and exclusion. One heard wings brushing against the water, wings brushing against wings. Each bird carried its unknown cargo, the majestic fleet of them following its prescribed fate. I longed to touch one—I was near enough—but felt certain if I were to alter my stroke the spell would be broken and the geese would flee so I swam as smoothly as I could among them, in Violet's green wake.

* * *

With the young man gone and summer's onslaught under way, I did my best to remain stable: I drank cup after cup of hot chamomile tea, I reread *Lolita*, I walked for hours on the side of the road, I weltered in my sorrow before the waterfall (which now struck me as an effusion of tears), I swam doggedly with Violet, I succumbed to working the Friday shift.

People came to the library in droves. There was now a waiting list for the computers, each patron was given a different color card specifying which terminal they had been assigned to. The director switched jubilantly to iced coffee, Kitty began wearing the silver and black striped halter top that had elicited several warnings from the library trustees (we were not to expose our shoulders or midriff, though contrary to my own instincts, the showing of feet in sandals was permitted), there were crowds of children at story hour, the Saturday crafts migrated to the back garden where the forest green umbrellas were raised and the striped awning unfurled once more.

Four young shelvers were hired that summer to alleviate the increase in circulation, two of them fairly attractive university age boys in whom I could not muster a speck of interest. I had thought that the young man might open within me a hidden floodgate or inspire a new predilection, but those two boys gave the lie to all that. His absence only made more explicit my need for Violet. Like a pet, I watched the door for her, eager to be fed any morsel pertaining to her son, but she was too busy for the library. Business was brisk and the weather was fine. She had time for swimming but no time for books. In summer our priorities diverged, making mine a double abandonment.

And yet, in the days following the young man's arrival in California, I was surprised to find that I did not feel—as I had so feared I would—abandoned. Instead, as if waking from an exhaustingly vivid dream, I struggled to verify whether my experience had been real. I went over the chain of events in my mind and couldn't help but wonder how well, if at all, I could trust my own memory. My state of bewilderment and ecstasy and terror was not one that lent itself to fact-finding.

To muddle matters further, I had, during the past year, read an abundance of novels on the subject of older women and younger men. (Where can one expect a librarian to turn for guidance if not to books?) As I recalled some minor details (his habit of removing my shoes last for instance) and even some minor events (the alleged phone call), I began to question whether I was recounting the history of my own affair or that of a literary characters or some mad amalgamation of the two. Had I manufactured false memories or had one woman's middle-aged modesty eradicated her belief? For if I was to believe in my own story, I was to believe in my own desire and desirability.

When the desire to hear his voice came upon me I found myself watching films featuring the aforementioned film star whose face threatened to supplant the young man's face in my memory, a phenomenon I worked conscientiously to counteract. As the swarthy chainsaw of the actor's voice cut through me (the memory of the young man was indeed both painful and exciting), it became my habit to close my eyes and summon the young man's face.

Such climactic moments aside, July was dull, the days wearisome and unsettling as long London bus rides to the outskirts of the city, the nights akin to journeys I made with my mother across the moors to visit her invalid sister whom she deeply resented. Poverty, darkness, estrangement, little to see or look forward to. Not even the rumbling of a school bus in the distance to prick up my ears. And yet I confess the island was astonishingly beautiful at that time of year. Yellow lilies (their color reminiscent of the irises that grew wild at the edge of the rushy pond) had opened in the garden; tomatoes, Sun Golds and Early Girls were ready to be picked; blueberries grew plump and wild just down the road; the apples were beginning to show; the cove where I took Maria for picnics, Ice House, and of course the sea, had never been more blue. But the island of my mind was such a horror.

As the temperatures reached into the high eighties, my sense of disbelief receded and I began to anticipate his return. I tried to stop myself—it seemed pure folly to wait for a seventeen-year-old, purer still for Violet's son—but even in the sweltering heat, I felt a chill at the back of my legs when I thought of him. The attic had become unbearable, hotter than the outdoors, especially at night, by which time it had absorbed all the heat of the day and stood emanating it. Unable to sleep, I had little else to do but perspire while I imagined our meeting. That year the apples fell early, when they were still green. I would hear them dropping in the cool dark.

As the temperatures climbed higher still into the nineties and the young man's return date drew frighteningly near, I was filled with fear that the dream had been real after all. I thought I would explode with panic at the idea of him arriving. It seemed unlikely that he would want to see me after whatever life-altering experience he'd had on that dirty river and less likely still if he were to grant me an audience that he would still desire me. Thanks to Violet I wasn't forced to question his very existence but the only proof of our relationship was my own desire, the phone call, the British edition of Salinger, and eventually a letter.

He wrote to me one night from inside his tent which I hardly dared to imagine, having once, as a young person myself, known the intoxicating intimacy of a tent's interior. In a clearing, near a wood, near a body of water, the flaps of the tent open enough to allow a breeze, shut enough to ensure privacy. The night lit by stars, the only sounds those of animals and birds and insects and the crushing of grass and leaves beneath one's prone body when one turns to face one's companion.

He had written the letter on a page from the journal Violet had given him and I had the small hope that he might think of me each time he encountered the missing page. Though he received an A- in English he was not fond of writing. (A- was in fact his lowest grade. Despite his unusually high grade point average, he insisted his true education had been "waiting on fools" at P.I.P.) He had expressed frustration with the composition element of the class and had warned me not to expect letters. And yet, he had expended the effort to write. The page was stained by rain or water from his canteen or perhaps dew. His handwriting was, as it had been that first day, quite ordinary, but at the sight of it I felt again an unstoppable surge of pride, as if I had been the one to teach him the alphabet, printing, the writing of cursive. It was a side to him that I rarely had the privilege of seeing. Each letter was small, carelessly formed, there were loops in places where in my own there were none. To me, it was a beautiful sight to behold, a youthful accomplishment. He said he missed me but devoted the bulk of his short letter to praising the river and the land.

There was no mention of other people though I'm certain he was living among others, other volunteers and their guides. I was convinced there must have been a Sophia or a Rosamond, if not an irresistible Kamala, beside him. To my suspicious eye, what was missing from the letter, seemed to reveal as much about his new life as the brief, pastoral descriptions. What may have been a sincere effort to include me, to convey that which I could not experience firsthand, had the effect of delineating the distance between us, between the place near a river where he spent his days and the place surrounded by the sea where I existed with, to be fair, my equally unmentionable husband and child. He said he was writing by the light of a headlamp, a modern Ishmaelian image to be sure, and I was torn between my longing to imagine him and a fear of my own imagination.

At the sight of his handwriting my doubts dissolved, though I sensed they might return like headaches to plague me. Some part of me could always be persuaded that his existence, its intersection with mine, even my own existence, were impossibilities. Writing was not his strong suit, he had not lied or exaggerated there, still the content of his letter mattered less to me than the fact of it, the fact of him standing next to a river tearing a page out of the journal I had seen with my own eyes, and then the fact of him sitting down, perhaps against a tree whose leaves were a bright, summery green, to form thoughts of me and write them down.

As his return date drew near, I pored over the "newspaper" (cruel misnomer!) in search of news of him. I scoured the sports highlights, honor rolls, graduation, and wedding announcements, even the police log. Religiously, I read the column that corresponded to his hometown in search of any mention of him or his mother. Such columns recorded the migration patterns of locals young and old and their achievements in the greater world; they documented their slightest movements with the avidity of ornithologists observing rare birds. Still I found nothing, not even any mention of P.I.P., which would have been a consolation. (Such columns seldom chronicle the lives of shy, private people; there is no way for the columnists to acquire their information.) A few journalistic facts would have perhaps tethered my brain more snugly to reality. As it was, my imagination roamed between the realm of sexual excitement and the realm of pure terror. One moment, I was convinced he would look past me at the dock to greet a slight yet sensual Sophia or a Rubenesque Rosamond, the next moment I was so inflamed by memories of the loft as to require a shower on those already sweltering summer afternoons.

* * *

August 14th was the day of the *Akihito futuna*, a fish that exists in a single river on the island of Futuna. The day seemed made for us. When at last it arrived, I brought Maria along with me to meet his boat, for the nursery was closed in summer and there was little hope of finding a babysitter during the high season. Though I confess I didn't actually phone anyone. In fact I made no effort whatsoever to free myself from her company because greater than my desire for privacy was my need for a companion and no one but Maria could have safely accompanied me on such a deviant mission. No one except Violet perhaps, but then I was a greedy one, wasn't I? Firmly, I told myself she'd be too busy waiting on fools to tear herself away.

There was already a crowd waiting outside the terminal when we arrived. Another smaller crowd had formed near the dock. I felt the need to be separate from both groups, to eliminate myself from view. For the first time, I was not afraid of being seen with him. Rather, I was terrified that he would not appear and that I would be seen weeping in public with Maria at my side. We sat at the bus turnaround on the bench that was nearest the ferries and watched the boat arrive.

The first passenger off the boat was a Kamala of about sixteen. Dark-skinned, wearing a white sundress, she led the procession like a queen and I had to wonder if the young man was trailing like a slave not far behind her. It was a noon boat, full of exuberant, hungry-faced people. There were women wearing the Indian tunics and dresses made of hand block print voile very much in fashion that summer, men wearing the usual oxford shirts and boat shoes, children wearing backpacks in the shapes of animals and sandals with Velcro straps, some bounding, much to their parents' dismay, ahead to the parking lot, some asleep in their mothers' arms or on the backs of hired helpers, some riding like little kings and queens on their fathers' shoulders. But no seventeen-year-old boy wearing a blue backpack filled with Californian treasures for his favorite forty-two-year-old librarian. How unlikely it would be to see such a figure striding down the gangplank toward me. It was not the stuff of literature much less the stuff of life.

"What are we doing?!" Maria wrapped her arms around my waist and jerked me to one side so that I nearly fell and scraped my leg on the low brick wall in attempt to recover myself.

"Just a minute!" I snapped urgently. I polished my glasses on the cuff of my blouse then replaced them before looking again.

There was no sign of the young man nor of Violet. I was nearly relieved. Had he come, I would have had to introduce him to Maria and vice versa and I had not prepared myself for such a reckoning. (She may have said about him what she had said about a friend of Var's: *I don't believe in him.* And then how would I have managed?) I hadn't even brought a gift. Certainly I was ill-prepared to encounter the young man; I couldn't begin to consider the problem of Violet.

The passengers began to disperse—some climbed into waiting taxis, most of which were shabby-looking vans, many were whisked away by friends or family in sparkling cars with plush interiors, a few stepped into open convertibles, and some strolled directly from the dock into town, all of them moving away from the boat and into their lives, their futures, their fates. At last, only Maria and I stood stalled at the dock.

By then I had given up looking on the sunny side of his disappearance and was entertaining the notion that a significant percentage of travelers missed their boats and had no choice but to wait for the next one. This was a comfort. Why, he could jolly well be on the other side of the water, sitting as I was, waiting for a boat, the two of us together on our island of waiting, while the rest of the world receded like waves around us.

Steamship Authority clerks have a reputation for rudeness but I found both the male and female clerks to be touchingly compassionate (I alternated between them in part to save myself some embarrassment, in part due to the requirements of the fluctuating lines). Each seemed to realize fairly quickly (perhaps well before I did) the direness of my situation. Neither showed any sign of impatience when I persisted in walking up to the counter to inquire after the next boat et cetera. The woman offered Maria a red lollipop and the man joked with her at length. (Maria had a knack for accomplishing more than I did, even on errands that were designed for my own purposes with little if any regard for her agenda.) Between arrivals, when I was not quietly pursuing the kind clerks, I scanned the terminal nervously for Violet, half hoping to see her so that I might then see the young man, half glad she was nowhere to be found. Her absence made it a possibility, however small, that I had come on the wrong day.

At last, I was not surprised when he did not appear on the day he had promised. I had, as much as was humanly possible, prepared myself for such a disaster. In the manner of a children's librarian, I had, in a persuasive, calming voice, told myself a story complete with lavish illustrations about the young man's journey. *Once upon a time there was a young man who loved a woman he could not have and so he left the small island where they lived and set sail to find happiness elsewhere.*

He promised to return, if not to claim her as his own then to bring her news of elsewhere. I did not blame the woman for doubting the young man's promise nor did I blame the young man for failing to return. It was just the way the story ended.

* * *

Days went by without any news from them. Jealously, I imagined a cozy mother-son reunion, a bejeweled Kamala alongside him. I felt excluded from their sudden change in plans. Finally, one late August afternoon, Violet came to the library. She did not return or borrow materials but simply asked if I would come to her house for tea. There was something about her manner (shy, polite, with something held in reserve) that was endlessly appealing though she might have used any manner in the world and I would have complied. I was wildly curious, but refrained from asking any questions with the exception of: "Where is your house?" At this she looked surprised and then smiled the most painful smile I think I have ever seen upon the face of a pretty woman as she jotted down directions distractedly on a scrap of library paper using one of our tiny pencils. Her script was nothing like her son's. In its legibility and precision it reminded me of my father's Japanese which I had always tried and failed to imitate. I was more than primed to follow its clear instructions.

There was no easy way for a nondriver to get to the two-hundred-year-old house. I suppose one could lug one's bicycle on the #4 then disembark at Tea Lane and ride one's bicycle the remainder of the way, but I had two misgivings about such a scenario. First, I have always deplored the moments during which one must install one's bicycle onto the grille's contraption; one often holds up traffic fiddling with the clanging bars and rusting slots. Second, there are only enough slots to accommodate the wheels of two bicycles, the system is first come, first served, so in theory it is possible (though unlikely) to be denied a space, possible to be marooned with one's bicycle no closer to one's destination than before, and so I cycled the entire distance.

I arrived in a shimmering cloak of chamomile-scented perspiration and stood panting in the shade of an apple tree for several minutes before leaning my bicycle against it and proceeding to the great front door. He had told me about the historic door. His grandfather had built it using the wood from a single oak that he had felled himself. It stood as yet another proof of the self-reliance and ingenuity of which the young man was a direct descendant. I literally rang the ancient bell that was mounted to the wall by pulling its soft, braided rope and could not help but think of Melville's sailors as I touched it, of all the tough, worn-out things that had outlasted them. I felt a bit ridiculous ringing a bell; it rang out like a farmer's dinner bell or a church bell making public a private occasion. Violet appeared at once. As she said hello she placed her hand on the bell to silence it. She paused ever so slightly in the doorway with her hands clasped in front of her before leading me into the foyer. I wiped my feet cautiously on the black mat within.

The house was mysteriously cool, and dark as a temple. There was no air conditioner, I was sure of that, both were allergic to conditioned air. Wooden shutters covered the insides of the windows. The orchard on the south side must have cooled the house considerably and God knows what other old-fashioned energy-conserving tricks his mother had been taught by her Calvinist parents and theirs before them and so on. The house was smaller and far less fine than I had imagined but it was pleasingly *wabi*. The floors were old wood, not shiny but clean. Most of the furniture was dark wood and the walls had been painted cream. I saw, at the end of the long dim hall, through a half-open door, a slim river of light, and thought at once of the voluminous library.

Violet led me to a parlor off to the left. As we entered we passed a large, oval mirror from which I shamefully averted my eyes. I scanned the room for signs of him. I looked for childhood photographs, trophies on the shelves; I studied the walls in search of a high school diploma but found nothing.

She showed me to a small, exquisitely set table. In the manner of a well-trained servant she pulled one of the chairs out and I sat down in it. I felt my own eagerness and curiosity to be too visible on my face.

"Thank you for coming." Like a fishing line her words seemed weighted, designed to sink then catch.

"Of course."

She served cream tea, the jam of which was beach plum. When I told her it was delicious she winced the way her son so often did when I complimented him. Without a doubt the scones were her own; they were warm and the scent of them hung in the air. When I felt I could not scan the room any longer without appearing paranoid or deviant, I rested my eyes upon the table to find the very same red and white cloth he had served our many lunches upon. In the anxiety of being seated I hadn't noticed it. The sight of the familiar hand block pattern caused my heart to quicken; it was nearly enough to bring tears to my eyes but I steeled myself against such an onslaught and was grateful in the end that I had.

Violet was silent. We were in a room whose windows, from a great distance, looked out at the sea. The blue like an eyebrow upon the land's green face. There was a fireplace, a daybed covered by a quilt of creams and whites, a tiny end table adorned by a milk glass lamp; there were rugs the color of harissa and books on the floor. The objects seemed to know things. For years they had existed in the room with mother and son. They knew the answers to my questions.

Something in her demeanor had changed since the last time we'd met. Could it be that I'd been wrong and she really hadn't known until now? I feared everything about her. I feared her silence, her high cheekbones, her pale skin.

The suspense was difficult to bear. Violet began chattering softly and incessantly about shop inventory, pending orders, the high price of local produce, her eyes fixed on some unknown point in front of her as if I weren't sitting right across from her. It frightened me, the way she went on delivering what seemed to be a monologue mumbled by a woman in crisis to herself.

To avoid her sudden outpouring, I busied myself with the scones and stared at her sweater. It was the same cotton sweater she always wore. Once rifle brown, now a shade of cocoa, its cowl hung down limply to reveal a portion of her pale neck. She must have worn it every day since the day I saw it for the first time. If I hadn't been so incredibly lazy when it came to learning how to knit, I'd have had the cherry sweater wrapped in a box for her now. It would have come in rather handy at that moment, providing comfort to her and an easy topic of conversation.

It was not until I'd devoured two scones and a full cup of tea with milk added beforehand (my mother too had always added the milk beforehand) that I learned both the reason for my visit and the reason for her son's failure to return. The two reasons were in essence the same. One rainy afternoon, in some still wild part of Northern California, while swimming with friends, he had dived into the river, struck his head on a rock, and had not recovered.

I tried to look her in the eyes after she said it. I was frantic for a look from her, a signal to confirm the validity of her statement, but she would not engage me.

Instead she tugged at a loose thread on the hem of her sweater as she muttered to me in the parlor's dappled light. She rambled on quietly citing statistics, explaining how very common it was for a head injury to result in death, and I, in response, looked down at my hands and began to pick at the edges of my fingernails in an attempt to shield myself from such information, wanting her to speak instead of her son in particular, to hear some detail about him, however gruesome, that I could, in the way of a cool pillow, rest my feverish cheek upon.

Indeed I suddenly felt hot, quite ready to explode in firework fashion. A dangerous spark was traveling upward through my body, burning a path through my heart as it went. I feared that when the spark reached my head it would go off. And yet I felt this to be a wrong reaction. I felt desperate to stop the fireworks of my own grief. I felt there could be no one sadder in the world than the mother of a dead child. If it had been my Maria I could not have sat before a stranger and served them tea. Violet did not need my blinding display of grief coloring her sober parlor, singeing her red and white tablecloth and clean walls with its sorry sparks. She deserved, at the very least, my silence.

"Violet," I said softly. I could say no more than that. I touched the soft wrist of her sweater with my fingertips, from which she very discreetly recoiled. She began, as the two of them so often had at the library counter, to look swiftly from object to object, her birdlike gaze never alighting upon any one scone or spoon or saucer for more than a half-second. The rest of her was still but her eyes were trembling.

"Violet," I said again. She looked at me then as if she had suddenly remembered my presence but then she returned to looking at the many pieces of the service and at the remains of our tea.

I didn't dare move. I didn't dare speak. I felt held there at the table by the strength of her sadness.

It would have wrecked him to see her in such a state. How he had adored her. But I could not bring myself to say this. At first I too looked down at the service. I tried to stay with her there but in the end I could not and I allowed my eyes to stray from the table to a dark hallway in the distance. I spent the long minutes wondering where it led.

"Would you like to see his room?" she asked.

"No!" I answered, perhaps too vehemently. "I mean, only if you'd like me to." I was desperate to do something for her though I did not want to see his room in her presence. I feared it would cause the launching of the fireworks.

"No, I just thought you might like to."

"Thank you. You're very kind, but I don't think I could." My God, what had he told her? For all my fantasies of late night mother-son chats, I was mortified by the very real possibility that he had confessed to her.

"Thank you for coming," she said and began very slowly—as if the announcement of her sadness had made her limbs heavier and difficult to move—to rise.

I joined her, relieved to be released from the table.

"It's you I have to thank," I said. "I don't know how you managed," I glanced at the remains of our tea. "It was lovely, really lovely, thank you."

"Oh, it's nothing. I'm trying to keep busy."

"Yes, of course, that makes sense." I too would soon find this necessary.

"And anyway, I wanted to thank you, May." The sound of my name's diminutive issuing from her nearly killed me.

"Thank me?" I asked. "Why, whatever for?"

"Well, I don't know how to put this, but…" She pressed her hands together and held them in front of her mouth. "If it weren't for you, my son would have died without…" The torch she had been bravely holding out to me flickered out.

Oh, mistress of discretion, oh, purple heart, oh, Violet.

I rather despised myself for what I said next. "I'd better be going," I lied. "I have asthma and I feel an attack coming on." No doubt I seemed like someone who would have asthma though inexplicably I did not.

"Will you be okay on your bike?" I despised myself too for winning her concern when she herself must have needed it so badly.

"Yes! Exercise nearly always improves my condition." It was ludicrous but I simply had to get out and could think of no better excuse. I nearly ran out of the house and through the orchard to retrieve my bicycle. Dwarfed by the enormous doorway, she waved and watched me go.

I whipped rather dangerously around to wave back at her as I pedaled off in a sad fury. It's a wonder I didn't slam into a tree or go down in a ditch, so agitated I was on that terrible ride back to the apartment. It was only when I was at last alone with the news Violet had given me that I was able to selfishly consider its implications.

I had never been so relieved to arrive at the apartment. Everything looked the same as I'd left it. The bathroom was filthy, Var was in his room, the kitchen counter was covered in dishes, the floor covered in toys, *For Esmé—With Love and Squalor* was on the dresser, his letter still underneath a loose floorboard at the bottom of the closet. In the apartment, the young man hadn't yet died. The AC—whose roar I usually resented for its power to obliterate thought—and I had never been more compatible. While I had craved solitude in the presence of Violet's grief, once alone I craved distraction.

"I'll go get Maria!" I called out as I ran down the stairs just a few minutes after I'd run in. Fetching Maria was something I could do.

As I fled the apartment, I slammed the door with such force that one of the panes of glass cracked and had to be mended later that evening with tape. The tape was an atrocious shade of blue, not unlike the tape the painters had used to seal off the gray house. With its jagged traverse of the broken pane, it looked like the only river on a blank map. But at the time I kept hustling. I left the glass in pieces on the ground.

I couldn't get to the nursery fast enough. I arrived early and didn't care. I shadowed Maria on the playground. I had endless amounts of patience for her antics; my appetite for diversion was insatiable. I lifted her up to the top of the monkey bars then stood ready to catch her at least fifteen times. I did the same for Sophia and Charlotte. I twirled them on the tire swing, I petted and fed the rabbit, I caught the chickens and put them in their house, I climbed under the play structure and wove bracelets out of reeds, I dug a hole in the sandbox and filled it with rocks, I chased all the remaining children around the perimeter of the yard. I exhausted myself acting like a five-year-old, letting Maria's chatter fill my brain until bedtime, until at last we both succumbed to that corpse-like stillness of sleep. My only comfort as I felt myself slipping away was the thought of working at the library next morning, the promise of that trusty encyclopedia of diversions not far off.

* * *

It seemed imperative that I tell Siobhan before she heard the news elsewhere. I didn't think I could withstand her broaching the subject at a time of her choosing, perhaps when I least expected it and was in no position to cope. I had my opportunity during the lunch hour, while the summer patrons were out getting their green salads and sandwiches.

"Do you remember that young man?" Reluctantly I said his name in full to avoid identifying him in any way connected to myself. I stood at the window watching the crowd cross the street. Behind me the computer, beeping each time she scanned a book, sounded like a heart monitor.

"Of course I remember him. How could I forget?"

Fumbling for the words I should use to pronounce his fate, the words that would hurt my ears the least to hear, I felt a sharp needle of pain at the thought of never again feeling his voice drag its dark chain against me. I turned away from the window and stood next to Siobhan at the counter.

"He passed away," I managed, recalling with some relief the

words my father had often employed—*dead* being too final, the heavy thud of a noun too grim, *passed on* implying too great a distance, a place beyond me, the word *away* being beautifully, stubbornly indeterminate, a word that could mean anywhere, the verb *passed* tolerable, it at least implied an action and therefore a life.

"What?!" she said shrilly.

"I won't repeat the words," I said.

"You can't be serious! But how? He was so young!"

"Outdoor accident."

"What?"

"Diving, a large rock."

I sat down and began researching request cards. I wanted to help someone, to meet a need. Siobhan sat down next to me and took a portion of the cards. We worked in silence for several minutes. It was a relief to be granted those minutes.

"Imagine if you had," she said.

"I did."

"You didn't."

I wrote the two words down on the back of a card for emphasis and slid it next to the card she was working on.

"Oh, May." Her sigh was that of a mother whose child has failed an exam. "I was afraid of that." She wrote on the card and passed it back to me. *At least no regrets.*

I recycled the card and stood at the window again. The parking lot was peculiarly empty. Our patrons were picnicking in a field or had brought their provisions to the beach. They would spend their afternoon eating asparagus sandwiches with wild blueberries, gazing raptly at the sea. The confession I had sought so keenly was now of no interest to me. Siobhan, of course, was not to blame. Though the patrons too would soon exhaust me, in her company I prayed for their return. What I craved were exchanges with strangers, the light stamping of books. Anyone but someone who knew me; anyone but someone who knew.

"We're going to have to delete his record," Siobhan said gently, though I knew for a fact this was not entirely true. Four years prior a library staff member had passed away and her record remained untouched. The director had made it clear we were not to delete it and so our colleague's name remained in the system, at once a false indicator of her continued existence and a true token of her persistent presence among us.

The sight of Viola's name in the database plucked a chilly string in me as much because I had loved my former supervisor as because she happened to share a name with my father's reader who, during a certain period of my childhood, would startle my mother and me with telephone calls at home. So the name Viola had held for me the music of three deaths, and now, in a roundabout way, a fourth.

"But," I began, then thought better of it, striving to leave the impression that although the young man and I *had*, we were not close. "Yes, of course," I said, acknowledging obliquely that it would never do for a library database to be cluttered by obsolete records. Such a state of affairs would have been nothing less than a librarian's nightmare.

"Do you want me to do it or…"

"Yes!" I could never accept such a murderous task. Once, when looking up a patron I had met the phrase *PATRON IS DECEASED*; I did not feel prepared to meet those three words again.

I kept the fact of the young man's first account, established safely under his father's name, to myself. He would be my Viola but no one would know. I could, when I felt the need, view the three items on his record and pretend he was not only very much alive, but also very young. It would be as if his second record, the one I had entered myself in what was to be the last year of his life, had never existed, as if our first encounter (and therefore those to follow) had never occurred. It was a comfort to me when I had little else, the idea that he was on-island somewhere, aged six or seven, being driven by his mother to school, to soccer, to P.I.P., just another child with a library card who had not been in lately, simply too busy being a child to stop in.

* * *

It was the library's busiest summer on record. Checking out books to patrons while trying to smile, answering the phone in as cheerful a voice as I could manage, I thought I would faint from grief and exhaustion. I could not sleep. News of the young man's death reached the public. Patrons marveled at how unlucky the young man had been, they were bent on illustrating how lucky we, who had not leapt to our deaths, were to be alive. I did not feel lucky but of course I did not express this. I became garrulous as one who wants to speak but has nothing permissible to say. I mirrored their marvelous expressions like a circus monkey so that by the end of each day my facial muscles were as sore as my feet.

At the apartment I was safe from any mention of him. No staff member to inquire sympathetically about whether or not the young man I had pointed out to them was the same young man who had died. No unsuspecting patron to select me at random as the staff member who would become audience for remarks about the injustice of being killed while on holiday or the tragedy of dying young, expressions of horror in the face of Mother Nature's many hidden perils or the brutally irreversible blows of fate. I wanted none of it, none of the fears and marvels that had turned him into a figure of terror or regret. I loathed their invitations to join them in their figure making.

In the apartment, no one knew he had lived or had stopped living. It was back to the frozen sea. I stood dumbly shivering upon it, hardly believing that the last several months had been real, the woman at the waterfall me, the woman in the gray house me. Though I must have, I don't remember cooking or cleaning or caring for Maria. I only remember standing upon the black ice empty-handed, yes, axeless, no way to break it, the summer heat strangely useless in this regard. I stood until I could stand no longer.

Each day, when I went into the bedroom, I saw that the donated calendar was still on June. The room seemed empty without him although he had never been in it. I did not bother to shower or clean my glasses or wash my face or even eat. I had no appetite. I only put on fresh clothes to avoid suspicion. I feared scrutiny of any kind and wanted only to be left alone to grieve. I had counted on summer's onslaught to distract me from missing the young man but I had not counted on him being Missing. Given this sad miscalculation, said torrent of distractions did not console me. Indeed, I was inconsolable. In none of the novels I had read did the young lover die. I had no instruction manual. Buoyed as I had been by love, when love was removed, I collapsed.

* * *

During my illness, which had few symptoms but despair, fatigue, and a high fever, Var and Maria were often absent; it was August after all. They belonged to another sparkling yet faraway world: the busy, moving, healthy world of post offices and grocery stores, summer camps and swim lessons, barbecues and visitors. I lay prone, motionless, dreaming, an island of sorrow surrounded by a sea of happiness. I was not at all easy to rouse, having fallen down roughly and reeled into a pit of sadness. Fate's logic had defeated me. I, in my filmy glasses and dirty white flannelette, could not comprehend how it was that he, of the *Treasure Island* vision and the raspberry Tootsie Pops, had beaten me to the grave.

To my knowledge, Var did not so much as peer through a spyglass in my direction though I suppose he may have done so as I slept; I spent much of my time sleeping. What right had I to expect him to care one iota for my comfort or happiness? Siobhan crossed the dark waters to bring me a pot of expertly prepared *makhlouta*, the smell of which immediately caused me to be sick. Afterward, she sat down on the bed and lingered while I feigned sleep. The director brought me a bouquet of damask roses with a card signed by all the librarians, a reminder that my grief was likely nothing in comparison to Violet's. Flowers, like so many things, now reminded me of death. Though daily I chastised myself, I didn't call her.

Maria came ashore on occasion to give me a drawing she had made or to tell me a story about a mother who did nothing but stay in bed all the time. Insofar as anyone could that summer, she was the only one who brightened the somber picture of my world as I saw it. She was not a sun, there was no sun in that melancholy picture, but a fish or a bit of coral, a spot of red or orange in one of the darkest coves of the sea. If she had not slept in my arms each night, I might have died of that double sadness.

When I was awake I felt too tired to read, the muscles in my arms too weak to hold a book upright, my mind alternately too frantic and too frail to follow a line of text. Instead I lay beneath the small constellation of plastic stars that were jaundice-yellow against the snow-white sky of the ceiling, and thought about books I had already read. I remembered books I had read in the loft with the young man and books he had read while lying next to me. I remembered the way he had chewed so intently on his fingernails while reading *Moby Dick*, as if trying to taste the experience. I thought about the sailors whom he had loved and admired. For them the real was not what happens but what is about to happen. The months I spent with him were my last voyage into that kind of experience. Like a sailor, I lived for what would happen next, trusting completely that whatever it was would be worth the effort, the anxiety, the agonizing wait. Now I had ceased to be one of them. Now the real was not what was going to happen or even what was happening but what had already happened.

As for the young man, he died being one of those sailors. Now instead of envying him his capacity for the future, I pitied him his never being able to recount it. Yet, like Ishmael, he had dreamed of strange bedfellows and harsh seas, tough ropes and blackened pulleys, rusty winches and greasy buckets. Whatever California's version of such things might be, whatever great whale the Pacific Ocean concealed, surely it was beautiful and perhaps the discovery of such a beast was worthy of a young man's life.

When I was not trying to recall books or our reading of them, I ruminated, as I suppose most grieving people do, on the ways in which I might have prevented his death. Not once during our last few weeks together did I plead or beg or bargain. Never once did I ask him to stay. So deep was my sense of obligation to what I perceived as his future, so terrifying my guilt at what I had already done, it hardly occurred to me to do so. As it was, I felt I'd gotten away with murder. I was like one of those miscreant patrons who keeps a book for two years—my item was long overdue, I was lucky to have had it at all, others were waiting, the item deserved to circulate. I had been given so much time I couldn't imagine asking for more. But if I had, he might not have died.

If he hadn't died, would I strive so to remember him? If instead he had grown into a frightfully attractive priest or an unknown filmmaker, the sensitive husband of a Rosamond, the father of a baby Rose or a junior Pip, might I have been more likely to write our affair off as a mistake best forgotten? Wasn't the fear for a woman of my age that I was, by loving him, keeping him from living his life? If one knows that there was to be no life but the one being lived, can one feel guilty for having lived it? Indeed one could even argue, as Violet plainly had, that by loving her son when I did that I made richer his short life; had I denied him he would have died without having loved.

Indeed his death tampered with the ethics of our affair. What meaning, right or wrong, had the memory of my pleasure, now that he was dead? What significance had our transgression in the wake of his death? Lying grief-stricken in my bed, it all seemed innocuous, my memories of our time together nostalgic details of a lost world, the fleeting materials of one young man's only love. Was I a fool? Were these the demented ruminations of a brokenhearted librarian in denial of her worst crime? Or was I right to feel as I did in that fever of mine: *His death makes me glad that I loved. His death makes me gasp with relief that we loved when we did.*

The fever did pass. After two weeks of convalescence, my body had had enough of immobility and despair. Though I myself was still bereft, my body was ready to get out of bed. It had had enough of idly watching the remaining apples turn from green to red through the spotted windows. It wanted noodles and tea and a shower in the marred, tiled room. I can't say I concurred but I let myself be moved from one part of the apartment to another; I conceded to my body's will to live.

* * *

On my first day back at the library, the director requested that I relieve the children's librarian so that she might take her lunch. I strolled rather unsuspectingly toward the children's room. Upon entering it, upon seeing the reading rocket, the stencils, the Stevenson, I burst into tears.

"Are you okay?" the children's librarian asked in an irritated, rhetorical manner, the phrase less a question than a statement designed to shush me. When I failed to cease crying or to answer, she added a bit more kindly, "What's wrong?"

Oh, how I had waited for someone to say those words! I stopped crying at once.

"I'll tell you," I said, "if you promise not to say a word." By which I did not mean not a word to anyone else but not a word to *me* for I was entirely too fragile to entertain feedback. In a whisper, still short of breath, I told her my whole woeful, ecstatic story.

After a brief but solemn pause she said, "Wow." Her blue eyes behind their round silver glasses looked wet and impressed.

"Please don't say anything!"

"Oh, I won't, your secret is safe with me." Her hands were folded and resting in the lap of her red linen pants. She looked hungry, most certainly ready to take lunch.

"No, I mean don't say anything to *me*."

"Oh, whoops. I guess it's too late for that. That little *wow* just slipped out."

"Please!"

"How about this. Since we're in confession mode, how about I make a confession?" She scanned the room. For better or worse, we were alone.

"Okay." What else could I say? One of the perils of confessing is that one runs the risk of inviting one's confidante to confess.

She leaned forward and put one hand on either side of her mouth as if mimicking one who is soon to yell and then whispered, "I don't really like children all that much!" (Did she honestly think she'd been keeping that a secret?) "And if I have to wear that Corduroy costume one more time I'm going to slit my wrists!"

I confess I laughed then for the first time since the young man's death. Perhaps that's what she had been intending, I couldn't tell. Was I self-pitying to have expected silent sympathy, if not a little grief counseling? (I had, after all, demanded her silence. And I had kept her from her lunch.)

While her confession lightened my mood for the moment, my transaction with the seasonal Japanese restaurant worker later that afternoon deepened my despair. I retained a first-person memory of how attractive he had been in years past, and I could, even in the present moment, see that he was an attractive man (his thick hair impossibly lustrous, his eyes so black as to be blue), but I felt nothing in my body. My pulse was faint, my heart sluggish, my thin blood had slowed to a trickle. One did not express one's loss of feeling outright—one continued to play the role of concerned and interested librarian—but the message *I have died a thousand deaths since last we met. I am dead and without desire.* was clumsily conveyed.

Soon after, the children's librarian resigned from her post in order to run a Guatemalan orphanage, making it both difficult for me to confide in her further and tempting to wonder if my confession had sent her running for the border. In truth, she was probably just glad to bequeath the furry, sweat-soaked costume to the next child-loving librarian. Though I imagine she must have, if only for a moment, said a prayer to God, asking that it please not be Mayumi Saito.

* * *

"You know you never say his name," Siobhan remarked one September evening while we were lingering on the front steps of the library. "Why don't you ever say his name? Is it a habit left over from your secret-keeping days? You can relax with me, I know everything now, remember?"

"To name is to kill," I said, though I longed to hear his name uttered. I studied the flecks in the concrete, the nearby soil of the flowerbeds, Siobhan's sandaled feet; I had adopted his habit of never focusing my gaze on a single object for very long.

"What am I, chopped liver?" she held a hand out and glanced upward as if testing for rain, afraid, I think, I had lost my mind.

"No, definitely bangers and mash. But that's different, you're still alive."

"But he's already dead! You can't kill him again, can you?"

"Perhaps not," I said doubtfully. "But I'd rather not risk it. To be quite honest, I tried never to say his name when he was alive."

"But why?" I saw her pale green eyes swiftly assess me. Grief must have been cruelly imprinted upon my middle-aged face or in the way I barely held my body upright—my back rounded, my shoulders hunched and drooping, my feet heavier than they had ever been during pregnancy—because she ceased to question me further.

"There's his memory to consider, you know. It's a living thing." It was difficult to convey why I remained so devoted to the memory of a high school student with whom no future for me existed, more difficult still to explain why when he died (and therefore became even less of a prospect) I became more captive still.

"I'm worried about you, your lowness" she blurted out in a shrill voice. When Siobhan was anxious she always grew shrill.

"Pem, that's not funny anymore," I sighed.

"Watch it. You're killin' me!"

"Ha ha."

"I'm not joking! If to name is to kill I don't want to be named either. Funny how all the plants in the world have names but they keep on growin'."

"That's not what I mean and you know it."

"You've got to get over this."

"I am. I will. I'll be all right. It's just difficult. I was just beginning to cope with his being gone—that was difficult enough—and now I have to cope with him being dead. It's only been a month or so, for God's sake. If Nick dropped dead this evening do you think you'd be finished grieving in a month's time?"

"But Nick's my husband."

"Tell me you didn't just say that."

"I didn't just say that. Husband being beside the point, I was referring to time spent with a person."

"I ought to get going," I huffed and wiped my brow with my wrist. "God, I loathe this humidity!"

"Did I say the wrong thing?" she asked. "I mean, just sayin', you only knew him for about six months."

"Darling, if I could approach my situation with your highly practical sensibility truly I would. Unfortunately the notion of time only worsens matters for me."

"But have you read the theory about grieving and time? It's something like, you need a month for every year you were with the person to recover from the loss of them."

"I believe that was in the context of breakups not corpses, love." She seemed not to hear me; she was as focused on fixing me as I was on being broken.

"And if you only knew him for six months well that would mean technically you could get over it in two weeks."

"Pem! You mustn't continue!"

"Okay, I'll stop. I'm just worried about you. Maybe because I was in the dark for so long I just don't get what you're going through."

"That is a distinct possibility. In any case, I love you but the *Kokeshi* King beckons." I pulled out my running shoes and began to put them on.

"Uh-oh, I know I've put my size-ten foot in my mouth when the *Kokeshi* King beckons."

"Indeed." I stood up to go.

"Wait, I almost forgot! I brought you something." From her worn madras tote bag, Siobhan produced a large bar of imported chocolate. Valrhona dark, not the sort he ever brought me, but still the sight of it was like a hand around my throat.

I smiled the young man's pained smile and kissed her sunburnt cheek. "Thank you," I whispered and then rushed toward the museum path, not wanting to cry in the presence of one so intent on happiness.

* * *

Walking among the statues of women and birds, I thought of the silent pledge I'd made when the young man announced he was leaving: *I too will leave this island.* If then the idea had been my only solace, now it was what saved me. I decided to honor my pledge. I would put my unmentionable sadness to use. I would board a light aircraft and take to the skies; I would watch the island grow smaller beneath me. I would live in another time zone, sleep in a strange bed, I would stare at indecipherable street signs without straining to read them. I would eat foods I normally only dreamed of in the company of people I loved but rarely saw. I would do what he'd done. I would leave.

Upon arriving at the apartment I locked myself in the bedroom and googled "Japanese language programs." I clicked on "The Yamada Institute" then "Japanese Language School" then "Clear History." I was beginning to think I could no longer stay on the island. Yet I had no desire to go to the mainland either. I wanted to go somewhere that felt like home but I was not sure if such a place existed. Japan at least was homey if not home. There were the many aunts and uncles who had fawned over me as a child and whom I knew would be just as eager to lavish affection upon Maria. I wanted to speak

Japanese, to hear the sound of others speaking it. I wanted Japanese ways of thinking and being, I wanted Japanese food, cherry trees, the Pacific Ocean. I wanted life on an island other than the one upon which for the first time I felt stranded.

At eighteen I spent a summer in Tokyo, in part because I had grown up with a coffee table book called *Tokyo: The Most Beautiful City in the World*. During grade school, I often pored over its color photographs and imagined myself there. My father made arrangements for me to study Japanese while living with a local family during the week and with Aunt Tomoko on weekends. I have never been lonelier than I was in Tokyo, though it was, as the book promised, a beautiful city, and though he never said so, my father was bursting with pride upon my return to England. How he loved to hear me speak Japanese and how deeply disappointed he was (though he never showed it) when I discontinued my studies.

After spending time in a foreign city I was no longer afraid of American cities and moved to New York. How provincial and cozy it seemed to me in contrast to Tokyo—a city made of antique buildings bearing perfectly comprehensible signs in English, its busy streets and many skyscrapers populated by people who spoke English or who were at least accustomed to hearing its alien sounds spoken. It was in this comfy American context that I found myself better able to discover cultures other than my own: the Portuguese-speaking *Igreja Católica Apostólica Brasileira* where I met Var, next door to the public library where I checked out British novels, across from the Chinese restaurant with its menus printed earnestly in F.O.B. English. It never dawned on me then that New York too was an island. The pattern was set unconsciously.

I felt a new curiosity about death, as if it were a place I had never traveled to, the only place where I might possibly find the young man, a place that might feel like home. This curiosity, which might be more aptly described as longing, collided with my efforts to care for Maria. There was no way to accomplish the two things at once. Between my longing for death and my longing for Japan, the latter seemed the more life-affirming destination.

I stood in the doorway of Var's room, feeling faint, a bit torn, and watched him carve a sash for his *kokeshi.* "I've got to get off this rock," I said, using a touch awkwardly the young man's phrase yet feeling for the first time I understood its meaning. How much larger the impossibility of being with him seemed on this particular island. It was as if he existed somewhere else in the world and if I were to leave the island I might find him.

"Why? What's wrong?" Var asked. I had at last shocked him into inquiry, though I no longer cared if or what he asked. To make matters worse, he placed his large, soap-scented hand on my shoulder. It had been years since he'd done that. I felt at once disturbed by his return to that old gesture and lulled by its deep familiarity. For a moment we were having one of our vintage, quiet chats that had been a signature of our university years together. When I searched his face for a change, it only looked more familiar and kind, the way it had then. "Is there someone else?" he asked. I thought of confessing to him, in the spirit of honesty or to establish a closeness between us, but decided it was a selfish impulse, that the truth would only wound him unnecessarily. Then again, perhaps he knew already, perhaps he had sensed it and had been waiting for the trouble to pass.

"No," I sighed, dismayed by the awful truth of my answer. If only there were. The Varian phrase "A day late, a dollar short" floated cloudlike across the sky of my mind and then out of sight. "I want to learn Japanese," I said. "And I want Maria to learn it too. There are no Japanese here. It's depressing." Like me, Var spoke only English and had learned about his dark ancestors from an American university.

"What about Chieko?" he asked.

I sighed again. I suddenly felt very tired and wondered if I truly had the will and stamina it would require to leave the island. "You know what I mean," I pressed on. "Chieko's down-island. Besides, even if she lived downstairs, I wouldn't expect her to be my Japan." One Japanese British wash-ashore plus one Japanese Brazilian wash-ashore does not a Japantown make.

"I know," he said sheepishly, as if he had known all along I could not be persuaded and had tried anyway to persuade me, as if he knew that if there had been a Little Tokyo down the road I would still go.

Var consented to Maria and me spending a month in Japan, enrolled in a reputable Japanese language academy, while he stayed behind. We would stay two weeks with my father's youngest brother Tadashi and two weeks with Aunt Tomoko. To this day I feel grateful to Var for his lack of interference.

It seemed wrong that I should leave the island without first checking on Violet. For all I knew she lay shivering in a bathtub or slumped in a chair, for all I knew she'd taken her own life. But every time I approached the phone I began to shake. More than once I lifted the receiver then dropped it clattering to the floor. If I had known she would call I would have sat calmly by the phone waiting for her ring. Instead I approached the phone repeatedly. I held the receiver intending yet unable to complete the call. Until, as sometimes happens to one in the habit of holding the phone, I pressed the button to engage it and she was there. The phone never rang. It merely acted as a conduit, a tunnel that had always been there waiting for us to enter.

"Mayumi?"

"Violet." How quickly her voice stilled me.

* * *

When I told her I would soon be leaving for Japan she suggested we meet. I couldn't refuse. My desire to see her was stronger than my fear.

Her face, very white with a round, red mouth, brought to mind the Japanese flag. She stood leaning against the café, wearing a tan P.I.P. shirt. The cursive lettering, the twin plums on their stem, looked as if someone had drawn them on with a dark chocolate pencil, an edible pencil. Her arms dangled like a girl's from the cap sleeves.

"You look so thin!" I cried with alarm, even before we embraced and I felt the skeletal fact of her.

"So do you." I nodded but the weight I'd lost was nothing in comparison.

The café was crowded, clamorous. I felt immediately our choice of such a public location had been a mistake. It was not the time or the place for any confidence. I could see that Violet would not have the opportunity now to say, when did it begin, were you ever going to tell me.

She exercised an excessive amount of politeness upon me, every gesture, every word, another stone she placed on the wall between us. If these stones were her protection she could have them. I would have given her much more had she asked.

"Which table would you prefer?" she asked.

"Anywhere is fine." She stood in the doorway waiting for me to choose. How many of the people within that small room knew?

The lone waitress burst out of the kitchen like a cuckoo and fluttered over to us. She greeted Violet by name and showed us to a window table.

"Would you and your friend like some water?"

"None for me, thanks, but my friend might like some," Violet winked. I thought fondly of Siobhan, of my abiding affection for lady winkers.

"No, thank you." Like a criminal I felt pressure to conform.

"Thanks for coming on such short notice," she said.

"Don't be silly. I'd meet you anytime."

"You would?"

"Yes, I would."

Violet clasped her hands and tilted her head slightly to one side to rest upon them. She gazed at me as if I were a place in the distance.

"So you're leaving."

"Yes. But only for a short time."

"Let's hope the weather's good."

"I'll be back before you know it."

"You don't really know."

"Okay."

"What about your family?"

"I'm bringing my daughter along. The relatives are thrilled. They haven't seen her since…" I winced at my own mention of traveling with Maria, my living child.

"You're smart to bring her."

"Yes, well, she's only five."

"I take it your husband isn't coming. You do still have a husband?"

"Yes, I do. And no, he's not coming."

"Still, it's smart of you to bring her."

"I don't feel very smart."

"Well, you are. I'm the one who was stupid."

"Violet."

"Don't." She held up her hands.

I ordered a salade Niçoise and she ordered the lamb burger, together we ordered a side of cooked greens; together we experienced a momentary surge of appetite. We ate the greens diligently as if they were medicine but left the rest of the food untouched.

"I have something for you," she said and set down a small, white box, the sort that typically holds jewelry. My first thought was that she was giving me something of his: a pair of cuff links, a tiny toy, a ring.

"Did you know that my son always wanted to go to Japan?"

"No, I didn't know that. I had no idea."

"Ever since he was a little boy he'd wanted to visit every island in the world. But he especially wanted to go to Japan. He loved Kurosawa, he loved Misumi's *Lone Wolf and Cub*."

"But I…" I didn't want to pick up the box.

"It isn't much," she said, picking it up and setting it down again. "It isn't heavy."

I had the bitter thought that we were at last having lunch together. And in a restaurant no less. Despite everything, Violet had kept her word.

"So will you do it?" she leaned closer. I had never seen her looking so greedy. I couldn't answer. I was determined never to cry in her presence. What right had I to sadness in the face of her loss?

"It's the least you could do for me, you…" she cut across herself.

"Of course I'll do it!" I spat. I swiped the box and thrust it into my bag. I couldn't bear to see it sitting amidst our lunch things, to think, even for a moment, of what it contained.

"Do you know what he would have said right now?"

"No," I said. I dreaded what she would say next.

"Let's make like a tree and leave!"

I smiled faintly. "How silly of him," I said.

"Oh, he was always silly, you didn't know that?"

Her life had been one in which everything had a season. Winter was South America, spring was cheese-making and placing orders, summer, all day, every day, was the shop. Fall was the winding down, the diminishing of hours, the mark-downs, the clearing out and then the darkening of windows. If her life was a calendar, every page was now torn.

Her son's death was like ink from a bottle spilled on a good dress. How or why, it didn't matter. In seconds the dress was ruined. The stain was fast, one couldn't stop it spreading. Violet could wash and rewash the dress, it would never be the same and there was no replacing it for it was not a dress but her life. This was the way it looked now.

There was surprisingly little to take care of before we left. Filling out the online application was terrifyingly easy. I could not help but think of the young man and his well-meaning summer program as I clicked the green "Submit Your Application" button and waited for that simple gesture to take effect. Within minutes a post appeared in my inbox confirming the receipt of my application. One week later my application was accepted. I made the necessary arrangements with Maria's school. The second month of kindergarten seemed as good a time as any to miss. I made arrangements with the library director to take the many vacation days I had accumulated. Even post-fever, I still had plenty of days remaining. It was an excellent time to take a leave. Nella's replacement had been hired; by the day of our departure summer would be done and the library would be quiet again. Our passports were already in order due to a trip we had planned but never taken to Aunt Tomoko's the previous Christmas. We brought almost nothing with us save one carry-on apiece, filled for the most part with gifts for our relatives and teachers. Paper-wrapped soaps, jars of honey, chocolates, tea, little bits of the island were all we carried. And then we were gone.

* * *

One earnest person can silence a crowd of comedians. In part this is due to the reverence even jokers have for truth but it is also due to the short life of sentiment and its incompatibility with laughter. A child too possesses this silencing power. Indeed Maria cured me of some of my sentimentality with regard to the young man. On more than one occasion, during our month in Japan, I tried obliquely to speak of him and was met with resistance, if not her outright refusal to grant me an audience. There was little room for the dead in the living world of her childhood. When I spoke of America or of the past, she would hold her arms out and shout, "*Dako! Dako!*" or "Pick me up! Pick me up!" and I would obey, though she was almost beyond a weight I could safely manage. When, without explanation, I wept, she took me in her arms like a little mother. She said to me in a low, storytelling voice: *I used to be your mother. You used to be my little girl. I remember living inside you. It was so cozy, I didn't want to leave.*

If we took in any particular sights, I've forgotten them. (Typical of me to make of myself an island wherever I am.) I bought a postcard for Violet but didn't send it, such an act seemed violently casual, that of a carefree traveler dropping a line. We studied our Japanese quite diligently. I remember Aunt Tomoko's country rice (whose surprising secret ingredients were mushroom-soaking water and a dash of oats) and her blood-cleansing burdock rolls, the cousins helping us do our flashcards for hours, teaching us silly Japanese songs, the *an pan* from the bakery next to Uncle Tadashi's, Uncle Tadashi's stories about my father as a boy, always with a book in his hand, his refusal to look up from it even when answering the door. Like Melville's nursing whales, I lived a double life. One self—hungry, wanting to live—drew mortal nourishment from the country rice, the kindness of my loved ones, while another self—absorbed by grief—feasted on memories of the young man.

On our last morning I walked alone to the sea. Afraid as I was of being seen, I went early, when it was still dark. Although *early* is a culturally relative term; to my dismay there were already throngs of people strolling the shore and a few robust swimmers. Most of them were elderly, one, two, three, even four times the young man's age, and yet they had risen early, they were swimming, they were strolling the shore. He would have liked to have seen them—miraculous—the way they all cleaved like the earth to the sea. He would have found it a beautiful thing.

I hadn't dared open the small box Violet had given me, having felt terror at the mere thought. I put it off till the last. I removed my sandals and waded in up to my knees for I had a fear of my own weak flinging, a fear of him falling short of the sea. When I withdrew the clear plastic bag from the box I felt assaulted by closeness. It seemed that I had, by keeping him hidden in the depths of my suitcase, squandered my time, that I should have slept with him nightly while I'd had the chance. Was it depraved of me to first smudge a bit onto my tongue and try to taste him? Once I had flung him away from me, I thought how anticlimactic it was that I should travel so many miles across foreign soil only to place him in the same sea I had looked upon as a child from the ferry. Perhaps someday he would reach Alcatraz. Who knew where the wild currents would carry him.

* * *

Var met our boat, ignoring my request that he permit us to ride the bus. I claimed it would be easier and less costly for him to wait at the apartment though truly I did not wish to encounter him anywhere near the dock. I did not want him there, like water diluting my strong drink. If I was going to be drunk with grief, smelling the sea air, hearing the boat's blasts, I wanted to drink alone. I looked, bleary-eyed, for Violet in the crowd, but she would have had no way of knowing our return time and what on earth would I have done had she appeared?

"Papa!" Maria screamed at the sight of Var. He rushed forward to take our cases—he normally never takes my case—but

Maria intercepted and insisted he pick her up. So he picked her up along with her case while I took my own. He looked fairly relieved to see us, or perhaps he was only relieved to see her. Like a sailor charged with counting heads, he touched my hair lightly. It had grown, a few short waves curled across my forehead. My hair was more like the young man's now. As we walked to the car I looked down at the street. I watched the silver foil from a chocolate bar dart brightly across the black lot.

The apartment smelled strongly of cigarette smoke. Like a dog who, when left alone for too long, reverts to bad habits, Var had resumed smoking. How could I blame him? Isolated from the truth, he was a creature attuned to suffering without knowledge of its particulars, a stray roaming loose upon the frozen sea. Each puff of smoke that issued from his bristly muzzle resembled the vapors one sees issue from the mouth of anyone crossing an ice field. Eventually the apartment did grow colder. Before long we could all see our breath, which made us look like a family of smokers. Var found a smart black space heater at the dump and repaired it using a chopstick and a broccoli elastic. He had the matchless resourcefulness of a castaway. In this way we were oddly compatible. If I had once felt like an island explorer, I now felt shipwrecked.

I was struck dumb by the familiar orange and white package of rolling papers he often left on the dinner table, which he had, in our absence, taken the liberty of painting blue. (When I asked him why, he replied, "It was for the gnomes.") His tobacco, of course, was different from the young man's, but its scent when he first took it out of the pouch was darkly reminiscent of that other. The sight of Maria breathing in secondhand smoke enraged me. I yelled at Var about it. Likely he yelled back, but I heard all his criticisms as if from a great distance, across a tundra of sound, the pale conch of my ear still submerged in the rough black sea of the young man's voice.

There were nights I lay watching Maria sleep, listening to

the migrating geese. Maria beneath her eyelids, alone in a world of dreams, a fleet of ships sailing across the dark sky. The warmth made by each part of my body that touched hers brought me a little happiness. It was difficult to pry myself away from her and yet I did so regularly. Drunkenly, I wandered the apartment at all hours in search of something that might remind me of the young man, a memory to wet my parched throat. More than once I sat in the dark at the blue table to find Var's gnomes and *kokeshi* arranged as if for a child's play. I felt strongly he had arranged the figures so that I might see them, that each scene held a meaning intended for me. But I couldn't decipher them. Instead I moved the figures around in response or, in the case of the most puzzling scenes, I left them as they were.

Once we settled back into a routine, Violet was the first person I made plans to see. The disappearance of the young man from my life strengthened rather than erased my affection for her. It was wonderful to see her. Difficult and wonderful at once.

We met in the cemetery at Dead Man's Curve, which is perhaps a place less morbid than it sounds. There are few places outside the library for two people to meet. Of these, the cemetery is the most private and the most beautiful. Its autumn blooming cherry trees flower once in the fall and again in the spring, first pink blossoms then white. One can walk down the tree-lined lane and pretend to be in the Aritaki Arboretum. Maria and I sometimes brought our lunches there. I wished I could visit the young man's grave but he had gone to the sea. My own stone was on the west side waiting for me.

We sat at the end of the lane with our backs to the stones, looking out at a tilled field and a few gray shingled houses. A flock of geese cried unseen, overhead. The blossoms were pink as a sky above us. We sipped tea I had brought in a thermos. Violet, perhaps unthinkingly, brought a carton of Petit Écolier and I had neither the nerve nor the heart to touch one. She didn't say much, she was hauntingly like him. She listened, she let slip the occasional sharp comment or half smile. It was almost like being in his presence, the same eyes, different skin.

"We'll be closing the shop soon," she said. I flinched at her use of the word *we*. He was no longer part of it. *We* now meant Violet and the bars of chocolate, the crackers, the tins of foreign paste.

"When?" I asked, though I knew the date precisely, he always looked forward to P.I.P.'s closing day. He would write in chalk on the sign outside: *The End. Everything 50% off!*

"In a couple of weeks." With a trembling hand she poured the last of her tea into the dirt. "But we'll open again in the spring." She and the foodstuff would persist. The schoolboys in their brown and red sleeves, the pink blossoms, the black tea.

"Where's his father?" I asked, the question tumbled out, I couldn't stop it.

"Down-island," she said, the words two hard fists to my heart. I had always catalogued his father safely in one of the vowel states—Idaho, Indiana, Ohio, Utah—never in a consonant state and certainly not on island.

"But," my mouth protested even as my mind dashed to imagine the young man alive as a middle-aged man, the ideal age for a husband. I prayed I would never commit that sin.

Ineptly, I thrust a gift toward her, a *maneki neko* filled with flower kiss, elaborately wrapped. "It's nothing," I said. "Something for P.I.P."

She nodded. In Japan I had thought of her daily, each time Aunt Tomoko nodded her head.

I didn't understand how she was coping, how it was she could keep up the shop. Our griefs were dissimilar. In time he would become a boy I once loved in secret but he would always be her lost son.

As much in an effort to distract myself as to fulfill my

cherry-red dream, I asked Siobhan to teach me to knit. She was aghast. "You don't know how to knit?!"

"Oh, please," I protested. "You would never say that to Nick!"

Our sessions were harrowing and humorous if a tad humiliating, but in the end she made a woman of me. I was not, I confess, an apt pupil. My insistence upon perfection paired with my horrendous fine motor skills was vexing. Equally so was Siobhan's notion that I should immediately apply my newly acquired skill to knitting a sweater for Var. Though I kept mum about my plans for the cherry-red yarn, I was not above mentioning Violet during our lessons and Siobhan was generous with her commentary.

"Do you think she's angry with you? I mean on some level she's got to be angry, right?"

"You don't know Violet," I said.

"I don't need to, I have a son. If you think she's not angry you've got a screw loose."

"She isn't like you," I said. "She isn't a typical woman."

"What's that supposed to mean?"

"It means you're a nosey parker and not every woman is as same as the next."

If, I sometimes thought, boldly assenting momentarily to Siobhan's theory, *if* Violet had ever been angry (there was her unspent venom at the café to consider) then her anger, like iron, had been transmuted. If her anger and my guilt were the iron, death was the process, and we—did I dare think it?—were the gold. It sounded medieval and mysterious and not a little presumptuous but I believed in it. When it came to our friendship, there was something alchemical at work.

"Denial is more like it," reasoned Siobhan.

I was frightened of setting foot in the library again, as if, like no-man's-land, it might contain unexploded ordnance. I was frightened of meeting his ghost. When finally I met it there at the counter, I didn't ever want to leave. The library became for me a kind of holy place. I suspect Siobhan whispered discreetly, without incriminating me, my news to the staff, for they all handled me with care that year.

When at last I saw Nella for my long-awaited confession, I was like a young man who, one moment flushed and single-minded, the next moment shrinks at the prospect of ejaculation in the presence of another. When I asked for details of her resignation, she was evasive. We discussed instead the difference between those who frequent bookshops and those who frequent libraries (there are of course those who frequent both, who were we to make such arbitrary and uninformed distinctions, it was pure entertainment if not agitation on our part) for she had left the library for a bookshop whose back door faced the Steamship Authority. Any confessional impulse I might have revived was further quashed by her comment that she had seen Var several times entering the ferry terminal. She did not press me for an explanation and I was grateful, lacking as I was even a single fact pertaining to Var's mysterious comings and goings. More mysterious still, she said she had seen the young man in the bookstore just a few days before. Were it not for his mother I might have clung like a lunatic to that tale.

The following summer I took up bookmaking, a hobby that I must admit is quite common among librarians. When I have time, I print English translations of *tanka* on mulberry paper, though over the years I've become increasingly busy. Violet asked me if I would help out in the shop on weekends and I agreed. I enjoy the work, I enjoy arranging fresh flowers, harvesting vegetables, handling the many imports that remind me of her son, but likely I would have done anything she asked. We keep ourselves fairly occupied, especially during the summer months.

Liam, that once-young lover of all words equal or pertaining to marijuana, precocious connoisseur of smoke rings, visits the shop on occasion, always under the auspices of buying food for a party, but I'm convinced his true mission is to check on Violet. At first I felt his cloudy gray eyes rest too heavily upon me as if he knew my secret and would soon drench it with some horrifying truth, but I think I imagined this. He's become a fisherman who drinks too much during the winter, married to a rose-colored milkmaid who stops in for brown bread and cold cuts when her husband's at sea. What does he think of when he's alone on a boat, I wonder.

Angry or not, I am infinitely glad that Violet did not abandon me. She could have so easily abandoned me and for good reason. I would have had no recourse, no defense. It would have been a loss, perhaps even for her, and certainly a terrible blow for me. I've grown attached to our silent walks through the woods, accustomed to seeing her on the trail just ahead of me. She wears her poorly made sweater well, a bit of red in the trees for all seasons, bright for the world to see.

In the midst of my new productivity I came, at last, to appreciate passivity, to view it as its own kind of audacity. I admired the boldness with which Var stood idly by and allowed the corpse of a deer to sink slowly into the earth of the garden instead of sweating to dig a hole in which to hide its stinking flesh. To endure nature's onslaught without intervening requires a certain resolve. Passivity is also the cousin of patience, which is, I think, a distant relative of faith. Doesn't the act of waiting imply faith in the arrival?

In the years after the young man's death I spent many afternoons sitting under a tree in front of the apartment waiting for Maria's school bus to arrive. By then the level at which I was able to distinguish between the sounds of various engines rumbling down the state road was nothing short of professional. Though now I saw all vehicles as the same vehicle. The trucks hauling gravel, the buses hauling tots, the buses hauling tourists and townspeople—I saw all of them as small islands en route to the big island. If not today then tomorrow.

Waiting for the proper engine to deliver my child to me was a thoroughly frightening experience. Reckless driving, tropical storms, hurricanes, blizzards, all these were daily possibilities. I understood statistics; I understood that someone somewhere in the world would dive into water only to strike rock; I understood that someone's child would die before she reached home. I could not see a yellow school bus without thinking of him. Always when Maria's bus careened to a stop (for the driver in his garish Hawaiian shirts did rather speed) and its doors burst open I felt a wildly disproportionate sense of relief and gratitude that she had survived the perilous ten-minute ride. Always I held her a bit too tightly because always behind her in one of the bus windows looking out was his handsome seventeen-year-old ghost, my eternal reminder of the worst that could possibly happen to one's child.

Apollonaire's phrase "You will weep for this time in which you weep…" held true in my case, if only temporarily. Immediately after the young man's death I could go to the woods and find him. I had only to set foot on the path to the waterfall and I would drown in thoughts of him. As the years passed this changed. As the years passed, when I walked there in search of him I might remember something or I might not. What was more common was that my mind would be flooded instead with minutiae—what to serve with the soup I had made for dinner, when Maria would next be home for a visit, whether or not I remembered to turn the heat off at the library when last I closed. I would stroll along not noticing at first that the torrent of details from my daily life had blotted him out. Far from drowning in thoughts of him, my thoughts drowned him. Then I would wish for the sharp memory that had come with my early grief. I mourned the loss of it. *Shikata ga nai*, I thought. *It can't be helped.*

And then, I don't know exactly when, this too changed. One morning, it was as if he had died again; I felt everything afresh. Twenty summers have passed since that summer and yet I find it excessively easy to remember his moods, his darting, downcast eyes, the energetic, athletic hand gestures that incongruously accompanied his shy yet sly sentences, the clean laundry smell of even his filthiest clothes, the slow metal chain of his voice dragging its well-oiled length across the silent winter air, the hard-packed snow, my unclothed skin.

After all these years, that sleeping loft holds my desire. I no longer visit it, it isn't necessary. I love any loft made of crude wood. Barns, garages, bunk beds, children's forts, they all produce a similar effect. Now I fixate most not on any of his physical attributes (though he was rife with beautiful aspects) nor on any particular exchange that occurred between us, but on the very feeling of secrecy that I once found so constraining: the sensation of being alone and aloft with him, a voluptuous entity existing apart from the main.

I don't say his name. Not ever, not aloud. It's a trick of mine, very effective, a way I have of keeping him alive. If it weren't for my memory, that mysterious, benevolent under-self within, it might seem as if he never existed. As if there was nothing out of the ordinary about that year.

Sometimes months, even years, go by without anyone referring to the young man (our beloved Violet is maddeningly taciturn) and then it is up to me to conjure him. Though I've found that remembering him alone isn't the same as remembering him in the presence of another. In the end, without the sea there is no island. Being an island, one tends to forget this. When someone outside myself refers to him, directly or otherwise, they reanimate him for me. It is different than my solitary conjuring. It is a gift.

Why, it happened just this morning while I was helping Maria address her wedding invitations. She's going to be married next spring, under Aunt Tomoko's *kanzan* tree. I had hoped she would marry in the back garden as we did, if only so that Violet and I could manage the food. But she is a different young woman than I was, very much her own. We had got halfway through the addressing when she asked, "Have you ever been in love with someone other than Papa?"

"Yes, of course," I said rather perfunctorily, unprepared for the force with which the young man's image then assailed me.

"What was his name?" she asked, pursing her lips to a point and lifting her eyebrows slightly.

After a brief hesitation, wherein I slid an invitation into its proper envelope, sealed it, stamped it, and set it lightly on the pile, I smiled. "His name was Oscar," I said, selecting at last the name of a much older boy whom I'd loved as a child, a boy who was surely an old man by now if he wasn't already long dead.

ACKNOWLEDGEMENTS

A view of the sea to Thaisa Frank who taught me that stories are everywhere. Wampum necklaces to the lovely people of the Asian American Studies Center at UCLA, the MacDowell Colony, the Creative Writing Program at University of Houston, and the Fine Arts Work Center in Provincetown, in particular King-Kok Cheung, Jinqi Ling, David Wong Louie, Valerie Matsumoto, and Roger Skillings. A pair of large sunglasses to Elena Ferrante whose work led me to Europa Editions and in whose shadow I happily exist. A Muji travel diary to Sara Levine whose book *Treasure Island!!!* led me to Emily Forland. Tea Lane dahlias for Mayumi advocates Amy Hoff, Katia Merriam, Mathea Morais, Maia Morgan, Ann Quigley, Sarah Durham Wilson, and Emma Young. Blue hydrangeas for longtime encouragers Chi-Wai Au, Samantha Barrow, Susan Burmeister Brown Lauren Buckley, Kathy Garlick, Alice Y. Hom, Syma Iqbal, Brian Kay, Lilly Kuwashima, Robin Coste Lewis, Donald Nitchie, Suneeta Peres da Costa, Linda Swanson-Davies, Diep Tran, Eric Wat, and Meg Williams. A lei of green and white flowers for G.E. Patterson. Peonies for all the librarians. Not Your Sugar Mama's chocolate bars to early readers Heidi Ganser and Jill

Jupen and a hefty sack of black jellybeans for Beth Kramer. A lavender eye pillow to Laura Coit for reading and seeing so much. An endless roll of ferry tickets to Amanda Tseng, Danzy Senna, and Fanny Howe. A special ahoy to Sarah Bowlin. Many sunlit swims at Ice House to editor Michael Reynolds for steering me toward clarity. Sea salt caramels to agent extraordinaire Emily Forland for boldly and with kindness, staying the course. Daily swan sightings to Sue and John Coyle for their steady love. To Maceo Senna, for meeting me as an artist, an eternal walk down an ancient way and the same gold ring. A library in the woods to our daughter Xing for giving me Maria, a life beyond myself, and a life beyond the page. To my father, an island postcard: *Wish you were here.*

About the Author

Jennifer Tseng's first book, *The Man With My Face*, won the 2005 Asian American Writers' Workshop's National Poetry Manuscript Competition and a 2006 PEN American Center Open Book Award. Her second book, *Red Flower, White Flower*, winner of the Marick Press Poetry Prize, features Chinese translations by Mengying Han and Aaron Crippen. *Mayumi and the Sea of Happiness* is her debut novel. She works at the West Tisbury Library on Martha's Vineyard.